Her Morning Star

Violet Cowper

Contents

Chapter 1

When Melanie had stepped inside Viscount Howick's ballroom for the first time, her heart had been full of hopes.

This was supposed to be her first entry into society since the scandal – the nightmare that began that terrible morning more than a year ago, unspooling into days ahead and blackening them with ruin. Lady Evelyn's arm had been firmly, if rather stiffly, linked with hers, assuring her of the promised support.

Technically, the promise had been made by Lady Evelyn's uncle, but Melanie was sure that even such a headstrong lady as the raven-haired heiress was reputed to be would not defy Sir Owen in such a way.

The setting seemed so beautiful it could have been constructed by the gods of bygone antiquity as a platform for her triumph. The chandelier was blazing with light reflected in a myriad of crystals, the candles weeping with white bridal wax. Deities of old with soft curls and creamy skin ran across the ceiling. Melanie was unsure which myth these belonged to.

Melanie had been greeted warmly by the host, but his attention had turned to Lady Evelyn rather quickly. Melanie did not begrudge him his quick loss of interest. As Sir Owen Prynne's niece and the daughter of the earl of Marsden, Evelyn outranked her in every possible way.

Melanie had been staying with Evelyn as her companion for a year now, and in that time, their goals had been wildly different. Evelyn's was to keep her uncle's household in town while he was away in the north, canvassing for the next election. Melanie's was to glue her life back together.

Melanie positioned herself by the western wall, feeling like a callow debutante again, floating in an unknown world, unsure where salvation or disaster awaited, and watched the other guests dancing. She wasn't as sprightly a dancer as some of the girls, but she could have acquitted herself well in the country dances. The final notes of the gentle and conservative 'Flowers of Edinburgh' faded away, and her breath caught when the orchestra struck up a waltz.

She had been discouraged from dancing the waltz during her first and only season, and she had never been the kind of daughter who would require a stern ban to dissuade her from improper behaviour.

On the other hand...

Melanie hesitated by the wall. It was only fitting that her new life started with a new dance.

She blushed, gazing at the closeness of the couples gliding across the well waxed floor. She couldn't blame the matrons frowning on the benches: of course, they would worry with their charges pressed so closely against their gentlemen partners.

The movements of the dance seemed easy enough to remember, and Melanie would never allow anyone to think that she lacked bravery.

She straightened her back, seeing herself in her mind's eye: a chaste and lovely figure draped in a high-waisted gown of pale muslin – thank God for the Prynnes' generosity – that made her look like a classical goddess or a bride.

Or a sacrificial offering.

She silenced her inner voice and waited for an invitation.

The music started winding to a close. Melanie swallowed, her gaze darting back and forth across the ballroom with a growing desperation. She had never been a complete wall-flower; even during her frugal debut, her dance card had never lacked invitations.

You know why. You know why very well.

Is the scandal following me still?

Do you think the ton has much to talk about? Or do you suppose it is every day that a respectable gentry squire from Yorkshire divorces his adulterous wife?

This was wrong; this was completely wrong. This was sup-posed to be a thing of purity, the start of a new life –

The waltz ended, and Melanie smiled when the orchestra began playing another one.

This time, Melanie vowed, she was going to be bolder. She had never been a coquette, but she gave one of the gentlemen in attendance a lingering glance, as if inviting him to invite her. He nodded, as if acknowledging her presence, and then crossed the ballroom to where a lady in a plum gown stood.

Melanie's cheeks were burning. She cast her glance around the room once again, her sight attracted by a splash of scarlet – the uniform of an officer.

Doing her best not to bother anyone, she crossed the ballroom as though desiring to converse with him. Her over-fevered imagination made her believe several heads had turned towards her, and fear told her everyone's lips moved in venomous whispers.

The ballroom was grand, but crossing it felt as if she were walking on a tightrope over a churning mountain river.

The officer turned to her, regarding her with interest – although she also detected surprise in his eyes. *Of course, he is surprised. It is probably not every day that he sees ladies who are so bold as to offer themselves up for an invitation instead of waiting as they are bound to.*

Truth be told, she would have much preferred waiting.

They were now a mere three steps away from each other. Melanie looked into his eyes, pressed her fan against her chest, the white feathers brushing the bare skin of her décolletage, and unclenched her fingers. The fan fluttered to the ground.

'How clumsy of me,' Melanie whispered, feeling herself an utter harlot.

'It is nothing to worry about,' the officer replied courteously, leaned down, and picked the fan up. He handed it to Melanie, and she gave him the barest of smiles in case he was as timid as she and needed further encouragement.

He smiled with the utmost politeness. And then he walked away without a single word.

Had her gown burst at its seams and left her standing in the middle of the ballroom in nothing but her unmentionables, Melanie would not have felt more utterly ashamed. There was no greater way to tell her she was not welcome – except spitting in her face or strong-arming her out of the stone palace altogether. Or possibly both, in whichever order.

She had never been stupid. She knew when to acknowledge her defeat.

Her head hung low, Melanie went to the benches lining one of the walls and sat down among the matrons.

'I say, Lady Evelyn.' Charles Grey, Viscount Howick and the foreign secretary, was genial is always. However, there was no mistaking the worry in his eyes. 'I have heard about your dream of travelling, and I cannot say I approve of it.'

You are not my uncle, to approve or disprove my conduct, Evelyn thought. *Even Father has lost that right long ago.*

Aloud, however, she only said: 'I understand that Europe is clogged with armies and no traveller, however careful, is welcome there. But surely no army might forbid me to have my dreams.'

'We all have to wait in England until the Corsican ogre can be dealt with.'

'I am afraid to become too decrepit to travel by the time this happens.'

'You seem to have a poor opinion on our soldiers, Lady Evelyn.'

'Certainly not. Merely an accurate opinion on my own age. I am no debutante anymore.'

Evelyn was only two years away from the dreaded age of thirty. An age of full living for a man, certainly; a woman, however, would have done well to acquire a husband by the time disaster struck unless she wanted to be relegated to the dusty world of old maids.

Once upon a time, Evelyn had hopes of a great and passionate marriage.

Such hopes were dead and gone. Only her purpose remained.

'Surely not.' Lord Howick coughed politely. 'Where would you have gone if you had a full run of the world?'

'That seems like a fine parlour game to play.' Evelyn dodged the question and turned to the lady listening in avidly. 'I concede the right of the first answer to you.'

'Oh, France,' she replied.

Evelyn's blood ran cold. *She couldn't possibly know, could she?*

'But only if the Almighty had somehow granted me the power to turns the years back and travel to the time before that horrid revolution. My mother spent some time in Paris when my father had been to our embassy, and she said once there was no finer city in the world, nor a court more magnificent.'

For a second, Evelyn's body felt light with relief. It was merely a nostalgia for a more gallant age. It had nothing to do with her own plans.

'And you, Lady Evelyn?' the woman asked, her smile thin.

She had to think something up quickly. 'The East,' Evelyn said. 'I am not sure where. Perhaps Constantinople. Perhaps Lebanon. Perhaps Egypt.'

The last word came out quieter than the others with a barely perceptible pause before it – a stumble, a crack, and the blackness peered from within.

As if on cue, the eyes of the conversationalists lit up with pity.

Evelyn did not know if there was a reaction she hated more.

'I say.' Lord Howick raised his eyebrows 'Constantinople!'

'Don't blame her,' the female guest intervened, her own smile just as insincere. 'Lady Evelyn could have hardly helped inheriting her father's adventurous spirit.'

Evelyn had lived long enough to know that wasn't a compliment. The references to her father rarely were.

The scar beneath her string of pearls started itching again.

'Adventures have little to do with it,' she replied smoothly. Once, she would have lashed out; however, years as a hostess for her bachelor uncle's political gatherings had trained her well. 'The language lessons I have received I received from my uncle.' *My perfectly respectable uncle.*

'I take it you speak French,' the guest said in a tone just polite enough not to let the statement sound as dismissive as it was.

'As well as German, Turkish, and Arabic.'

'Arabic!' Lord Howick exclaimed. 'By Jove, why would a lady have a need of that? Or a gentleman, for that matter, unless he goes to serve in India. I've heard they speak it in some provinces.'

'My uncle says there is no such thing as a useless knowledge.' She sipped her ratafia. 'And I agree with him wholeheartedly.'

Thank God, they did not pry further than that. Not that her insinuations hurt Evelyn – at least not in the way they would have done only a few years ago when she was still smarting from every reference to her wild father.

Or to put it a different way, when she could still feel.

It did not hurt, truly. Not anymore. If anything, it gave her a peculiar power – as if she were floating above this bejewelled, bird-bright crowd, her true spirit too far away from them to be harmed, her body protected with an ice shield of grief.

They made keening goddesses in marble.

'London is not the safest place for a young lady alone. Too many temptations,' Lord Howick commented. His tone was warm and genuinely concerned; Evelyn could easily imagine how he had managed to win over the Whigs. It was not an easy thing to be foreign secretary after the great Fox.

'If you are referring to the gin, I have no interest in sweet oblivion,' Evelyn noted nonchalantly, as if referring to an after-dinner stroll. 'One's mind has to be kept keen, in my opinion. Besides, even if I were so inclined, my uncle made sure I had a companion to take care of me.' She did her best not to let her voice sound resentful. 'I am sure Miss Bright is going to keep my conscience on the straight and narrow path. She is sweet, and level-headed, and rather perfect. Sometimes it seems to me that she had stepped into the world straight from the pages of etiquette books.'

Which is why I cannot wait to part with her company. Where I would be going soon, I would need no companion, young or old.

Evelyn indicated with her eyes the spot where Melanie was, no doubt, receiving compliments from the young officers in attendance – only to find out she was no longer there. Feeling rather silly, Evelyn scanned the whirlwind of silks that was the floor in search of the familiar white garment and the golden head crowning it. There was no sign of her.

Finally, she spotted the colours she had been looking for –the colours of innocence – far away and half hidden, huddled among the benches where stout mothers were sitting.

'I don't understand,' Evelyn murmured, frowning. In truth, she did understand. She understood rather well – better than most women present, to be sure. She knew how a parent's shame could stain a daughter's future.

Compared to her own father's political proclivities and domestic habits, the Brights' divorce seemed to her a tawdry and paltry thing – something to drone on about for a year – that wasn't earthshaking enough to continue cutting the debutante of the family afterwards.

Evidently, she was wrong.

She looked again, noticing new details. Melanie Bright's gaze held no rancour – only the kind of Christian resignation advised by conduct manuals and preached to the mothers of dead children.

'Forgive me.' Evelyn turned to the host. A resolute plan was ripening in her head. She had no reason to bear Miss Bright any love; however, some things were, simply and plainly, not right, and the girl had clearly done nothing to injure her. 'I have a rather unusual request...'

How much time had passed? Forty minutes? An hour? Melanie was not sure.

There is nothing to cry about. Her fingers curled and uncurled in their pristine pale gloves. This was her own fault for having expected too much. It was the fate of every presumptuous, vain girl who wanted more than she deserved from the world than it was willing to give her. Every tale she had ever read pointed to that conclusion.

She should not have been expecting any better. She should not have been expecting the ton to forget and forgive her mother's sin. How could she blame them for suspecting the signs of the same wantonness in the daughter?

Her yes continued to prickle hotly with unshed tears, the unseen muscles contorting in a vain attempt to keep them in. Melanie couldn't even imagine the reaction of the good society if she actually burst into tears at the foreign secretary's ball. If she did, she would likely drown the last shreds of good opinion anyone had been holding of her.

'Miss Bright,' someone with a slightly amused voice called above her, sounding like a call from heaven, 'may I have this dance?' For all its velvet-like deepness, the voice belonged, unmistakably, to a woman. And not just any woman.

Lady Evelyn Prynne, the daughter of an earl and the niece to a great politician, was standing in front of her, her gown of dark verdant green making the pallor of her skin shine like a pearl.

'Lady Evelyn?' Melanie swallowed. 'I... I beg your pardon... What is the meaning of this?'

'Have you never seen women who have ill luck with partners dancing together?' The dark-haired heiress smiled as if the matrons regarding her with distasteful shock did not exist.

'Yes, but country dances most often. Not the waltz.' Melanie looked at her and whispered, 'Is that allowed? Would the master of ceremonies, I mean, the host, not look askance at this?' She could not have picked a worse moment to remind the world that her experience with genteel entertainments had consisted, before the catastrophe, of rare visits to the assembly rooms in Halifax, not of grand private balls.

'He graciously gave me the permission to help you when I asked him.'

'You've asked Lord Howick this?' Melanie couldn't help but feel slightly awed. 'For me?'

'I see no other lonely maiden with fair complexion in this room,' Evelyn teased her slightly, her eyes growing impatient. 'So, what do you say, Miss Bright? Does your dance card have a little room for me?'

Melanie knew she should have demurred. Even though this kind of solution would be hardly unheard of for a partner-less lady, she did not want to compound her already damaged reputation with new oddities.

On the other hand, she reasoned, Lady Evelyn *was* Sir Owen's niece and one with whom she was going to be sharing a long year. Offending her would not do. She rose from the bench, inclined her head, and said with as much ceremoniousness as she could muster, 'I would be delighted to.'

There were a few gasps and a flurry of whispers when Lady Evelyn led her to the floor. But the heavens did not burst open and the ground did not gape into a chasm to swallow the audacious sinner as Melanie had feared. She placed her right arm upon Lady Evelyn's left and felt her partner's hand grasp hers.

'Have you ever waltzed?' Lady Evelyn whispered in her ear, her breath suddenly warm against her skin.

'No.' Melanie shook her head. 'But I have watched. I have always watched.'

Their first few steps were careful and slow. Melanie had little experience with the dance just as her partner, no doubt, had little experience with leading as a man would. However, if their movements were over careful and lacked the ease of those of the men and women whirling around them, they were no less enjoyable for that.

'Have you read Lady Mary Montagu's *Turkish Letters*?' Lady Evelyn asked when the dance grew on them enough to sustain a conversation.

'Oh, many times!' Melanie exclaimed, inwardly chiding herself for such a burst of passion. 'Our subscription library must have tired of me. I have taken every account of foreign adventure they happened to host.'

'I suppose these were not numerous,' Lady Evelyn guessed, her amused tone returning.

'You would be correct.' Melanie blushed. She had never exhibited shame of her provincial origins and had never been one of those ladies who hungered for London; however, she did sometimes wish their subscription library was a little bigger and, they had two or three more in the vicinity. 'But I've read Hester Piozzi's memoirs of Italy, and Lady Elizabeth Craven's *A Journey Through the Crimea to Constantinople*, and Anna Falconbridge's recollections of Sierra Leone.'

'A good selection,' Lady Evelyn commented.

'I think they've been fortunate women to have seen so much of the world,' Melanie confessed. She had thought so a lot of times while walking in the pale greenery of her father's garden and imagining what it must be like to walk the deck with vast depths of the oceans churning beneath one's feet, or battle the merciless sun of faraway jungles, or ascend the Spanish Steps of Rome the way Hester Piozzi did.

'Mary Montagu had been well-positioned to see the world. After all, she was married to a diplomat.'

Melanie's heart skipped a bit. Had the Prynne heiress's dark gaze somehow plumbed her soul and fished out her desire? This had been her dream ever since she was old enough to think of her marital future. While other girls dreamed of catching the eye of a duke or a viscount, all Melanie prayed for was an ambassador husband. Naturally, he would also have to be wealthy, and handsome, and relatively young, but that went without saying. Many times while taking housekeeping lessons from her mother, she had fantasized about hosting foreign potentates, engaging an Italian cardinal or a French nobleman in a witty talk across the dinner table, her nebulous husband looking on with serene pride at his polished wife.

Of course, such dreams disintegrated into ashes with her mother's disgrace. Melanie had only one chance now to make them come true – and that was to make sure that Lady Evelyn Prynne enjoyed her company.

Melanie wouldn't have had this chance to begin with had Sir Owen Prynne not been her father's political patron. She knew she had to be grateful to her father. She needed to be grateful to him for a lot of things. Even if, somehow, the words of gratitude were blocking her throat like a sharp bone that could choke its victim to death.

'Speaking of Mary Montagu,' Lady Evelyn continued, 'do you entertain some intentions of following in her footsteps?'

'What do you mean?'

'I mean, I cannot whisk you away to Constantinople – but I can show you some Turkish baths in London.'

Melanie had to take a moment to catch her breath because her partner had sent her spinning with the lightest movement of her fingers. Her petticoats bared her ankles for a second. 'Turkish baths? Do you mean bagnios? Weren't they rather disreputable places?'

'That depends on the bath. I assure you ladies of quality need warmth and relaxation as much as the Covent Garden nuns do.'

Melanie did not know the term, but she counted herself as sharp enough to understand the meaning beneath it.

'Oh, I remember the baths passage in Montagu,' Lady Evelyn continued. 'She compared the Turkish and Circassian ladies there to statues of Eve and figures from Titian there, didn't she?'

'I believe so.'

'It was certainly a welcome change from all those gentlemen writers claiming Oriental women to be debased creatures so debauched that they had to have their cucumbers brought in only cut in slices, lest they set to any mischief.'

'What do you mean?' Melanie blinked, the ballroom spinning around her in glittering colours. 'What kind of mischief can one get up to with a cucumber?'

'I have no idea myself,' Lady Evelyn replied, palpably lying. 'I would have asked one of those writers, but most of them have gone on to a better place.'

Melanie decided to leave the subject alone. 'Would you come with me?'

'It won't be necessary. I can introduce you to any number of fine young ladies who would be delighted to accompany you.'

Yes, fine young ladies who would detest me at first sight, if not at the first heard gossip. It was palpable that Lady Evelyn did not feel anything particularly warm towards her unwanted companion either – but at least that had nothing to do with Melanie's family and everything to do, she suspected, with the intrusion she represented.

'But that was the purpose of your staying with me,' Lady Evelyn protested. 'For me to ease you back into society's good graces. How do you propose to accomplish it if you go everywhere with no one but me?'

'Not everywhere. Just to the bathhouse.'

Officially, they were supposed to be equal friends in the eyes of the ton. In truth, of course, Melanie was as dependent on Lady Evelyn's goodwill as pagans of old were dependent on the generosity of their marble deities; few would have claimed equality between a daughter of a minor gentry family and a grand lady of the ton. Melanie knew, even if she had to remind herself of the bitter truth of her position sometimes, that she would do well to refrain from having too many personal desires while in London.

'I am afraid I would have errands to run.' Lady Evelyn shook her head. 'I am sure you would enjoy the visit.'

'What kinds of errands?'

'Important ones.' The first hints of impatience in the cool exterior of the heiress shone through like red flashes. 'You would find them utterly dour, I'm afraid.' Lady Evelyn's hands were holding hers warm and firm.

'I have been asked to be your faithful companion while your uncle is away. What you are proposing is going to rather defeat the purpose.'

'Nonetheless, I am proposing it.'

'I would have to decline your proposal.'

'I'm afraid it is not up for negotiation. Unless, of course, you would want to trail me against my will.'

'What if I do?'

'Then I would be greatly displeased.'

Melanie knew what the words implied. She was not stupid. She knew her situation. Whatever amity arose in her soul in response to Lady Evelyn's audacious invitation withered in resentment.

The music, as if on cue, wound to a close.

'Are you going to be available for a second dance?' Evelyn asked nonchalantly.

Melanie had her own pride, however. She might not have been a diamond of the ton or even a lady from a family of immaculate reputation – not anymore – but she was a human being with a heart, and that heart demanded dignified treatment.

'Thank you for your invitation,' she replied, imitating her erstwhile partner's cool voice without meaning to. 'However, I am afraid I find myself fatigued.'

Chapter 2

The grandeur of the baths robbed Melanie of her breath.

The large stone building was crowned with five domes. There were no ordinary windows inside, but she had no need to squint. The openings in the roof let enough light through, and the pale marble that paved the first room seemed to emanate a glow of its own. Four cold fountains provided little streams of water running through the channels cut in the marble.

'Are you satisfied?' Lady Evelyn asked at her side. There was impatience in her voice, but there was also a kind of teasing as if she were enjoying Melanie's shock the way a friend or a guide might enjoy showing their companion some foreign wonders.

'It's magnificent.' Melanie exhaled loudly. 'Is that how real baths in Turkey look?'

'The proprietor had apparently spent some years there performing some minor services on behalf of the king and Crown at the sultan's court,' Lady Evelyn said with such nonchalance as if the man in question had been a grain merchant. 'I suppose he would know.'

To either side of the room, there were several marble sofas. Women lay upon them. Some were in shifts and stays, and some were naked as the day they were born.

Melanie froze, feeling both embarrassed at intruding upon them and self-conscious about being dressed from throat to toes. Lady Montagu, she remembered, immediately attracted the attention of the guests of the bagnio, who proceeded to call her charming and invite her into their company. No such attention was lavished on Melanie. For that, she was almost grateful.

One of the women turned her head, looking Melanie in the eye. There was nothing brazen in the gaze, certainly nothing houri-like; it was a mere curious appraisal. The lady's dark eyes reminded Melanie of someone else, and she averted her gaze from her face. However, in doing so, she met with the wide and lavish hips of the second guest of the baths, and from there, there was only one path available to her – namely, to lower her eyes and walk as quickly as possible to the next room.

Melanie regretted her decision as soon as she passed the threshold. The room was hot with steams of sulphur and made her clothes and underthings cling to her skin immediately. Worse, it was adorned with even more sofas and enjoyed by even more women – some reclining like Roman matrons, some sitting together, and some kneeling by the edge of the pool.

This time, they did stare. And this time, one did approach Melanie.

The black-haired, heavy-lidded woman with breasts resembling the shape pomegranates asked, 'Aren't you going to undress, poor things? The heat would do you in if you don't.'

Blushing, Melanie shook her head intensely. She couldn't help but redden at the notion of being looked at with the same curiosity at the appearance of a stranger as before, only now she would be naked for other women to appraise...

The dark-haired lady shrugged, as if saying 'suit yourself.'

'Are you sure this is the right place?' Melanie asked Evelyn nervously as the unknown beauty walked away. 'Is it supposed to be like that?'

'It is the best Turkish bagnio I have found this side of the Channel, and I had to make quite a few enquiries for that. Would you like to leave?'

Melanie wanted to make precisely this request, but something in Lady Evelyn's voice made her pause. Only a few days ago, Melanie had been rhapsodizing to her about the envy she felt towards the great lady travellers of past and present. What kind of an explorer would Melanie have made if she shrank even from a pale shadow of foreign customs, the kind one could see in a London bagnio?

Melanie recalled the conversation at the ball and the way Lady Evelyn's voice had warmed with interest when she told her of her reading habits. Other people tended to demonstrate wry amusement at her book-fed girlish fantasies of adventure, but there Lady Evelyn's voice had contained something almost like admiration. Did Melanie really want to disabuse her of that? It would be unwise, Melanie decided, since they were to spend months and months together.

'No. It is nothing.' She shook her head decisively and sat gingerly on the corner of a free sofa. Her stays were light, yet it was hard to breathe in the heat, and her clothes seemed more cumbersome than ever. 'Are *you* not going to undress?'

'I didn't think we would stay here long.'

Something flared up in Melanie's heart – not quite anger but a faint echo of it.

'What a fine opinion you have of my fortitude, Lady Evelyn.'

'It had nothing to do with you or my opinions of you. Merely with my own business.'

'Your errands?'

'My errands. But far it would be from me to make my guest uncomfortable. Would you mind helping me undress?'

Melanie dutifully stepped closer to her. She didn't have a sister, and doing this for another woman seemed strange. However, declining would have been downright rude.

In the steaming heat, her fingers slipped more than once on the hooks of the dress, and sometimes it required more than one attempt for her to undo them. The slow progress bared Evelyn's shift beneath. The shift was made of muslin, which did not surprise Melanie, and embroidered with a pattern of small berries, which surprised her. What kind of family would waste money on embroidering a garment which would be treated by the laundresses the harshest?

A family like the Prynnes, I suppose.

When the gown and the petticoats fell to Evelyn's feet, Melanie looked away swiftly and turned around as if herself in a hurry to undress. In truth, she was mortified of the prospect.

I am not going to undress completely in front of strangers. Ever.

'There is going to be no great shame if you were to disrobe down to your chemise,' Evelyn called out from behind her back as if having read her thoughts in the awkward angles of her arms. 'Girls in boarding schools take baths in their shifts and see each other wearing nothing but in their dormitories; it can hardly be considered shameless.'

'Have you been to a boarding school?'

'No. Father saw to my education at home.' There was a strange pause between the first word and the others, as if her admission of a rather usual arrangement were some Gothic confession. 'Let me help you,' Evelyn added decisively as if wanting to prevent any further questioning on this front.

Melanie did not turn around but felt the nearness of the other woman with her back, the warmth of her body close to Melanie's still-clothed skin. The heat of the bathhouse was causing a strange drumming in her temples as if the pulsing of her blood had gone frantic.

There was some relief in the fact that Evelyn's fingers were just as fumbling as Melanie's were at the same task, as the hands of any woman who had a maid and had no sisters would be. The dark and glamorous Lady Evelyn Prynne was not perfect at quite everything she did.

'Thank you,' Melanie mumbled, turning to face her reluctant saviour at last. With a force of will, she made sure her eyes strayed no lower than the woman's neck.

Evelyn's cheeks were bright with the heat of the chamber, and her hair, although still pinned in a simple bun, was touched with moisture that made it a little curlier.

'I find I am not in a mood for lying down,' she said. 'I think I shall go and find the kiosk with coffee – I've heard there is one and it is a splendid place for talking with the others. Would you like to come with me?'

Melanie had no love of coffee, and the notion of having to face and converse with barely clothed ladies set her heart aflutter with embarrassment. Besides, her rational inner voice added, given the reputation of the bagnios as an institution, it was very unlikely that all of those women were truly ladies of quality. What if some of them turned out to be merchants' wives or, worse, wealthy sin-peddlers of the frail sisterhood? It wasn't as if there was a way to determine their status by their clothes the way one could at a park or assembly rooms.

Melanie shook her head. 'I'd rather stay here.'

'If this is what you'd like.'

Melanie kept her eyes glued to the floor as her companion disappeared down the corridor. She folded her garments neatly and lay with her back on the marble and her folded garments under her head as if they were a cosy pillow. She closed her eyes and tried to forget she was not alone in this realm of sulphur heat.

Evelyn's heart was beating fast and not simply because of the lingering heat of the bagnio or the hurry in her steps. That was a close call. What on earth had prodded her to agree to accompany Miss Bright to this place instead of insisting on giving her over to one of her friends as a chaperone? It wasn't as if Evelyn were not in a position to insist.

Of course, she was not one of the people who particularly enjoyed being in a position of power, especially not over a woman already distressed. But so much was at stake here and so much to lose if her intention were to be discovered.

Her gamble had paid off. The timid Miss Bright did not look too closely at where her half-naked companion headed. Nor did she notice, having kept her eyes firmly on the floor tiles, that Evelyn had taken her garb with her. Now having changed into her clothes and running down the street towards the embankment, Evelyn couldn't help but feel a twinge of guilt over Miss Bright, dozing now in blissful unawareness on a marble bench.

She didn't like lying to the innocent, wide-eyed Miss Melanie Bright. But, had she known the truth, she would have buried her teeth in Evelyn's sleeve to keep her put. Once she finished shivering with shock, that was.

Oh, her shivering and her missish ways. What on earth had made her uncle agree to invite such a creature to their house and leave her to Evelyn's ministrations? Of course, obligations of patronage had to be respected, but surely there were other ways to mend her standing.

Evelyn hurried towards the arranged meeting place. She liked that they were meeting by the boat steps of the river even though the idea was not hers. The parks and confectioners of London where she could easily go had a thousand ears while the traditional coffee houses would never admit a woman; water, however, was a great equalizer – and a great silencer, too.

'Mademoiselle Prynne.' The man who awaited her kissed her hand. His hair was cropped short as though to make the work of a headsman easier. A remnant of a Directory fashion, most likely. 'I was very much intrigued by your letters. I am glad you agreed to give me the pleasure of your company.'

'Not as glad as I am to share yours,' Evelyn replied politely. She could be courteous when it suited her needs. She settled in the boat and threw a meaningful glance at the boatman.

'You need not worry about him.' The man who was, according to all appearances, a respectable émigré, spoke in his native tongue. 'I am yet to meet a man of such origins who spoke the kind of English understood in better houses, let alone French.'

Some time passed in silence as both took their seats upon the cushions, and the rower took off, letting the bustling city fall to the sides. Evelyn's hair still felt wet and coldafter the baths.

'I understood that you wanted to discuss your travel plans with me.' The agent coughed.

'Indeed.' Evelyn smiled. 'I have a notion to spend the coming winter in the south of France and then to continue on to Paris.'

'And thence to meet His Imperial Majesty, I presume?'

'Monsieur understands me well. I feel nothing but admiration for your master.'

The water was lapping against the sides of the boat, washing away the smell of coal that tinted the streets.

'An interesting position for an Englishwoman whose country is at war with mine. I hope you understand the risk you are taking by even meeting me here, Mademoiselle Prynne.'

'I know that the citizens of my country are now prohibited by law to mingle with the citizens of yours.'

'And the law is still in force.'

'I know that. But so do you or else you would not have taken the precaution of the boat.' *And, had my notion not interested you, you wouldn't have arranged this meeting at all.*

'Touché. But you haven't answered my question.'

'Not all of my countrymen think Emperor Bonaparte is an incarnation of the antichrist. Indeed, there are plenty of those who deem him to be a man of destiny.'

'Is that so?' The Frenchman's tone was nonchalant, yet the gleam in his eyes betrayed naked, predatory interest.

'Of course. There are even more of those who hail him as a liberator of Europe from the medieval shackles. Everyone knows of the day he threw open the doors of the Venetian Ghetto. Besides, Mr Pitt's campaign of terror on any organization dedicated to political liberty did not look good by contrast.'

'Monsieur Pitt was your uncle's closest ally, was he not?' the man asked sharply.

Evelyn was prepared for the question. 'My uncle was his, rather is his, I should say – Mr Pitt might be dead now, but his policies live on. But I am my father's daughter first and my uncle's niece second.'

Evelyn expected a painful tingling in the scar at these words or a suffocating wave of protest rising inside her. However, nothing of the sort happened; the frozen lake that was her feelings on the matter remained serene.

'Your father had been a truly original man.'

'Monsieur flatters us.' *Rather, Monsieur is being polite.* 'He celebrated the day Bastille was taken with tables spread for his tenants. The papers have dubbed him Citizen Prynne. He was indignant of the abuse envoys of the new republic tended to receive in foreign lands.'

'I see. And now his daughter wants to see the emperor to express her admiration for his reforms?'

'More than express an admiration. You were right when you said that my uncle was one of the closest confidantes of

William Pitt. I did much more for him than simply organize political dinners. At the very least, I sat with him as the mistress of the house and listened.' *And talked. Rather a lot. At least, in the past.*

'I see,' the agent repeated. 'I shall pass your case into the hands of Talleyrand. I have no doubt, however, that a French passport can be procured for you. The emperor is going to be very much interested in what you have learned at that eminent table.'

Against all odds, Evelyn felt not quite exhilaration but a kind of victorious light-headedness. Those who claimed that the loss of sensibility crippled a person, whether woman or man, were wrong. She would never have managed to preserve this nonchalant, fair, icy demeanour today had she not been a so-called cripple.

If this crippled state could bring her a step closer to her self-imposed mission, then, perhaps, it was better to never be whole at all.

Chapter 3

Normally, the presence of the foreign secretary at the dinner party one attended should not have been a point of worry for a young woman – even if the woman in question was almost past the marriageable age. But when Evelyn entered the withdrawing room of her host and saw the gallant Viscount Howick ready to escort her to the dining room, her blood ran cold.

Could his attention to her mean he might have suspected what she was up to? Could he have somehow heard ... But no, of course, that was absurd. With the situation being what it was and tensions running high, no one would be so courteous with a supposed traitor.

Since they were entering the dining room according to precedence, the dinner being rather formal despite merely preceding an outing to the theatre, Melanie fell behind. For the first time since the little debutante first entered the Prynnes' London home, Evelyn felt an acute kind of emptiness when she lost sight of the girl. Of course, it could not have been anything more than a fear of being left alone with her now adversary.

'You seem slightly pale, Lady Evelyn,' the viscount commented. 'I hope you are not unwell?'

'No, I am in perfect health.' She forced herself to smile and scolded herself in the privacy of her mind for wavering so. How could she hope to accomplish her mission if she was so bad at concealing her emotions? She knew the mission would likely result in her demise and felt no great grief about the fact, but she hoped it would happen *after* the success. 'Merely thinking about the play ahead.'

'Is the production so dire? I thought it was merely one of Smythe's early comedies.'

'This is why I worried,' Evelyn improvised. 'I've heard that her comedies are not where she shines. I have always preferred her tragedies.'

'The ones that tested the Licensing Act to its limits? I have always known you were something of a rebel at heart.'

The heart in question contracted in fear at this no doubt innocent remark. Fortunately, they had reached the dining room. Even more fortunately, their host was an old-fashioned sort who allowed no mingling of the sexes at the table and seated his female guests to his right side and the male ones to his left.

'You were talking to Lord Howick,' Melanie whispered as soon as the eel soup was served. 'I saw you.'

'Yes,' Evelyn replied tensely. 'So I did.'

'Did you happen to talk of anything ... pertinent to my situation?'

Anger born of quiet terror erupted in Evelyn's heart. Were this chit's thoughts really centred on no one but her own tragic self?

'No. Worry not, Lord Howick gave not a thought to your situation. He has rather greater problems on his plate at the moment.' Not the best metaphor given the circumstances, perhaps.

Melanie's pale throat moved as she swallowed. She leaned closer. 'I mean ... I mean my marriage prospects. I just thought – perhaps he could recommend an honest young diplomat working for him, and ...' Her voice trembled a little.

She was close enough Evelyn caught the scent of clean linen and soap. Melanie rarely used rosewater, Everly had learnt, and never more cloying perfumes. Evelyn wasn't sure how to respond. On one hand, she had better things to worry about than the fretting of her unwanted companion about her marital eligibility. On the other hand ...

'Melanie, listen to me. I swear, if I would be in a position to do so, I would put the question to him.' If she wasn't in that position, Melanie would be the first to learn about her disgrace. She now lived closer to her than either Uncle Owen or her brother.

Evelyn sat stoically through the buttered lobster and the stuffed pike. Before the fowl was served, she excused herself for a moment, citing the need of fresh air. Neither the guests nor the host expressed any surprise at her request. She must have really looked ill.

Evelyn walked down the corridor in a quick, soldier-like stride as if the open window was a redoubt she needed to capture. Once there, she took a deep breath. The spring air had a note of chill underneath it.

'I hope you are feeling better, Lady Evelyn,' someone behind her commented.

She spun around and came face to face with Viscount Howick.

'Are you feeling unwell, too?' She couldn't help but muster some sarcasm.

'Never better. Tell me, Lady Evelyn, how are you finding London this spring?'

She blinked at the strange swerve of topic.

'As usual. A juxtaposition of filth and splendour. The most vital place on earth.'

'To me, it's a city of great mixing. Just think of it – there are Whigs and Tories, northerners and southerners, the French who descended from the Huguenot silk weavers and the French who fled the revolution, the Germans and the Italians – even some Turks... and, like in a good novel, everyone has their own agenda. Everyone is out for himself.'

The wind on her neck felt uncomfortably cold. 'I didn't know you were a lover of novels,' Evelyn said neutrally.

'Oh, I am a great admirer of Miss Burney's talent. But, pleasant as it would be to discuss literary matters with you, I am afraid I would have to start an altogether less agreeable subject.'

Evelyn had no intention to dance about her doom anymore . 'I take it the boatman *did* speak French.'

'I would have been a poor candidate for my post if it were otherwise. Now, Lady Evelyn, is there anything you would like to say about your conduct?'

'It was not as it likely appeared to you.'

'I surely hope so, for, to me, it appeared as something even worse than the breaking of the law against fraternizing with an enemy. To me, it appeared like you were willing to commit high treason.'

'Before you hang, draw, and quarter me, allow me to explain my motives.'

'I was curious about them myself. It could not have been money. Your father's will left you well-provisioned, not to mention your uncle's ongoing care.'

My father simply had no time to revise his will. 'No. My reason was patriotism.' *My reason was wanting to go out in a blaze of glory – to bathe my life in fire before it was snuffed out. It is better than merely withering into the grave. But you don't have to know that.*

'How so?'

'I wanted to gain Bonaparte's trust and employ my new position as an agent for our country.'

'A bold statement. I hope you forgive me for not believing it immediately.'

'You can write to my uncle or to my circle. They would give you a detailed information on my character and political views.'

'Character can be concealed; views can be pretended.'

'Not for a decade.'

'If you truly think so, you would not have had a chance at Bonaparte's court.'

'Because I don't know how to stay quiet?' Evelyn bristled.

'Yes,' Lord Howick replied evenly. 'Precisely because of that.'

'So, what are you going to do? Put me away and throw away the key?' Evelyn gazed at the walls painted with serene *vert de mer*, breathing with the colour of the sea she might never see again now.

'It would have been a waste. Tell me, Lady Evelyn, is your desire to serve genuine, or were you merely attracted by the glamour of impersonation games at the imperial court?'

'All my desires are genuine.'

'A rare thing for a lady of the ton. If so, there might be a task more suited to your unique talents. Is it true that you speak many tongues?'

Evelyn nodded. 'Uncle insisted upon me learning them, given the growth of our political interests both in the West and the East.' That was not the whole story, not the whole reason, but Viscount Howick had no business knowing that.

'Is it also true that you have had a rather unconventional upbringing – some even might say a masculine one?'

'Father did not think it masculine.' *He merely thought it an upbringing fit for the future citizen of a frugal and virtuous Republic.*

'That is excellent. That means you are going to find yourself standing on firm ground while dealing with nationals of most countries we are concerned with.'

'What do you mean?'

'Not so long ago, a French agent by the name of Vincent Dubois was found dead in his lodgings just off Moorfields. His papers were not with him nor were they found in any of the inns or safe houses known to us.'

'So, you think I can locate them? Just because I won't find myself lost talking to his countrymen or the Germans?'

'Or the Swiss, or the Belgians, or the Austrians. There are more than two players in the game, and not every one of them announces himself. Besides, I have heard of you. Once you set your mind on something, you rarely leave a skill unlearnt or a task half finished. Which is yet another reason to employ you.'

'That, and the fact that our enemies are likely to underestimate a lady?'

'Precisely. An unintelligent frame of mind and, in our business, a dangerous one.'

'You are saying our business as though I have already agreed. I am not alone now. How am I to investigate without alerting Miss Bright?'

'I am sure you would find a way. Besides ...'

'Besides, I have little choice?' Evelyn gave him the bitterest grin she was capable of. It was one thing to fling herself into the roaring flame, for some heroic reason, of her own accord. It was another to be thrown there like a helpless babe.

'Your conversation with that Frenchman might be seen as treasonous in some quarters.'

'I take it you promise to keep it from these quarters if I take up your assignment?'

'You are perceptive.'

Evelyn's heart was a vat of boiling water, hot with rage. Rage at his trap, at the traitorous boatman, and at her own sudden powerlessness.

Is there a difference? You wanted a blaze of glory. One heroic demise is much like another.

Had Melanie not known of the lady's eccentricity, she would have thought the whole story invented.

At first, she had thought Lady Evelyn was lying, trying to cover up a more mundane sin – outings to masquerades, perhaps, or even a lover.

If the last year had taught Melanie anything, it was that even the most demure, well-reputed lady could have a secret vice, and Lady Evelyn Prynne was not demure.

'Why are you telling me this if the business is coming from such secret quarters?' she asked incredulously, leaning closer to her in the Prynnes' box at the Drury Lane theatre.

'So that you would know that I would have to be absent from time to time and did not have to worry.'

'Did not have to worry! How can I not worry when my friend—'

'Miss Bright' – Evelyn turned to her – 'if there is a thing I truly detest, it is hypocrisy and pretty lies. It's a shame that I cannot get away from either in society and politics, but I have expected better from you. I know you are not worrying about me because of some sudden, fast-grown affection of friendship. You are worrying about your family's plans to have you re-enter the good graces of the gentry and wonder if staying with a highborn lady would do anything towards that goal if said lady is going to get herself killed.'

'I thought no such thing,' Melanie proclaimed in the haughty tone of Clarissa confronting Lovelace. She could feel, however, a treacherous blush creeping up her cheeks. Were her intentions really that mercenary?

But a lady could not be a confection, living on fine sensibilities alone. Fighting for one's reputation could sometimes be a harsh thing – it required cutting off unsuitable friends and pleasing over-ardent suitors, for example. Oh, it was fine for a woman of the high ton to do whatever she wanted, provided her means and her husband allowed it, but Melanie moved in a different world, a punier world, a world of the countryside, a few thousand a year and the brewing of home beer in season.

No scandalous extravagances for her. A woman who forgot that was a woman who could end up worse than dead.

Just ask her mother.

'Can this enterprise really get you killed?' The full meaning of Lady Evelyn's words struck Melanie belatedly.

'Not if I am careful. But I imagine the late Monsieur Dubois moved in different circles to me.'

'Then why did his lordship give you this task at all?'

'To give me a chance to redeem myself, I suppose.' Evelyn shrugged.

'You seem very calm about the choice between a charge of high treason and a mission that – you've said it yourself – can lead to your demise!'

'My first task is not dangerous at all. I am merely to meet with a contact known to them, a man knowledgeable about the activities of French agents on our soil. Besides, there are worse things than death. Miles upon miles of meaningless years stretching in front of you, for instance. Can you imagine that, Miss Bright? Would you have liked to live that?' Lady Evelyn's smile was pure ice.

Melanie reached out and touched Evelyn's gloved hand tentatively. It was just as icy as her smile. 'Yes, if the alternative was no years at all!' Melanie whispered then paused, thinking of her own situation.

What if the social curse hanging over her never dissipated? What if she was never be able to marry and would spend the rest of her life as an old maid kept out of charity by relatives? Would she not sacrifice that kind of prospect for a glorious cause? No. Life, even the most grey and miserable kind of life, had value.

'It's not as if I am forcing you to investigate along with me. I have told you, Miss Bright, you yourself are in no danger at all.'

'I would be in danger if something happens to you – or if you get yourself into something unspeakable!'

'I would be careful with my disguise. No one is going to recognize me, much less trace me back to you.'

'You cannot know that,' Melanie argued with ferocity that surprised even herself. 'People can be very sharp-eyed.'

'I hope you are not suggesting I stop?'

'I have no such power.' The words themselves were demure. Her tone merely tried to be so.

'Then what *are* you suggesting? That you would come with me and make sure I do nothing stupid as a duenna in the southern climes might have done?'

Lady Evelyn's words were acerbic, but they gave Melanie a pause.

'Yes,' she said firmly before quite thinking it through. 'For your own good and for my own, this is precisely what I am going to do.'

Chapter 4

For Melanie, Vauxhall Gardens had always been a place of enchantment, conveyed into her world only in whispers: whispers about the splendour of its dining boxes and the Grecian marble lines of the Rotunda, whispers about the extravagantly expensive dinners where a roasted chicken could cost as much as two shillings, and whispers about the dark alleys where bold Cyprians approached gentlemen and importuned them for wine – or other things. ;

Indeed, it was that affiliation Melanie now feared the most. What could be more humiliating than to be taken for a woman of easy virtue? And what kind of a lady would visit such a louche place without a brother or a husband accompanying her?

'Vauxhall is no Gomorrah,' Lady Evelyn said, giving her a Venetian-style mask to conceal her face. 'There is a statue of Handel; fine musicians perform there all the time. My brother takes me there whenever the business of the estate spares him enough to come to London. I am yet to witness anything truly shocking.'

'I've seen some sheets of Vauxhall music at the printers, that is true,' Melanie conceded. 'But it's not its music that the place is famous for. Imagine what the guests would think of us – honest women, after all, have no need to cover their faces.'

'They can think us apple pies as long as they don't put us in the oven,' Lady Evelyn replied and wrapped her shoulders in a long cloak decorated with silver thread.

Melanie had worried about the cost of admission, but her host paid two shillings to have them both admitted. The Rotunda, white and glowing faintly in the moonlight against the dark trees, soon rose in front of them; however, it was not there that their path lay. They, according to Evelyn, were told to meet the man whispered to be of help in the Turkish Tent.

'It's not a real tent, of course,' Lady Evelyn added, walking down one of the narrower paths, while Melanie gazed at the gleam of chandeliers through the windows of the Rotunda. 'Merely a pavilion, the kind His Highness has at Brighton. You can consider this my introduction for you to the delights of London,' she added with a sudden warm mischief. The carmine lips of the mask hid her own, but there was no mistaking the brief smile in her tone.

Something made Melanie's heart skip a beat. 'Have you written to your uncle?' Her breathing grew shallow as she did her best to match her companion's quick stride.

'I decided not to inform him for a while. It would be better if he is not aware of the whole situation.'

'Why are you living with him?' Melanie was unable to contain her curiosity, even if now was an awkward moment for sating it.

'Because an unmarried lady cannot live alone unless she wants to be thought a lightskirt. I don't.'

'But – why not with your father?'

'Because my father is dead.'

'I mean ... I know that you joined Sir Owen's household before your father's death. Why?'

Lady Evelyn stopped and looked her in the eyes. 'Because my father flung me out of my own home,' she said sharply without melodrama or an attempt to embellish.

'Heavens, why?' Melanie gaped despite knowing, uncomfortably, how deeply impolite such probing was.

'I think you are asking too many questions. Here,' Lady Evelyn added almost hurriedly, 'we've reached the place.'

It wasn't hard for Melanie to imagine why Evelyn's father had flung her from their home. Many daughters faced the same fate for succumbing to a seduction. Melanie did not think it right because, for one thing, seductions could be somewhat forceful, as not all gentlemen, alas, always behaved as such; for another, being left without natural protection only pushed the poor things down the path of vice, and that was not anything a parent or a guardian should want.

Of course, such things did not only befall daughters. She shivered, remembering her sinful mother's fate. Whatever scandal her mother had been involved in when she was a headstrong young heiress still affected her, and Melanie vowed she was going to find out what had happened.

Melanie never would have guessed they had reached the Turkish Tent without Evelyn's announcement. The edifice in front of her didn't look even vaguely tent-like. She was no scholar, but she had read enough travel books about the lands of the Turks and their customs to know that their tents, even those belonging to the sultan himself, were not usually supported by twenty Ionic columns. Nor did they have carved domes or hothouse flowers festooning the place.

Looking around with amazement and curiosity, she stepped underneath the dome. After the fairy-like murk of the gardens outside, the blaze of the five chandeliers seemed sudden and blinding.

Lady Evelyn stood at the threshold, looking around. and then she pulled her to take her place by her side at one of the fourteen tables.

Evelyn and Melanie had barely managed to take their seats when a new figure entered the room.

Like them, he was dressed as if for a masquerade in a bright white aba with the lower half of his face covered. There was something perfect in the way their disguises complemented each other, making them seem like revellers who decided to stop in the pleasure garden en route to a costume party. In Hyde Park, of course, they would have looked ridiculous, but here, in this nocturnal, enchanted place, no one spared them a second glance.

'I hope you forgive my lateness and my garb,' Joseph Verney, the Swiss man whose name she had heard in the hushed corridor with vert de mer walls said, sitting down.

'No offense is taken,' Evelyn replied in German. She had no intention of letting the other people here overhear their conversation.

'The last time I've heard this language spoken was in my auberge in Valletta before the French came.'

The meaning didn't percolate into Evelyn's mind at once.

'Do you mean you used to serve the Knights of Malta?'

'I *was* a knight of Malta,' Verney corrected her.

Evelyn saw Miss Bright's eyes widen. *Of course, she would be entranced by the notion of sharing a table with a shadow of the gallant knights of old*, Evelyn thought with strange irritation. *Of course.*

'What are you doing here then? The Corsican is long gone from the island, and our governor there has a great respect for your order.'

'The order that once withstood the fury of Suleiman the Magnificent is no more. The order I knew, at the very least. The order I have once believed in.' There was a pause – a barely perceptible dark slit in the conversation. Then Verney filled it as if nothing had happened, his voice nonchalant. 'To answer your question, I am keeping a fencing school here. Officially. I do not lack for clientele, if that is what you wonder, and I am unlikely to lack for it while Eton and Harrow continue spitting young bucks out into the world.'

'Then why your other activities?' Whether speaking German or not, there was a certain level of discretion to be preserved.

'I wouldn't go so far as to call them activities.' Verney shrugged. 'Some of my pupils tend to mix themselves into all sorts of trouble – the sorts of trouble they wouldn't tell their esteemed families about. My having to drag them out of these has endowed me with some useful knowledge of the parts of London one wouldn't see in the daylight.'

'The kind of trouble that would lead one to know a French ... man of affairs?'

'Vincent Dubois was well-travelled. Although he was perpetually short of funds, there was no shortage of bright young men who liked to listen to him talk about Egypt and Syria and the lands of the Turks. Centuries are gazing upon us from the tops of these pyramids and so on.'

'Did he catch the illness that killed him there?'

'Illness?' Verney looked at her, slightly perplexed. 'Dubois died of a severe case of knife in the throat. Did your master not tell you that?'

Something bucked in Evelyn. She was not sure if it was the revelation of Dubois's gruesome end, the notion of being kept in the dark, or the implication of her having a master. In truth, Dubois's cause of death shouldn't surprise her. With the war going on, how else would Grey's man have dealt with an enemy spy? 'Of course, he did,' she lied smoothly. 'Just not about the exact method.'

'I see. He was sparing your maidenly sensibilities.'

'You would discover I have very few sensibilities to spare.'

'I am glad to hear that. The race for his papers is brutal.'

'There is a race?'

'Oh, yes. The French, the Imperials, some say even the Russians ... Everyone wants to know what it was that Vincent Dubois had discovered in the heart of the desert.'

'I hope he did not unleash some ancient Hittite curse,' Evelyn joked.

'No.' Joseph Verney shook his head. 'He unleashed a thoroughly modern one.'

'Do you happen to know anything about his last movements?' It was a good time to finally get to the heart of this meeting.

'I do.' He stared at her as though waiting for something.

From the neighbouring table, from a different world, Evelyn heard the clink of small glasses and a woman's laughter. Breaking the silence, she asked, 'Would you care to tell us?'

'Of course. Not for free, though. I'm sure you understand.'

The price Joseph Verney named made Evelyn wince; however, she had no choice. Besides, she realized she liked him. After the whimpering and the trepidations of her companion, it felt strangely refreshing to meet someone with a fierce and fearless outlook, someone who took life head-on and feared no death.

She feared no death either. Not anymore.

'I do, Herr Verney,' Evelyn said and drained her cup of scalding coffee.

'Your breeches are slightly wrong,' Melanie noted. Not satisfied with merely guessing the fact, she knelt by Lady Evelyn's feet and touched her buckskin-enclosed knees. 'For that matter, so are mine.'

She was right. Too long.

'I understand why you don't want to wear the linen ones,' Evelyn said, glancing into the bedroom mirror and touching the pristine jabot of her shirt. 'But remember, you are to be my cousin from the provinces. A kind of country mouse whom I am going to be showing the delights of the capital. Linen culottes would fit the image perfectly.'

A very distant cousin, then, Melanie thought. Now when they were side by side this way and looking into the floor-length mirror, it was utterly impossible not to notice what complete opposites they were: light and sweet against imposing and dark.

At least their mode of dress did not differ anymore now, not without Lady Evelyn's favoured riding habits to get in the way. Now, they were both dressed in a perfectly masculine fashion, sisters – or should it be brothers? – in the bizarre.

But it would have been completely impossible for them to enter the gaming emporium Vincent Dubois was said to frequent as ladies – unless they wanted to burn their reputation to the ground and dance upon the ashes. Melanie understood that.

Which did not, of course, mean that she liked the plan.

'Maybe they do fit the image, but they do not fit the person,' she said. 'Neither do yours. Would you like me to trim them a little? I am sprightly enough with the needle.'

In a moment as rare as a crack of sunlight through the winter clouds, Lady Evelyn's lips were touched by a warm smile. 'Thank you,' she said. 'But these belong to my brother. I suspect Paul isn't going to thank us when he comes down to London one day and notices that his town garb barely covers his skin now.'

The surprise must have reflected on Melanie's face because Lady Evelyn added, her eyes still sparkling with humour, 'Or did you suppose these were my own? That I was keeping a perfect wardrobe of masculine clothing for daring outings?'

'I wouldn't have been surprised.'

'I am not as wild as you think me to be, Miss Bright. Not anymore, at the very least. My uncle has purged some of my darker habits.' She said it with the same smile on her lips – only this time Melanie couldn't help but notice the corners of her mouth were slightly tinged with wistfulness.

Then she coughed, as if catching herself at something inappropriate, and looked back into the mirror so that now Melanie could only see her eyes in the cold reflection.

'I propose we assess each other,' Evelyn said. 'Tell me, do I look like a dandy about town? Or, at least, a man aspiring to be one?'

Melanie looked at her, quite unable to fight the mix of mortification and admiration. It was like being in the bagnio all over again. Of course, this time her companion was dressed in much more than a single chemise; indeed, it seemed there were as many garments that went into the making of a gentleman as they did into the making of a lady. Evelyn's stockings, woven in silk, were fitting her calves more snugly than the most daring muslin gown of Grecian silhouette. Her buckskin breeches had no soft curves to cling to as they would have had with Melanie – which was another reason why the looser-fitting linen was a better choice for her – but they still hugged her flesh a little too close for comfort.

Melanie quickly looked higher, where the glacial-white shirt hung thankfully loose of Evelyn's breasts – no tight binding could conceal this sort of generosity of nature easily. The waistcoat covering the shirt was verdant green, and the upper part of the outfit was crowned with a cravat of the same hue.

'You look wonderful,' Melanie whispered. 'A real young blade. Except ...' She stepped closer to Lady Evelyn – close enough to feel the heat emanating from her body and smell the clean scent of her skin innocent of all perfumest. 'Let me fix this.' She slowly unwound her cravat and retied it with a slightly different knot. 'Here. This is how it looked on that fashion plate.'

'You look through fashion plates for gentlemen, too? It seems there is no limit to your interests, Miss Bright.' There was no jab in Lady Evelyn's voice this time – only a slight teasing.

'I was looking for something for my father.' Melanie blushed.

'You wanted to make the Beau Brummel of Halifax out of him, I take it?'

'Something like that.'

'I've seen your father. You are quite ambitious.'

'With all due respect—' The moment of warm affinity was lost.

'You have taken his side in the matter?' Lady Evelyn looked genuinely surprised.

'What matter?' Melanie asked uncomfortably as though she did not know. Of course, she knew. The whole of London knew.

'The – never mind. I was cruel. I apologize.' Her tone did not sound apologetic; it seemed just as sharply firm and straight as the blade of a rapier. But Melanie knew what the polite thing to do was.

'I accept it,' she said formally.

'In this case, let me tell you that you make for a remarkably handsome country mouse.'

'If you are dressed as a rake, it does not mean you have to act like one.' Melanie blushed. From a man, that kind of compliment would have sounded morally doubtful, but coming from Lady Evelyn, it appeared not precisely innocent of spice but somehow harmless, like a warm spring instead of an unpleasantly scalding one.

Evelyn suddenly stepped closer to her, running her hands over the front of Melanie's long shirt and culottes. 'There is something missing,' she said almost coyly.

'What?'

'A weapon. These bright belts are not here to accentuate the beauty of our eyes.'

Not hers, that's for sure. To make Lady Evelyn's enormous dark eyes even brighter, only the kohl of the Arabs would do.

For Melanie's English rose-blue eyes, a belt would be more than enough. 'I have no intention to ever touch a weapon.'

'It might do you a good service. It is not Almack's that we are going to in these clothes.'

'I don't think the situation is going to turn that dire,' Melanie said nervously.

'Life is never short on dire situations, Miss Bright. Besides, I am not talking about a lifelong study. Only of a couple of hours a day to teach you the basics of sabre fencing.'

'Teach me?' Melanie stared.

'Of course. This kind of skill requires intuition. Otherwise, you would be as like to cut off your own fingers than to wound an enemy.'

Melanie had no intention of wounding any enemies at all; however, that was not the part that surprised her most. 'Who is going to teach me? Mr Verney? I am not sure if he would agree ...'

'I am sure he won't. The Knights of Malta have always been an orthodox lot, what with their warrior-monkish ways. No, Miss Bright.' Evelyn looked into her eyes. 'I mean to teach you myself.'

One could have knocked Melanie down with a feather. 'But how do you yourself know sabre fencing?'

'It's a long story. Are you familiar with General Miranda?'

'The Venezuelan malcontent?' Melanie racked her brains for the memories of his name in the papers. 'I think so.'

'You might call him malcontent; my father called him a freedom fighter, and so did I.' Evelyn bristled. 'He was our guest during his sojourn in England and agreed to give me and my brother rigorous lessons while he remained so. He has always been a brilliant fencer.'

'Why not only your brother?'

'General Miranda is a man of unorthodox ideals. He once told me that, once he liberated Venezuela from the power of the Spanish, one of the first reforms he is going to enact is the establishment of universities open to both sexes so that every youth and maid could be a useful and rational citizen.

'At one point, he infected me with such a fever that I started to believe that my future lay at the banks of Guadalquivir, not Thames. That came to nothing, of course. My family would have never agreed to let me go and enmesh myself in a fight for independence not my own; there had been limits even to my father's radicalism. Besides, I couldn't leave my brother to his fate after ...' Evelyn swallowed audibly, and Melanie watched her pale throat and the scar on it move up and down.

'After what?'

'It doesn't matter,' Evelyn replied with some brusqueness. 'What do you think about my idea?'

'I think it is ...' *An utter nonsense*, Melanie thought, but she couldn't say that aloud. Not to her. Not to a lady placed so much higher than herself. 'It is rather unwise. Imagine what my father is likely to say when I come back home and he sees me having a swordsman's calves and wrists!'

'Is he likely to look at your wrists, much less calves, so closely?'

Melanie grew quiet. Now that she thought of it, he was not. But that didn't make the notion of being taught sabre fencing – and by another lady at that – any less outlandish. 'I am grateful for your offer, but I have to decline it. I don't think these sorts of skills necessary for a lady.'

'You might not think them so,' Lady Evelyn replied, 'but where we are going, we will need more than ladylike skills to succeed.'

Chapter 5

'This is no Bolton Street, that is for sure,' Evelyn said, deliberately loudly, swaggering with her 'cousin' into the gaming hell by the name of Proserpine's Chamber. 'But it would do for the night.'

'Have you been to the club on Bolton Street?' Melanie asked her equally loudly, eyes wide.

Evelyn waited for a heartbeat's worth of time before dashing that illusion, as if there was some part of her that yearned to remain rakish and mysterious. 'No,' she murmured under her breath. 'I've just heard of it.' She led her through the hall.

Proserpine's Chamber certainly was different to the gambling emporiums of St. James that Evelyn had seen on engravings in scandal-lashing pamphlets. There were some pretensions to a theme, to the mythical antiquity of the name, like slender white columns rising throughout the great hall the size of a decent ballroom and the serving girls being dressed in stolas, their hair unpowdered and piled high. At first glance, it seemed the den of vice was an elegant kind of den. However, looking closer, she saw the columns could use some cleaning, the stolas some washing, and the decks of cards some changing. New decks had clearly been cut sparingly in this place, so as not to incur too much expense.

A great variety of games was played here: there was a hazard table, one for baccarat, one for loo, and one for *vingt-et-un*. In the corner, Evelyn even saw a group of men bent over a collection of plates and only realized what was happening when she came closer and noticed small, pale dots darting across the pewter expanse.

They were racing maggots.

'By Jove,' one of the jockeys exclaimed, 'that's cheating!'

'What is? We have all heated the plates.'

'I saw you drop a flake of snuff in front of my chap!'

'It was a perfect accident.'

'Not as perfect as the nose I'm going to give you!'

No bothering with pistols at dawn in this place, then. 'There is nothing to hear here,' she whispered to Melanie. 'We have to make enquiries.'

'Won't we look suspicious if we do?' The girl fretted. 'Du— The man we are talking about had just been murdered, after all, and here we come...'

'If we don't, all we are going to hear is tidings about the fish they have lost and the fish they have won.' Evelyn looked the hall over again and, glimpsing an opening, strode purposefully to a circle of men playing macao.

'Would you mind if me and my cousin join you, gentlemen?' she asked, making her voice a touch deeper.

'For sure,' one of the players said. 'We have two places left.'

'I don't think we've met,' his brown-haired companion intervened. To Evelyn's surprise, he was dressed even better than her – she could recognize a Saville Row cut. However, his shirt was crumpled and his sleeves touched with grey. Too much sweat in the candlelit, wax-weeping enclosure of the gaming hell; too little time at home.

'I do apologize.' Evelyn made a slight bow. 'I am Sir Peter Evans, and this is Martin, my Yorkshire cousin. He is on a visit to our fair town, and I've decided he should use the time to sample all its delights.' She gave the gamblers a grin she hoped would come off as rakish instead of desperate.

A couple of players straightened their spines when they heard the titled address. The brown-haired man wasn't as impressed. Nor was Evelyn intending for him to be so – she chose the modest knightly title instead of anything higher in the noble ranks to make it harder for others to sift through the lists.

'Then you've come to the right place.' The gambler grinned. 'Do you know how to play macao, Martin? Or you, Sir Peter?'

'I know a little,' Evelyn replied, just as she had planned to. She was not a bad player although not a master gambler the way some ladies of her circle were; however, it was better if these men thought her an easy prey to fleece.

The more relaxed they were, the more susceptible to questions they would be.

Five cards were dealt to both women, and the deck was cut, the cut card becoming the first one in the discard pile.

'Seven of spades!' Evelyn exclaimed, looking at it. 'Not a bad start.'

It had been decided Melanie would speak as little as possible, so as not to betray her own more high-pitched voice in an inopportune moment. Therefore, the younger woman simply nodded and smiled, surveying her own cards.

The candlelight forced the shadows into bizarre angles, and when Melanie nodded, Evelyn's gaze was drawn to her neck and the shadows there. Now that the younger woman's hair was not crimped and constructed into a fashion-plate confection but hanging in a simple, loose ponytail, Evelyn's attention was curiously more drawn to the shadowed world of her neck. Merely a patch of it was bared by Melanie lowering her head over the modest fan of her five cards, but that patch seemed to capture Evelyn's gaze.

'Sir Peter?' The brown-haired man coughed. 'It's your turn.'

She didn't have to pretend confusion in this case and threw the first card that seemed appropriate out upon the table.

'An ace!' One of the players whistled. 'My, but you are playing boldly, Sir Peter!'

Evelyn glanced at the remaining four cards in her hand and found a perfectly acceptable nine of spades, which would have been just as suitable for the turn.

But then, I am not here to win anyway, she consoled herself. *I am here to win these men's trust.*

Evelyn and Melanie diligently lost the first round, and the point went to the brown-haired man who got rid of his cards first. The next time, Melanie was lucky and got rid of her cards first, earning a point for herself. She laughed, pretending boyish exuberance over an early win, and threw her head back. Her eyes sparkled as if with a genuine joy, and her lip were parted slightly.

This was the first time Evelyn had heard this sound of unbridled gaiety from Miss Bright. In every other instance that Evelyn could recall, Melanie Bright had been as demure and decorous as a marble statue or an ink-and-paper creation of conduct manuals.

But here, it would have endangered their disguise for her to be so. Demure and decorous young men did not go to tawdry gaming hells.

If there is a word to describe Miss Bright completely, it would be diligence.

'I say,' Evelyn exclaimed, throwing half a guinea on the table, 'tonight doesn't seem to be the night for me.'

'I hope it doesn't mean you're going to leave?' one of the gamblers asked with naked hope for more lucre.

'No, I won't. Let no one say Sir Peter Evans ever backs away from a fight.'

'Then why are you here?' the soiled fop asked leisurely, dealing the cards, his eyebrows arched. 'Why not somewhere at sea, sinking Boney's galleons, or whatever it is he sails on?'

The question would have been natural enough if asked differently, but from this man, there was a strangely vicious edge to it. One that Evelyn had no choice but to ignore.

'Why, I have a younger cousin to tend to,' Evelyn quipped, hugging Melanie's shoulders with one arm and drawing her a little closer, almost toppling her from the chair. Melanie's shoulders were narrow under her touch, the bones thin as those of a bird. 'He has no one else to properly debauch his tastes and morals, after all.'

That provoked a bout of laughter from the small gathering.

'Your cousin's a pretty thing,' a player observed. 'I bet the ladies are throwing themselves at him day and night. Do they, Martin?'

Melanie raised her cards higher – clearly in an attempt to conceal her blush. She probably did from the others, but Evelyn, who sat just to the right of her and could gaze at her profile freely, noticed the slow creep of warm blood up her cheeks. 'I have never been – propositioned by a lady yet,' Melanie mumbled.

'We can fix that. Do you want us to call one of Proserpine's maidens here? She might brighten the evening for you.'

'My cousin's sole passion is travelling, actually,' Evelyn intervened.

'Must be a hard thing with Europe closed now.'

'The bloody war.' Another player sighed. 'Have you seen how they raised the prices this month? Those bloody profiteers, swaggering around now, dressed as if they were gentlemen. They weren't so bold before.'

'And they won't be so bold after,' the brown-haired man supported him. 'Once the war is over, everything is going to come back to its natural order.'

'Maybe it would be safer for Martin to go to the East for a while.' Evelyn steered the conversation back to its original topic. 'Cairo, perhaps, or Constantinople. He hasn't seen those yet, and they are perfectly open to travellers these days.'

'Cairo? Or, worse, the capital of the Turks? Don't do it, pup. Without a good cicerone with you, they are going to strip you naked for the velvet and throw you into the Bosporus on the next day after landing at the Golden Horn.'

'Where can we find a good cicerone?' Melanie asked quietly.

'There was a chap who used to frequent this place,' the well-dressed gambler said, holding his cards close. 'His name is Vincent Dubois. I haven't seen him here for eternity, however.'

Is. They don't know Dubois is dead. That will make everything easier.

'Perhaps he went abroad again,' another player ventured.

'So soon after coming back? No, something isn't adding up.'

'Where did he travel?' Evelyn asked quickly, unable to disguise the avidity in her voice.

Melanie tugged discreetly on her sleeve, probably urging her to be less direct. Evelyn ignored her. It was never in her nature to be quiet and unobtrusive, and she was not going to start now when the prize was so close she could almost feel its scent in her nostrils.

'Lebanon, as far as I know,' the fop replied. 'Macao,' he added, signalling he had only one card left.

Evelyn smiled a genuine, victorious smile. Tonight, she was going to take the prize. Every prize she wanted. 'Double macao,' she said and threw a seven of hearts and a seven of clubs upon the table.

For a moment, silence reigned. The men looked at her, then at the cards, and then at the pile of guineas gleaming to the side of the playing area. Evelyn supposed they were imagining a farewell to the coins glinting in the candlelight.

The brown-haired popinjay threw his remaining card down and rose, throwing his chair back violently. 'You are a cheat,' he accused Evelyn. 'I know how many sevens of clubs there were in that deck! You couldn't have had one.'

'Then your mathematics might not be your stronger suit,' Evelyn replied acidly, rising in turn, her hand hovering – just in case – over the hilt of her sabre. 'Any more than gambling is.'

'You are going to be cutting your witticisms to the Lady Proserpine in person.' He drew his own weapon, shifting to the combat stance. The men around him backed away, but no one intervened.

'Only if you would accompany me to her husband.' Evelyn positioned her feet in the correct duelling pose without much thought.

The fop didn't need any further provocation. He lunged straight at her, only a swift movement to the left saving Evelyn from being speared through the heart.

Evelyn had exuberance aplenty in her blood tonight, but he had quite as much rage. His extravagant betting on this turn of macao must have come not from lavish funds but from desperation over their dwindling. Evelyn was not going to let herself be run through for the sake of someone else's financial embarrassment.

The blades struck against each other, filling the air with thin, almost silvery metallic clanging. The players at other tables stopped their games and rose or at least turned, watching the fight.

A step, a lunge, drawing back, and sidestepping an attack. A step, a lunge, drawing back, and sidestepping an attack. The pattern repeated over and over, but Evelyn felt no tiredness. On the contrary, her veins sang with life. Here, on the edge of death, she felt alive. She felt sure.

Melanie exclaimed something behind her back, but Evelyn could not afford to pay her attention. She kept her focus on her enemy and was rewarded with scoring a hit, and below the knee, his leg blossomed with crimson.

The elation lasted but a second. The next moment, Evelyn's arms were grabbed from behind and pinned to her back too quickly for her to take action. The sabre fell out of her slackened fingers. 'What is the meaning of this?' she demanded, turning her head and seeing a grim man with broad shoulders. Out of the corner of her eye, she could see her opponent being disarmed and grasped in place by a man who could have been her captor's brother.

The man behind her said, 'Mr Congreve doesn't want trouble. If you have a quarrel with that fellow, take it outside.'

Mr Congreve, what a name to choose. Why not Sheridan? Why not Shakespeare? Evelyn nodded, her blood slowly cooling. She had gotten the information they came here for. She would have dearly liked to continue the quarrel in question in the street, but she suspected Miss Bright would have vapours if she tried.

'You both are going to pay for the damage.' The guard nodded. 'Look at those chairs. Do you think Mr Congreve found them in a cesspit or something?'

'He is a government agent,' her opponent suddenly exclaimed, pointing at her. 'He pestered me for the whole game about the men who come here and their movements. No one has seen him here before either! I realized there was something wrong with him at once. That was why I challenged him. Why should I be made to pay for protecting this place from this man's perfidy?'

'You didn't challenge me. You attacked me. If we are to speak of perfidy, start with your own.' The retort sounded childish to her ears, and the guard certainly wasn't listening.

'A government agent, you say?' Evelyn's captor gave Evelyn and Melanie interested looks. 'I'm not going to take a wine-soaked gambler's word on its own. I wasn't born yesterday.'

Hope flared in Evelyn's chest, but then the gambler raised his voice. 'Are you really going to risk them bringing the dogs of law here? Wouldn't you rather deal with them just in case?'

The guard fell silent. Then he jerked Evelyn's hands towards him and said, 'Let Mr Congreve decide this. You are coming to him.'

This was all Lady Evelyn's fault.

Rarely did Melanie feel her thoughts boil with such anger, even if it needed to be kept beneath the surface.

If only this woman knew what discretion was, what modesty was. If only she knew when and where to stop. If only she wasn't so determined to show off, they wouldn't have been in this pickle now. Did Lady Evelyn really need that final flourish of winning since the sum she staked upon the outcome of the turn wasn't even that great? Couldn't she notice, the way Melanie noticed, their partner in the game was a tawdry rake down on his luck, who would be desperate to win the money? Hadn't she noticed the absence of any jewellery upon him and the pale marks upon his fingers that rings would have once made – the rings he had likely already pawned? Hadn't she noticed the lack of shine on his St. James-made boots?

Lady Evelyn just had to provoke him after they'd already had the information they went there for, and then, instead of trying to calm him with words, she whipped out her sabre and clashed with him as if she were a wild rake herself!

Hoyden was not a strong enough word. Melanie wasn't sure any word would be enough. She thought back to the spectacle of that brawl. The sabres ringing against each other, the chairs falling, the cards falling from the table in a sudden snowfall – and Lady Evelyn Prynne in the middle of it all, her cheeks burning, her dark eyes blazing, and her strikes both precise and quick...

Melanie's thought process was interrupted as the brawny guard flung the door open in front of her. Acknowledging it with a nod, as though he were a footman opening the doors to the dining room – a lady should always be polite – Melanie walked into Mr Congreve's study.

Straightaway, she was struck by the garish opulence of the room. It held a desk made of amboyna and side tables of calamander, armchairs of kingwood, and boxes of Spanish cedar. Melanie thought of her father's study and its furniture of pine and fir and the scent of these woods, gentle as the taste of water.

Here, the smell that rose from the exotic wood was rather musky with a hint of heavy spices. Or, perhaps, that was the result of its unholy marriage with Mr Congreve's eau de cologne.

The owner of Proserpine's Chamber was as impossible to miss as the desk at which he sat – if only thanks to his eyeball-tearing scarlet waistcoat.

'What is it?' he asked, raising his gaze from the ledgers in front of him.

'We brought these.' One of the guards pushed Melanie into the room roughly. The other did the same with Evelyn. 'Henry Agnew said these men were from high up and wanted to tattle on you.'

'Henry Agnew says a lot of things. Mostly those that allow him to avoid his debts.' Mr Congreve, if that was his real name, looked at them, and then his flint-hard grey eyes widened slightly in surprise. 'God and all his saints preserve us. Are you two blind? These are not men at all. These are girls if I've ever seen one – and I've seen many.'

'Girls?' One of the guards looked at them with astonishment. 'But I'd have sworn—'

'That's because you have your eyes on your backside. Have you never seen a Covent Garden nun trying to sneak in here to ply her trade?'

'We are no such thing!' Melanie's cheeks heated with indignation.

Mr Congreve looked at her with a kind of cold disdain. 'I don't think I gave the harlot permission to speak.'

Lady Evelyn slipped out of the guard's grasp and lunged across the room to the desk. She gave the owner of the gaming hell a resounding slap. No one calls her a harlot in my presence,' she said, standing tall. 'No one.'

'Melanie could only look at her with molten admiration. A dangerous silence hung over the room. Mr Congreve's cheek flamed from the blow, and he stared at Evelyn, his gaze heavy and hard.

'I was of a mind to simply leave you with a reminder not to cross on my girls' territory and let you go,' he said. 'Shear your hair to make you remember it for long enough, perhaps. But for that, they are going to find you with the spring tide. Both of you.'

In the space between one breath and another, Melanie's heart froze in terror. Lightning-fast, Lady Evelyn reached into her right boot and produced a dagger. One of the guards sprang toward her and attempted to grab the dagger. Evelyn stepped back, moved forward, and jabbed the man in the ribs. He grabbed her arm and yanked, but she managed to escape his grasp.

The second guard grabbed her wrist, struggling to get the weapon away from Evelyn. He laughed and tightened his grip. Evelyn's hold on her dagger loosened, and it tumbled to the carpeted floor. The first guard picked up her dagger and swung it up toward Evelyn's throat. She sidestepped the attack, and the blade was buried in her shoulder. The air filled with the metallic tang of blood.

While the guard was occupied, Melanie jumped to the guard's side and drew the pistol from his belt. The cold of the weapon against her palms was frightening and foreign. She clutched it with both hands, raised it, and pointed it at Mr Congreve while keeping an eye on Evelyn. One of the guards had retrieved the dagger, and he pushed the point of the blade against Evelyn's scarred throat while the other guard held her.

Melanie had never seen a look of such utter terror on the Prynne heiress's face. Without hesitation, Melanie put her finger on the trigger. 'Let her go.' She heard her own voice as if it was reaching her from some distant glacier. It was not shivering, either.

'Or what?' one of the guards asked, his grin white as the ivory knickknacks around them.

'Or I shoot.'

'Do you even know how to shoot, little thing?'

'Of course, I do. We Cyprians have to know how to protect ourselves, living outside of the shelter of a husband's home.' She was embroidering freely now as if writing one of those barely truthful travel accounts she had always scoffed at but devoured nonetheless.

'You will never pull that trigger,' he said, but his tone was far from sure.

The gun in her hand was growing heavy, but Melanie only gripped it more firmly. She was not a warrior, she was not even a headstrong heiress, but she would be damned if she allowed these men to harm her friend.

'I will,' she said and moved her finger slightly, completely unsure if she was doing anything right.

My friend. Is Evelyn Prynne really that – my friend? Not my benefactor, not the woman I have to please under all circumstances, but a friend?

Yes. Melanie kept her aim steady. *Danger makes us all equal beneath the mountain sky.*

To her astonishment, the guard obeyed her and stepped away from Evelyn. Immediately, the other woman's hands went up not to her shoulder but to her throat – touching the old scar.

Melanie did not need Evelyn's direction to grasp her hand and run.

Rain washed her blood away, but like in some nightmare sequence, crimson bloomed on Evelyn's upper arm again and again. There was no time to think. Barely stopping, Evelyn bound it tightly with her soaked handkerchief. *Was it entirely clean? Might it make things worse?* The crimson bloomed through it, too.

The water and the cold were shocking after the indolent warmth of the den. Evelyn could still hear the shouts of the astonished players in the wake of their dash back through the hall. She clutched her companion's healthy arm, and they plunged themselves into the gaping mouth of an alley.

The cobbles were slippery and shiny as glass beneath her feet. The furious rain was turning the world into a waterfall. At first, she saw flashes of amber where the water was cut through by the linkboys' lanterns; then everything went black. They were going into the depths of the world which light had never penetrated.

Crooked alleyways were writhing around her. The upper levels of old medieval houses, far from the classical edifices of St. James, were protruding above, half blocking the sky. Evelyn was aware of the wheezing in her breath and the hardness in her chest, and she hoped it didn't mean anything bad.

'Look!' Melanie exclaimed.

'What?' Evelyn rasped. 'They—'

'No. This.' Melanie pulled on her arm, forcing her to turn back a little. 'Look. This plaque.'

Evelyn had to narrow her eyes a little to make out the dark bronze plaque through the darkness and the torrent. *Dr Meryon. Medical services.* Raising her head, she made out a sign with a pestle and mortar creaking in the wind. 'This seems too good to be true,' she managed to say.

'I hope you don't think it a trap?'

'No, but it can become one. Do you really think Mr Congreve can't offer this Meryon enough money to give us up? Judging by the state of this plaque ...'

'And judging by the state of your shoulder, you won't make it home unless we do something!' Melanie exclaimed and, pulling on her arm again, dragged her to the doors.

Evelyn wasn't sure what made her obey – the crying pain in her shoulder or the sheer astonishment at the girl's forceful insistence.

'Open to us, please!' Melanie shouted, banging on the door with her little fist. 'A woman is wounded!'

Ever the polite little lady. Evelyn winced.

After a few harrowing heartbeats, the door opened, revealing a young man – a younger man than she had expected after seeing a physician's plaque – in a nightshirt standing on the threshold. 'What is it?' he asked sleepily. He visibly took in Evelyn's bloodied form, and his eyes went wide. 'Get in quickly,' he commanded, stepping aside.

We could have been a burglar's decoy, Evelyn thought. *We could have been criminals ourselves.*

Of course, the ready admittance didn't mean he wasn't going to sell them for coin later on. Their best hope lay in the hope that the rain would wash away the bloody trail her wound left in its wake quickly enough for their pursuers to lose them.

He led them quickly through the smallest withdrawing room she had ever seen. It was shrouded in darkness – the candles having been long since blown out although a faint whiff of cheap tallow still wafted in the air. The physician opened a door at the back – probably the chamber where he usually saw his patients. He lit the tallow stubs there quickly and expertly – so much so that Evelyn couldn't think but wonder how often he suffered such nightly invasions.

'This wound did not reach the bone,' he proclaimed. 'But it's still dangerous if—'

He didn't get to finish the sentence. From beyond the small room, from where the entrance door was located, a few forceful knocks sounded.

Evelyn froze. *Here it comes.*

Out of the corner of her eye, she saw Melanie blanch with horror. The younger woman's fingers were still grasping the palm of her healthy hand, wet with the rain and the sweat of combat. And the sweat of fear.

Whom was she trying to deceive?

'What do you want?' The physician's muffled voice reached them through the closed door of the patients' room.

'We're looking for two women. One dark, one all doll like. The dark one has a gash in her shoulder.'

Evelyn thought they could hear the beating of her heart through the walls.

'I haven't seen any women tonight. This is not this sort of house.'

'I'm not in it for jokes, Wharton. You know who I work for. He is going to make it worth your while.'

No. They were not going to take her and skewer her like a pig. Evelyn looked at the small window in the room, and gripping Melanie's hand, she all but dragged her to it.

'What are you doing?' Melanie whispered.

'Getting out of here before we are both killed.'

'You aren't going to make it! Look at your shoulder—'

'Do you think I have a better chance against those ruffians?' Evelyn hissed. 'See that stool? It should be enough for both of us to reach—b'

She realized that Melanie wasn't listening to her. She was listening to the man beyond the wall.

'I have more than enough,' Dr Wharton's voice came through clearly, for he must have raised it. 'There are no wounded girls in the house. I know whom you work for indeed. Even if there were, I wouldn't have given them up to you.'

'Then you won't mind if we came in and looked, will you?'

'If you want to. But I've just treated a patient with smallpox tonight.'

'How do I know you are not lying?'

'Be my guest, if you want to check. But if you catch the pestilence yourself, don't come to me for treatment. My house is going to be closed to you.'

The next sound Evelyn heard was that of silence and then a slammed door.

When Melanie helped Dr Wharton strip off Lady Evelyn's waistcoat and shirt, she gasped at the sight. The wound glistened darkly in the candlelight, the bleeding showing no sign of stopping.

'Hold her,' the physician told Melanie. 'This may hurt.' He took one of the jars upon the many shelves, slathered his fingers with a green ointment, and rubbed it into the gash.

Melanie held her. She held her tight. Contrary to what Dr Wharton probably expected, Evelyn did not thrash all that much. Instead, she howled. Melanie could find no other word for this wild sound that seemed to belong in a dark forest.

Evelyn's throat was arched, and white, and pale like moonlight itself.

'I know it hurts,' Dr Wharton murmured soothingly. 'But you need this unless you want your wound to fester.' He paused, turning to Melanie. 'I take it you haven't brought any lint with you?' he asked almost with resignation. It seemed they were not the first patients here who brought no supplies – or, perhaps, could not afford them.

She shook her head apologetically.

'It's no bother,' he assured her. 'I could find some ...' He rummaged through the shelves. 'No, no paper left for plastering. But, perhaps ... ah, yes, here it is.' He produced what looked like a rag, grey with washing. 'This should do.'

As the cloth tightened around her wound and the pain abated, Evelyn quietened and was now sitting with her eyes closed. Her face was utterly white, her raven hair framing it darkly.

Melanie did her best not to look at what was below her neck, at the soft outlines in the shadows. Her gaze still strayed there – she would have said, to her shame, but the utter terror of the evening had burnt that emotion out of her. It would need a rest and a morning light to regrow.

She thought of the opulence of the bagnio, of Lady Evelyn's silhouette she could glimpse under her chemise. Back then, it seemed to her the height of embarrassment, the most mortifying situation she could have found herself in.

She was naïve.

'I have a double bed,' Dr Wharton continued. 'You can spend the night there.'

'You really don't have to ...' Melanie started.

'It's a trifle. I will not die if I spend one night on the sofa.' He looked at Evelyn, evidently judging her finally capable of rational speech. 'May I ask what was the reason for the attack? A wild customer?'

Evelyn looked straight at him. In the half-darkness of the room, her great eyes seemed like twin black moons. 'I am not who you think I am,' she said. 'Once I am home, I promise, you are going to be rewarded for this.'

Once I am home. Rationally, Melanie knew that, now that they were in relative safety, it would happen very soon. A sedan chair would likely take them to the Prynnes' house tomorrow morning. But, in her heart, home seemed terribly far away.

Once I am home. Melanie recalled the terrible helplessness that gripped her in Mr Congreve's study. How like the help-lessness of being an outcast at a ball it was, but at the same time, how much worse. How infinitely, infinitely worse.

She recalled the deadly weight of a pistol in her grasp. If not for that weapon, she and Lady Evelyn would have likely been on their way to the Thames embankment now, their bodies lifeless in someone else's grip.

Melanie remembered Evelyn's offer of private lessons. She had no intention of transforming into a Scythian Amazon, but perhaps, having the means to protect one's friends was not such a terrible thing.

'Thank you,' Evelyn said in the darkness of the bedroom.

'For what?' Melanie raised her head. She had decided not to undress for the night, and it was not simply a matter of modesty. The draughts in this house were too strong.

Lady Evelyn seemed to have agreed on the same as though they exchanged thoughts without a single word needing to be spoken. Melanie couldn't help but feel pleased the stubborn heiress decided to see sense in this matter; for once, she was followingMelanie's advice and not simply the voice of her own reason.

'For saving us, of course. If you hadn't picked up that pistol, we might have died.'

'It was on the spur of the moment.' Melanie blushed. 'I was barely thinking.'

'It's all the more commendable, if that was your first thought.' Evelyn lay down next to her, drawing a single woollen blanket over them.

Melanie wrapped her arms around her. After all, the night was likely to be cold, and it would be better for both of them if they were to seek warmth in each other's bodies. There was a warmth in her companion indeed – a kind of condensed heat, burning through the young woman's skin. Without thinking, Melanie entangled her limbs with hers.

Yes. This certainly felt much better.

'I was surprised you were in any way inclined to follow me to Lebanon,' Evelyn said. 'Much less to save me from captivity.'

'I would have done the same for any fellow human being.' No sooner had the response left Melanie's tongue than she realized its falseness. No, she wouldn't have done the same. She wouldn't have thrown sense and propriety to the wind for any person – not, perhaps, even for some of the friends from her old life before the tragedy struck. There was something in this dark-eyed woman, with her stark-raven hair and intense pallor, that made her suspend her usual mode of thought.

'You are a better Christian than I am, in that case. Do you truly take the maxim of loving your enemies to such an extent?'

'Why would you be my enemy?'

'Well, not me, perhaps. But you surely have reasons to resent my uncle, don't you?'

'I don't know. Do I?' Melanie frowned. In the murky air of the bedroom, she could see the perturbed glitter in her companion's eyes.

'Are you telling me you don't know?' Evelyn asked.

'Don't know what?'

'That my uncle was the one who helped your father with the act that granted him the divorce.'

'Sir Owen did this?' Melanie froze.

If she stopped to think about this for a second, it seemed clearer than day, clearer than the spring sky. Her father had never been a grand figure even in his own county; how else would he have been able to secure the expensive and tortuous legal separation but through his old friend and political patron?

Melanie had never quite believed the divorce was going to go through. In the beginning, of course, she was quite sure even the fight between her parents was merely a temporary thing.

When she came down to breakfast that memorable morning all those months ago, her hands had been cold and her head buzzing with questions. All through the preceding night, he remained in her room, sleepless, standing, listening at the door, hoping to catch something of what was being said – or shouted – in her parents' bedroom just across the corridor. She heard something resembling *disgrace*, *wanton*, and even an unspeakable word she had only ever encountered in its meaning of *lazy*, but that now, she strongly suspected, was taking on a different meaning entirely. It was like being locked in one's room while the city outside one's window was being sacked or Vesuvius was erupting and thinking herself somehow safe from the calamity. It *was* a calamity – Melanie felt that in her bones. However, once the pale, soothing rays of the morning sun streaked across her bed, a new hope bloomed within her: a hope that whatever happened in the night would have settled down by morning like a storm.

The hope shattered as soon as they settled for breakfast. Her father had been there, his silence stone-like, and one of her two brothers, too, the older one being away in the militia and spared the grisly hours of the bedsheet scandal. Of what Melanie had not yet learnt was a bedsheet scandal.

Her mother's chair gaped with absence.

It was not at once that Melanie mustered the courage to ask a direct question. By the time her father's plate grew near empty and she decided his spirit must have been somewhat mollified, she enquired, her voice a touch tremulous:

'Is mother unwell?'

Her father looked at her, and for a second, it was a glare of the kind she had never seen from him. Then it softened, as it always did when met with the gaze of his dutiful only daughter. 'Your mother is away, Melanie.'

'Away?' It seemed impossible that Mother was going to leave to make any call, even the shortest one, without either saying goodbye to her daughter or offering to take her along. And at this hour? 'Do you mean ... on a visit?'

'On a visit to her family, yes. She left at dawn.'

Stranger and stranger.

'Is she going to stay away for long?'

'Forever, if father has any say in it,' her younger brother piped up – and almost earned a cuffing on the back of his head. Nonetheless, he had all the glowing smugness of the man of the world he fancied himself to be at sixteen.

'Forever?' Melanie's head spun in a sudden vertigo. 'What do you mean? Why?' Some of the words, the hideous night-time words, flared up their heads in her memory again, like some ugly hydras.

They tried to whisper the truth to her, but she turned away from it and looked at her father with wide eyes full of frightened innocence.

'Me and your mother are going to be separated,' he replied crisply, looking up from his plate.

'By law?' This time, both Melanie and her brother looked at him with astonishment.

'If I have anything to do with it, yes.'

'But Father,' her brother said, 'we are going to be in the papers!'

'She would deserve it.'

'Father.' Melanie's palms grew cold and clammy. 'What has mother done?'

For a second, silence reigned over the profusion of porcelain and glass.

Then Melanie's brother – her wily, well-informed brother, a boy from whom the world required no frightened innocence – turned to her and said:

'Haven't you seen it yesterday?'

'I returned from the hunt ball very late.' She remembered the twilight hours at the ball, her father tiring of the cacophony and leaving her in the chaperoned care of her Aunt Annabel. One dance after another, all in a glittering succession, the hour when her brilliant fate seemed to be sealed for the future. Wasn't she, after all, the belle of the ball, the Evelina, the Belinda of the evening?

'It seemed,' her father said, 'when your mother pleaded headache to remain home, she called a physician indeed but with other concerns on her mind.'

The truth was already crawling out of its lair, its tentacles covered with slime and whispering secrets.

'You mean ...'

'I mean,' he said, his voice was heavy and measured, as if he were dropping boulders, 'that I caught your mother with him in a rather obvious situation.'

'No!' Melanie gasped audibly. 'That – I mean – there must have been some mistake ...'

'As I said, the situation had been rather obvious.'

'How ... how obvious?'

'Horizontally,' her younger brother said with mischievous relish, a still-child privy now to adult secrets and delighted by the fact.

The world swam in front of her eyes.

'If you faint, I can hardly call a doctor to your bedside.' There was a familiar twinkle in her father's eye now. There was an amusing touch to his tone. There was something from the life she remembered. Except, of course, now her life had been cleft in two.

For seemingly no reason at all, Melanie remembered the morning of her first bleeding, not so many years ago, and the sight of her white linen nightgown stained with crimson gore. All her life had been made of white linen – examples of Christian fortitude and ladylike modesty, the quiet pride of being far from both the purple excesses of the ton and the mud-coloured vulgarity of the newly rich, the pristine virtue of chaperoned walks, and the innocent excitement of the first season.

Not that Melanie was ignorant that other colours existed in the world, but she drew some private relief from living in a separate dimension from them. Except now the red of ugly, illicit, physical passion had seeped into their little universe and stained her mother's heart – God forbid, even her body. Except now the gore had spread everywhere, and it made Melanie want to cry for the damned spot to be out of her hand, for she had done nothing, nothing at all –

But it didn't matter what she had done or not done. What mattered was her proximity to the crime.

She remembered the day of her first blood and her mother's soothing, sensible voice explaining to her the matters, showing how to fix a thick bundle of cloth in the shameful place between her thighs, telling her she was not dying at all but becoming a woman.

Melanie used to think that, for her mother, being a woman meant chaste love and duty and moral inspiration of others. Apparently, she was wrong. Was her mother already carrying on her affair those years ago? On the day when she stroked Melanie's hair and bundled the offending nightgown away, did she also think of her lover, come evening? The very thought made Melanie sick. More than ever, more even than on the day that followed that first bleeding, she felt *unclean*.

She rose from the table abruptly. Her first thought was to sequester herself in the library and lose herself in the accounts of some great journey to the West Indies. But this sort of lazing about now struck her as doubly *unclean*. After all, that was the kind of thing a slattern would do, lie down with a book when there was household that needed running. The kind of slattern that would eventually betray every duty of a wife, even if she was herself a wife to no one yet.

Melanie spent the rest of that day seeing to the making of spruce beer. When she came back from the outhouse, her cheeks pink and her hair slightly wet from the effort, she caught her own reflection in the mirror, and it seemed to her the very image of country industriousness – less Melanie than what Melanie ought to be.

When she came back into the house, her father smiled for the first time since the morning, put his evening newspaper away, and called her his buzzing bee. When he did, a pleasure akin to warm honey pooled itself within Melanie's chest.

She pulled herself from the memory. 'I do not blame Sir Owen,' Melanie said, turning to her companion. Her cheek rested against the waterfall of Lady Evelyn's dark hair, spread out upon the sheets. The texture against the tender skin of her face seemed more prickly than silky. Paradoxically, she liked that. 'I definitely do not blame you. My mother was, after all, guilty of ... of what served as the grounds for divorce.'

'Next you are going to say your mother deserved it.'

'Well.' Melanie froze. No one had ever placed her in front of such a stark question before. Indeed, all they did was expect her to acquiesce to what was happening, to remould her flesh and bones to fit the new situation. 'I – I won't be quite so harsh ...'

'I do hope you won't be. If you ask me, our divorce laws are ridiculous. A man is able to cast his wife out of the home she had run for God knows how many years and separate her from the children she bore him for the crime of adultery, yet she cannot disentangle herself from the marriage even if he keeps a whole regiment of mistresses. I know my uncle, for instance, has never lived like a monk.'

'Your uncle is a bachelor,' Melanie reminded her. 'He is within his rights.'

'He would have been within his rights even if he was married. There would have been no punishment for him – certainly none like the kind that befell your mother. I don't think that is just.'

'That's different.' Under the shared coverlet, Melanie was starting to get uncomfortable. 'A wife is bound to be the source of moral instruction in the family. How is she going to bring up her children if she breaks her marriage vows?'

'So, men are incapable of moral instruction? If so, it makes me wonder why most of our schoolmasters are of the masculine sex.'

'That's different,' Melanie repeated, feeling the argument slip away from her.

'Moreover,' Evelyn continued, undaunted, her irises heated in the darkness, 'if that all were true, we would have had to scrutinize the members of Parliament, not ladies of the manor. After all, they are responsible for the moral guidance of the whole nation, not just one family.'

'Well, maybe we should! I would have never supported a man who deceives his loyal wife. I won't support a woman who deceived her loyal husband, either.'

A woman. How distant this term sounded, almost disdainful. This was not the tone Melanie intended, but that was how it came out.

She didn't see it that way; she truly didn't. Her mother had never been anything but gentle with her, anything but patient with her only daughter.

Perhaps, that was part of the reason her betrayal rankled so much. Mud was all the darker when it was staining the robes of an angel.

'How do you know your father was loyal to her?'

Melanie's heart skipped a bit. 'I have no intention of – listening to such things!' she all but hissed, disentangling her limbs from Evelyn's. The warmth of her flesh was gone, and there was a slight regret, as though something faint and fine was extinguished in a moment.

'What are you going to do, tell Dr Wharton about my infamy? You know I am right. Deep in your heart, you know it.'

Melanie did not reply. She willed herself not to. She turned away, staring into the blackness of the walls.

'Have you truly hated your mother so much that you seized on the reason to blame and abandon her when it came?' someone called out from behind her. Melanie turned, quietly furious. Did this impudent heiress really know no rules of civil conduct, no tenets of genteel intercourse?

Suddenly, Melanie remembered this night, and the blood blooming on the other woman's shoulder. *Genteel intercourse indeed.*

'It was not my decision to abandon her. Father forbade us to correspond with her.'

For a moment, there was silence, and Melanie even wondered if she managed to finally come up with a triumphant argument. Then Evelyn spoke up:

'My father never forbade me to speak with my mother, of course. That would have been impossible – they were not separated. He applied a different tool. He spoke of her ways and habits with disdain, taking me in as his confidante. All her desires were pronounced affectations, all longings a sign of spoiled childhood, all modish turns an aristocratic frippery.

'I was so much better than my mother, he said. Me and my brother Paul were strong and forest-spirited children, right out of the pages of Rousseau; she was the relic of the old world that was soon to roll into its well-deserved grave. And I have never refuted it. I have never defended her. Never, until her illness – the illness that killed her because my father thought it unpardonable to break with his habit and take a carriage to find a physician. I have only realized how wrong I had been when standing over her grave. I have no reason to love you, Miss Bright, but I am grateful to you ...'

'For tonight?'

'For tonight and for coming with me at all. I am grateful to you, and this is why I don't want you to live through the same pain.'

'But you do not understand,' Melanie heard a hint of distress in her own voice, 'I have no choice. He forbade me to write to her. He is going to find out if I disobey...'

'How? Is he going to come to London to give you a talking to?'

'I am not going to live in London forever.'

From the other side of the coverlet, Melanie heard nothing more than a sigh, and then a tired voice:

'You are right, Miss Bright. You are not.'

No other words passed between them for the rest of the night; however, Melanie still could not quite find sleep and lay there in the stygian dark, listening to the silence.

Chapter 6

'I take it you are a Catholic?' Evelyn asked the young man sitting opposite her. Despite Dr Edmund Wharton's nervous demeanour, there was no skittishness in his movements. He was eyeing her withdrawing room with fascination, but that was understandable. Evelyn could remember the way she herself was astonished by the urbane luxury of her uncle's household – Sheraton and Hepplewhite furniture, Worcester porcelain on display, and Grecian couches and chairs with the legs of griffins – when she first came here, fleeing from her father's house.

'How did you guess, Lady Evelyn?' the physician asked, his freckled cheeks flushing with a sudden blush of surprise, with the usual ease of gingers.

'You said you went to the University of Gottingen, on the Continent. Of course, it might have been because you failed to pass the exams into Oxford or Cambridge ... or it might have been because both of them only accept students of Anglican persuasion.'

'You have guessed right.' He nodded. 'I must add that I feel no shame about my faith. In my opinion, it is the government persecuting it that should feel abashed.'

'You are a brave man to say so to the face of your prospective employer. How do you know I do not share the same prejudices?'

'I recognize your name. One of the society pages mentioned you once making a fuss at a dinner party by defending the writings of Abbé Raynal.'

'Do you mean his case for abolition of slavery? Let us say I am not ashamed of my own faith either, even if it makes me few friends.' She didn't need many friends either. Sometimes it seemed she needed no one at all. 'Dr Wharton, it might be that me, and, Heavenly dove willing, my friend are going to be travelling to Lebanon in a short while. I would be very grateful if you could accompany us as a physician.'

Dr Edmund Wharton had the good graces not to stare at her. He could not, however, conceal the surprise in his voice:

'To accompany you? But, Lady Evelyn ...' The titled address came after a pause. He still seemed astonished by the fairy-tale-like transformation of his midnight patient from a battered Cyprian to a lady of the ton. 'I would have thought that your uncle has a personal physician of his own?'

'My uncle does. But my uncle might never learn of our little adventure before our departure.'

'Ah. I see.'

'I am afraid you don't, Dr Wharton.' Evelyn could guess his thoughts by the sudden flush on his cheek–. 'It has to do with foreign affairs, not with boudoir passions. I can assure you I am not going across to another continent in order to chase a lover.'

'You have a frank tongue, if I may say so.'

'Of course, you may. I have never refused compliments.'

He took a careful sip of tea. 'I hope you understand, Lady Evelyn, that, if your esteemed uncle disapproves of this journey upon your return, and he is likely to do so, my own reputation would suffer as much as yours.'

'I know a man who is going to take care of that.' Evelyn wasn't sure Lord Howick was going to be thrilled by her request to write to her uncle and absolve her absence in the name of services to the nation. But then, she wasn't here to thrill Lord Howick. She was here to accomplish a task. 'I assure you even if our ways are going to part upon my return, you are going to have the best references I can come up with.'

'Lady Evelyn, may I ask you why? It seems an excessive generosity for merely binding your shoulder.'

Evelyn winced a little at the reminder. Her shoulder was healed now, after a week of staying in bed, and as far as the ton knew, she had been unwell with a spring cold. She was glad to be whole again. She hated feeling helpless.

Besides, the wound was a handicap to the start of the lessons she promised Melanie, and she fully intended to fulfil every promise she made to Melanie.

'It is not for the shoulder,' she said. 'It is for having honour.'

'In that case, you overestimate my possession of honour. I have not a drop of noble blood in my veins.'

My father had his brimming with it. Did it help my mother and brother?

Evelyn couldn't say that out loud. She regretted the fact.

'I promise you you would be able to attend to the noblest patients of the land after we are back from Lebanon.'

If *we are back from Lebanon. But I suspect he understands this one without my needing to say it out loud.*

'Would I still be able to treat my old patients from time to time?'

'Of course. It might cause comments, of course, but I don't think anyone would try to actually prevent you from doing so. Most of your colleagues would have preferred to make their fame and fortune by attending exclusively the denizens of St. James.'

'Let us say I am not like most of my colleagues,' he replied rather stiffly. 'I do not believe that the right to be treated well should be reserved for the select few. I am no wandering saint – I do need to eat and keep a roof over my head. But I make a policy of never refusing a plea for help.'

Heavenly dove help me, a genuine idealist.

Evelyn felt tired, and strangely old. She wondered what it must be like, to view the world in such a clear divide of black and white and with such a staunch commitment for it to remain so.

She couldn't say she didn't pity Dr Wharton. She couldn't say she didn't envy him either.

'If we go to Lebanon together, are you going to pause to treat every unfortunate you encounter, too?'

'I will be honest with you, Lady Evelyn. If someone would ask me for treatment, I would find it very difficult to refuse.'

'I see.'

'I take it you have made your decision.' There was a kind of resigned sadness in his smile.

'I did,' Evelyn said, rising from the floor. 'I am going to ask your patients some questions. Then, if I am satisfied with their answers, I would tell you which day to pack for.'

Melanie didn't at first understand what the fresco on the walls was supposed to represent. Bathed in the pale, golden light of the morning sun rays as the mural was, it transfixed her with beauty and froze her thoughts.

Melanie had never been in the room Lady Evelyn suggested for their first lesson before; somehow, the door always stayed closed to everyone. Now, standing in the strange hexagonal chamber, looking around, Melanie could understand why it must have been opened only for special occasions.

She just never thought a fencing lesson belonged to those. Apparently, in Lady Evelyn's eyes, it did.

She came closer to the mural, trying to understand the subject. Melanie could glimpse the four gates surrounding the city, and beyond –

Beyond stood the most magnificent temple she had ever seen. Dwarfing the settlement, broken as a cake and white as a Christmas snow, the edifice rose in the splendour of columns.

'The Temple of the Sun,' Melanie whispered in awe, growing excited. 'I've read Volney's 1784 description of it – I would have never imagined I would ever see it like this...'

'The early inhabitants called this place Heliopolis in the days of antiquity,' Evelyn commented, coming closer. 'The City of the Sun.'

Under careful attention, the golden vision crumbled into details. Melanie could see now the untidy, overgrown gardens of the new Baalbek, the paltry houses, and even the barking dogs skulking in the alleyways. What would the ancients have said, she wondered, if they saw the city now? The Temple of the Sun was still burning nobly and bright above it all, like a broken lighthouse.

'I do hope you acceded to this lesson because you truly wanted it and not because you simply tried to avoid wounding the person proposing it.'

'Have you ever done such a thing?' Melanie asked, surprised. She would have been hard-pressed to imagine the proud heiress acceding to anything she truly disliked.

'I might have,' Evelyn said after a brief silence. 'It was soon after I came to live with my uncle. I went to see Lord Romney's military review unchaperoned. It was a splendid event – six thousand volunteers from Kent alone – with scores of bright young men dashing across the field and swiping the heads of turnips off with their swords and the Duke of York presiding over a feast in the tented encampment. Uncle was quietly furious when I came back. I thought – I thought nothing of the possibility that he might be.

'Remember, it was not so long ago that I had been running wild in the forests of our estate and taking fencing lessons from a Venezuelan independence fighter. Had uncle spoken to me about maidenly modesty, about Christian deference to one's guardians, his words might have fallen on deaf ears. However, he had spoken to me in the language of power. He told me that, in the world where I am to find myself now, noisy defiance does not win the day, that, if I truly want to be his helpmeet, learning about the highways and byways of politics would not be enough – I would have to make sure there are people who would listen to me.

'There is power to be derived from conforming to the outside rules, he told me, even for a woman. Perhaps, especially for a woman. He told me to look at the Duchess of Devonshire and see what a great influence on the affairs of the nation she had because she always made sure to be a gracious hostess and adhere to decorum. She even managed to get away with her decidedly unorthodox domestic arrangements. And I listened. I listened ...'

'What kind of unorthodox arrangements?' Melanie asked, both dreading the answer and hearing her own voice shiver in eagerness to hear it.

'She lived in a kind of menage with her husband and her best friend.'

'You mean her best friend was her husband's lover? But that's terrible!'

'Not only her husband's lover, if the gossips are to be believed.'

It took a second for the implications to sink in. 'Is such a thing possible?'

'Physically, you mean? Of course, it's possible. Our travellers have often speculated whether women in Oriental harems might not amuse themselves with each other in the absence of their lord husband. I would take it with a grain of salt, after all. Foreign men have never been allowed to speak with the women in question, and their imaginings on the subject have often proceeded from regions other than their brain.'

Melanie decided not to ask any more questions on the subject, lest her blood heated with embarrassment to the point she'd spontaneously combust on the spot.

Instead, she turned again to the fresco.

'Baalbek is in Lebanon, isn't it?'

'To my knowledge, yes. This is partly why I thought to set our lesson here. To get us used to the landscape, as it were.' It was hard to discern whether Lady Evelyn was earnest or joking.

'Not to rob me of my breath?'

'Perhaps that, too.' Lady Evelyn came closer.

The grass on the mural was strewn with stones and cornices, broken columns and mutilated capitals, as if it had been the setting of some titan's rage.

The morning air was silent. Melanie walked around, touching the wall as if she could feel a shattered stone beneath her fingers sometimes, discerning the lush vegetative patterns that once adorned it. There were tablets in the shape of lozenges that must have once adorned the very roof of the temple. Melanie knelt down, gazing at them. She could see some people and guessed at some of the mythological figures they portrayed – Diana with her moon and bow and Leda with her swan. Shards of a vanished world.

'Makes one think, doesn't it?' Lady Evelyn's cheeks were slightly reddish, as if she were a maiden blushing at her first ball. She must have already gone through some exercises before Melanie's arrival. There was something preternatural about her figure, dark against the young sun. 'Let us begin. The habit of two hours every day has to start somewhere.'

'Every day?'

'What, you weren't expecting to become a master swordswoman from one lesson only, were you?'

I wasn't planning on becoming a master swordswoman at all, Melanie thought but did not say. It would have sounded petty after Evelyn went to all the trouble to set up the lesson.

'What does this court make you think about, you said?' she asked, hoping to divert her attention for a while and delay the inevitable.

'Oh, the usual things. The fragility of mortal bones.' For a second only, Evelyn's nonchalant tone deepened, and she blinked in a rather strange way, her eyes growing distant and glassy. 'Imagine all the empires that worshipped on this spot. They must have all considered themselves to be immortal.'

'The Romans were famous for their pride,' Melanie agreed.

'Not just the Romans. Before them, the locals worshipped Astarte here and Tammuz, her dead consort. It was only much later that the gracious Hellenes transfigured these into Aphrodite and Adonis. The goddess of old was made of far less gentle stuff. She sat on a throne flanked by lions and was served by youths who poured the blood of their manhood into her vessels.' Without a further word, Evelyn offered Melanie one of the sabres, hilt first.

Melanie took it. 'Is that how one holds it?'

Evelyn shook her head and covered her gripping hand with her own. Evelyn's skin felt dry in the heating air and possessed heat in its own right. 'No, no,' she said with sudden softness, moving Melanie's fingers in what was less a direction than a suggestion of a caress. 'You do not have to grasp it as though it were a pestle to your mortar. Hold it firmly, yes – but lightly. Imagine it were an extension of your hand.'

Melanie felt her breath catch. 'Like this?' she whispered, relaxing her hand slightly.

'Much better.'

While the morning sun glinted upon the steel of the sabres, Evelyn spent a much more considerable time setting her companion in the right stance with her left foot behind, perpendicular to the right, and no more than a foot's length behind them. Melanie could feel small bouts of impatience bursting behind her words like fireworks, but it was only once or twice that she let them through and then suppressed them quickly enough.

Melanie wondered what Lady Evelyn might have been like in those wild years as her father's daughter, deprived of genteel education and left to scavenge her own knowledge in the world. She imagined coming upon her in those dusky years on an impossible visit in some shadowy growth – a Miranda recognizing a Caliban. Would she have recoiled from the vision? Or would she have come closer to look into its dark eyes?

'Now let us work on your inside guard,' Lady Evelyn said, her back straight, every inch dictated by her uncle's polish. 'Raise your wrist like this – not the whole hand, only the wrist. Blade up. Like that. Make sure it covers the high line. Wonderful. You are a natural. They should consider your application to the militia together with your brother's.'

'Hardly.' Melanie was flustered, willing every muscle to keep the guard up exactly as she was told. 'How many types of guard are there?'

'Three main ones: inside, outside, and medium. There is also the hanging guard, but it's rarely used except for defence.'

'Tell me.'

'I've heard it's a rather vogueish move in some military gymnasia or, at least, had been so since Schmidt's *Fechtkunst* was translated into English. You raise your hand almost to the level of your head and point the sabre downward, at your opponent's left hip. Like this.'

'It doesn't seem too hard,' Melanie observed.

'That is because you had stood in it for exactly a second. A guard is supposed to be easy on the wrist, or else it is going to do your enemy's job for him by tiring you out. Use it only to retreat under after you've made an attack.'

'I will make sure to do so,' Melanie commented with all the dryness of someone who knows full well they are never going to find themselves in such a situation.

'Splendid,' Evelyn replied without a hint of irony. 'Let me show you how to make the attack in question. Lunge by stepping forth with your right foot and extending your left leg back like this.' She showed her, moving quickly, with an impossible, metallic grace.

For a second, time seemed suspended as Melanie watched her. The older woman's leg straightened in parallel to the ground and quivering slightly, as though a violin string a moment after the music died.

'Try and repeat my movement.'

Melanie did so, feeling acutely aware as never before – not even when climbing the wall – of the screaming inappropriateness of her outfit, of her current activity, of this situation. There was some obscene, rank physicality in the position – legs spread far, sword extended – that made her think, once again, of the red stains on white linen.

'You have a wonderful posture,' Evelyn commented. 'Would you like us to try and spar?'

'Spar?' Melanie froze. 'What if I hurt you?'

'Don't worry, the ends are blunted. I just want to look at your footwork and your defences.'

'But I could still bruise you.' Partly, Melanie meant Evelyn could bruise her . But only partly.

'I am not going to hurt you,' Evelyn added in a honey-soothing whisper. 'I promise that to you, Miss Bright.'

'Melanie.' There was a warm wind upon her skin, and her whole being seemed to be open to it. 'I think, given everything we have been through, you can call me Melanie. As befits my friend.'

'Your friend?' Lady Evelyn smiled with only the corners of her mouth. 'I think I like the notion. Now, *en garde* ... Melanie.'

The younger woman shifted into the position hurriedly, her limbs obeying with the readiness of someone who had spent years following the instructions of a dancing master. When she did so, Evelyn was already in position.

They started with circling each other warily, as if unknown magic had transformed them into animals armed with sharp claws, alert to each other's scent. Then Lady Evelyn began her attacks.

They were carefully couched, ballet-like, child-like attacks – even Melanie, with her almost non-existent expertise in the art, could see that. Still, she couldn't miss the excitement burning in her opponent's cheeks, the breath growing shorter not with exertion – they had, after all, barely started – but with desire.

Melanie parried, taking the attacks upon the forte of her blade, or stepped out of their range.

'You are a nimble thing,' Evelyn called out. 'I have noticed that in that ballroom. I should have guessed you are going to be good at this, too.'

They were circling the hexagon of the room. Melanie took great care not to extend her sword arm too much, to keep her footwork pure, and to keep her grip light. It felt as if her mind was fractured into a thousand pieces.

'Are you afraid to hurt me?' Evelyn asked. Her dark eyes were glittering, and Melanie wondered if she had missed her sabre lessons during the genteel years of living with her uncle. 'Don't be. I know how to evade a novice's thrust.'

'But ...'

'But what?' The older woman inclined her head, opening her arms and her chest for the attack. 'Despite what I said, this is not a ballroom. This is not a place for maidenly timidity.'

Everywhere is a place for maidenly timidity, Melanie thought. Blood was thrumming in her head. 'I cannot,' she said aloud. 'I am giving you all I have.'

'Not quite everything. Perhaps, it is not about being careful?' Evelyn taunted. 'Perhaps, you simply lack the elan for this art?'

'I lack nothing.' To her inner mortification, Melanie ground her teeth, and she moved forwards. All the irritation that had been simmering beneath the surface since the day she had been introduced to the stately heiress burst forth, like a red rush of blood. How dare this woman look down upon her for knowing her role, her place, her lessons. How dare she despise Melanie's ways when her own father's name was a byword for political scandal. How dare she—

Without so much as a thought, Melanie rushed into a quick, sharp lunge and extended her sword arm forward. Had this been a real fight, her opponent would have already been impaled upon the sabre.

Had said opponent not been as quick as Evelyn, that was. The dark-haired lady merely retreated two steps, raised her own sabre, and, as soon as Melanie returned to the inside guard, executed a quick attack. Melanie felt a brief, ringing pain in her wrist, and the sabre clattered out of her hand and fell upon the polished floor.

'You are disarmed,' Evelyn said, the point of her sabre hovering gently a centimetre away from Melanie's chest and her beating heart. Slowly, with mesmerizing care, she raised her sword and tipped Melanie's chin up with the flat of the blade. 'You are disarmed, and therefore, you are dead.'

Lady Evelyn lowered her arm, and breathing heavily, she stepped away from her. 'But, for the first time, you were brilliant,' she added. 'I am going to make a swordswoman of you if that is the only thing I am going to accomplish on this journey.'

'You would need my agreement for that.'

'Am I not going to receive one?' Evelyn raised her eyebrows. 'I was under the impression that you've enjoyed our lesson.'

'It was difficult.'

'All worthwhile things in life are. Had your first sewing lesson not been difficult?'

It was obviously a mere figure of speech; however, Melanie actually thought back to the day when her mother had put a needle in her fingers for the first time and showed her how to attach the thread. It was a thread of verdant green. Other women – more sensible mistresses of the house, perhaps – would have started with the plainer, cheaper black or white. However, Melanie's mother was of the opinion that, since a child's mind was easier to capture with the displays of the bright and the beautiful, it would be more humane and more practical to make use of this quality instead of trying to override it.

Sun was streaming through the windows of their drawing room, and it felt as though Melanie's feet did not touch the floor. Her heart purred and curled like a kitten when her mother first praised her clumsy attempt at a cross-stitch.

Melanie recalled all the whispers bandied about behind her back by the genteel society of the country. All the venomous euphemists dissolving in the perfumed air and all the epithets hissed between the teeth. She suddenly imagined facing one of those respectable matrons or sanctimonious young wives with a sabre in her hand, heated and poised, and calling them to answer.

Say what you whispered aloud, loud and clear. Then let us see how pure your soul is.

'You are under no obligation to go to Lebanon with me,' Evelyn said, pacing the room, the bed strewn with ghosts of diaphanous dresses and ruder silhouettes of riding habits. 'In fact, I'd rather you didn't.'

'Why?'

'For one thing, you don't speak the language.'

'You do, and I promise not to stray from you a step.'

'For another, you don't know the customs.'

'I have read so much about them in my adolescence that I might be better acquainted with them than many others.' Melanie caught herself before saying than you. Despite what happened on the night of their mission into the gambling den, she was still a disgraced daughter of the gentry and her companion a great lady. It would not have done to forget that.

'Still, the streets of Beirut are hardly your usual milieu.'

'They are not yours either.'

'I can protect myself, if needs be.'

'But not keep yourself out of trouble. That is what you need me for. I have already told you that when you just accepted this mission.'

Is it truly the only reason?. Keeping her out of trouble? Do you truly derive no thrill from the prospect of adventure to the lands you used to dream about?

Melanie had dreamed of visiting them properly and re-spectably, as a diplomat's spouse, but that most likely would never happen because of the scandal.. She has always been too reasonable and level-headed to seek empty excitement.

The fact had not changed over these last few weeks. Not a step.

'Why would you care?' Evelyn asked. 'Have you grown to like my company so much?' It was not hard to discern the sarcasm in her voice.

'I have never stopped liking my duties.'

'It is the duty of a host to protect her guest, not the other way around.'

'That depends on the host and on the guest.'

'Have you forgotten the reason for your coming to London in the first place? You did it to cleanse your reputation under my wing, to re-enter society, perhaps to be introduced to some eligible suitors. Even if our lie about going to the Lake District to make picturesque sketches would work and the absence is not going to damage your standing more than it had already been damaged, you are still going to lose precious time.'

Melanie opened her mouth then closed it. She could not find a reasonable argument to counteract this one, and she was not the woman for witty retorts. Instead, she simply said, 'Perhaps, I have grown to care about you. Perhaps, I want to protect you from danger.'

'Perhaps, I do not need protection.' Evelyn came closer and grasped her wrists lightly but firmly. 'Perhaps, if you attempt to restrain my attempts to fulfil my task, I am going to restrain you, rather literally, and leave you at the nearest inn.' She raised Melanie's arms above her head and pressed her backwards until Melanie's back was flush against the wall.

Melanie's breath caught as she looked up into her companion and tormentor's dark eyes. A barely visible smirk was playing on Lady Evelyn's lips, suggesting the threat was in jest – but only suggesting.

Melanie's instincts screamed for her to retreat, to dissolve into fumbling pleas for forgiveness. Melanie's memory insisted that was the only way to salvage the situation. Melanie's heart prompted her to raise her head and look Evelyn straight in the face as if they were equals. 'I have saved your life in that gaming hell,' she said in a tone that, mere weeks ago, would have seemed shockingly harsh to her ears. 'I hope you don't think me outrageous for expecting a measure of trust and gratitude.'

'I do trust you. It is because I trust you that I want to shield you.'

'Then you are not going to tie me up in a foreign inn.'

'Why so?'

'Because, I suspect, you have come to care for me, too.'

For a second, neither moved. Then Lady Evelyn released her wrists, allowing them to flip back to Melanie's sides as though some sweet tether running through them had snapped. 'Perhaps, I have.'

Melanie said not a single word in return but rejoiced silently, for in that tone, she heard defeat.

Chapter 7

Melanie's first impression of Beirut was that of blue and white, as if the city was painted upon the Delftware that used to be modish in her grandfather's day. The watercolour sky, infinite in its blueness, was merging with the Mediterranean Sea, and the white glitter upon the waves was of the same intense hue as the walls of genteel local houses. The mulberry trees rising above the garden walls were ripe with pale blossoms.

Melanie felt sorrowful that her beloved Lady Mary Montagu had never written a word about this place. Wouldn't that have been wonderful if people at home could conjure up in their minds the colour of the Beiruti sky?

The journey, involving them catching a ship to Malta and later south to Lebanon, had been much less eventful than Melanie had expected. Indeed, she suspected, it would have been much more dangerous had they tried to jostle their ways into one of the once safe countries of Europe, now burning with war.

'I think staying with one of our countrymen would be dangerous.' Lady Evelyn gave her verdict – clearly a fruit of many pontifications within the depths of her mind. 'It would be better if we try to mix with the locals. There are merchant khans in the city, and a good local garb can be bought at the market.'

'I thought the Ottomans were our allies?' Melanie asked. 'Isn't it an Ottoman territory?'

'The Ottomans may be so, but we are not in Turkey proper. The Arab lands have always had independent minds of their own and rarely liked what their overlords in Constantinople told them.'

'She is right.' Joseph Verney nodded. 'Besides, these provinces are rife with spies. French ones and every other kind.'

Melanie was of two minds about allowing a strange man, who used to be a knight of Malta but now kept a mere fencing school, travelling with them when they had no chaperone but each other. However, Lady Evelyn had insisted that, having picked up plenty of Oriental languages during his years of serving the Maltese Cross, Verney would be a helpful companion on the journey.

Melanie kept silent, as she often did, and did not speak aloud – did not even allow herself think overmuch about the fact – that his presence felt like a violation of their sisterly adventure.

While according to Verney and Evelyn, their language skills had been more than a little rusty, it did not take them long to find a merchant khan by merely asking the people in the street. After their meagre luggage was hauled upstairs and Dr Wharton left to tend to his residual seasickness in his room, Melanie was told to wait for them to return from the market and the door of her own allocated chamber was closed.

It was not locked, and Melanie spent the first hour running through the khan like a giddy little girl who discovered a new place of amusement. Every corner promised surprises. The first-floor gallery was supported by six elegant columns with blue tint, and a carved wooden ventilation shaft was set into the vaulted roof, filling the corridors with a pleasant breeze. She had discovered five rooms on one floor and five on another, all their doors reinforced with iron bands and their handles made of copper set to shine by the constant touch of human hands.

All this beauty had a distinct air of being tarnished, faded, diminished over the centuries, but still, the beauty was there.

Melanie spent time imagining how she would have set the description down had she been a literary traveller like Lady Montagu – how she would have painted with mere words the pallor of the marble, the frugal comfort of the rooms, and the pious carvings upon the wooden walls.

At least she thought they were pious carvings. She could understand not a word. Lady Evelyn and Joseph Verney would have been able to read them with ease. That was, after all, the reason why they left her behind and went to the market together.

Melanie imagined them walking together in the sunlight, touching the spread of Eastern cloth in front of them, arguing with the sellers – haggling over the price together, even – giving as good as they got, the way Melanie herself would have never been able to. She thought of their equally dark heads bent together, examining the goods.

He might be infinitely removed from Lady Evelyn's circle, but he still had much more in common with her than Melanie did, and there was nothing Melanie could do about it.

This onset of strange, mournful jealousy was interrupted by the sound of light, decisive steps in the corridor.

'Melanie? Are you awake?' Evelyn said from the other side of the door.

As if she could have fallen asleep! The melancholy turn of her thoughts forgotten, Melanie opened the door and was confronted with the sight of her friend with her arms overflowing with what seemed to be, at first glance, misshapen cuts of white cloth. 'What is this?'

'The kind of robes that the Bedouins of the nearby tribes tend to wear. According to the seller, these would protect us from the sun and allow us to move much better than our native frocks. Of course, the same seller also claimed his wares clothed the Emir of Afghanistan, so ...' Evelyn raised one eyebrow, as if inviting Melanie to decide for herself.

When the cloth, now recognizable as a simple pair of wide trousers, a robe, and a bright sash – the single splash of colour, and something resembling a medieval coif was spread upon the mattress, Evelyn turned away, allowing Melanie the privacy of changing alone.

Melanie slipped out of her gown and dressed quickly as directed.

With the bright day outside, the inside of their temporary accommodation was penetrated by latticed sunlight, rendering the garb shining white. On the other hand, the cotton had been bleached under the merciless summer sun of Lebanon for many years; how else would it be?

Melanie was now dressed in a long cotton shirt, a waistcoat, a single sash of bright blue, and – the source of her current distress – breeches.

'They are hardly the same kind of breeches that Beau Brummel wears.' Evelyn pointed at the breeches. 'Look how wide they are. Why, one would have to labour long and hard to find your shapely legs in them.'

'You must have found them if you think them shapely,' Melanie said, to her own mind, reasonably.

A glance in the mirror soothed her somewhat. While the trousers were unmistakably themselves, the long robe could be, if one squinted, taken for a shapeless sort of gown.

Melanie recalled the night of their disastrous mission to a gaming hell and how uncomfortable she felt in her dandy-like garb. This was different. There were no tight breeches or stockings but free and flowing lines such as one could find in a skirt. At the same time, Melanie could not quite force herself to deny that walking in this outfit was somewhat easier than in her usual clothes.

'I want you to teach me Arabic,' she said, turning to Evelyn abruptly. 'Could you do that?'

As soon as the words were out of her mouth, she froze with belated shock. Was it really her mouth speaking? Where was the anxious desire to please the great lady of the ton, the eagerness to go along with any scheme of hers for the magnificent prize of her uncle's benevolence? She spoke to Lady Evelyn as if they had been merely...

Merely friends.

Lady Evelyn laughed. In contrast to her stark beauty and boisterous spirit, her laughter was quiet and not without a strange, uncanny charm. 'Very well! Last time you wore the garb of a gentleman, you acceded to your fencing lessons; now, in the robes of a Bedouin, you are burning with a desire to learn Arabic. I think, once we are home, I shall dress you in French frocks just to see what happens.'

Melanie laughed along with her and walked to the window. She wanted to bathe her face in sunlight, to feel the afternoon breeze through her robes. She all but pressed her nose against the fine wooden lattice and turned back instantly, full of excitement. 'There is a caravan in the courtyard. If Dubois had really gone to Lebanon, he would have sailed into the same port as we did – maybe he even stayed in the same khan. I think, if we want to find any traces of him, we should start with asking the people who have their own reason to travel.'

Evelyn all but ran down into the courtyard, the tiredness of the long trip to the market forgotten, replaced by excitement. Joseph Verney and Melanie accompanied her.

Before addressing the leader of the caravan, who was in conversation with the khan's delighted proprietor, she paused to take the colourful spectacle in. The leader in question was unmistakably Arab; however, the string of well-dressed if dust-stained merchants alighting from their steeds was as varied as the sand in the sea. There were the fair-skinned Druze, the folk of the mountains; the Christian Maronites, sometimes accompanied by their wives; and the Turks, tall and proud, the bright sashes cutting across their robes reminding Evelyn of her own. Except, of course, the sabres hanging from these most likely had seen far more practice in the outlaw-infested wilderness such caravans had to travel through.

'Forgive us for the intrusion,' Evelyn addressed the leader in Arabic, 'but we have only arrived in this land recently. Where is your road going?'

'To the port at this stage,' the man replied shortly. 'We are bringing the perfume from the Mountains of Sour to the court in Constantinople to adorn the sultan's ladies.'

'Your way must have been long and perilous.'

'Not as perilous as it could have been,' he demurred politely. 'Emir Bashir of the Druze is a friendly one these days. The days of the over-proud Fakr-el-Din are past.'

Out of the corner of her eye, Evelyn noticed how intently – almost avidly –Melanie was listening to their conversation despite not understanding a single word of it. Was she trying to tease the meaning out from the melodic strains of Arabic, like one teases threads out of a tangle?

Evelyn felt a rush of protective tenderness towards the younger woman. Melanie Bright had been raised to never leave the confines of her family's native county, apart from for a season or two; here, thanks to Evelyn, she had to adapt herself to a language foreign to her and a culture unimaginably distant. Not that Evelyn had any doubt about Melanie's aptness for adaptation, but, somehow, it felt strangely dishonest to tax this aptness any further.

I really should start teaching her Arabic as soon as possible.

In her white Bedouin robes, Melanie was looking even more diminutive than she did in a proper muslin ballgown.

Her hair was hidden under the chequered coif, but single threads of blonde have escaped from beneath the cloth, and were now burning up gold in the afternoon sun.

Evelyn blinked, willing herself to return to reality.

She knew the pull that had just tugged at her. She knew the disasters that started with it.

'Do you sometimes take travellers along with you? Travellers who are not traders?' Joseph Verney asked the caravan leader, filling in the lull left by Evelyn's mental absence.

'All the time. Pilgrims travel with us to the shrines of various saints very often. We know it's not right to worship dead men who used to be ordinary humans once, but ...'

'But they pay for their upkeep.'

'A man must eat. Not all voyages are profitable.'

'We are looking for one particular traveller,' Evelyn intervened. 'He might have concealed himself in the guise of a pilgrim and has probably used a false name. We know him as a Frenchman under the name of Vincent Dubois.'

The caravan leader looked pensive for a moment. 'I don't think there was any Frank in my caravan for a long time. I'd have remembered it.'

'Do you happen to know anyone else who might have conducted him through the country?' Evelyn asked, not wanting to acknowledge defeat. *These outlaws that these men fear do not only prey on merchants. It would have been common sense for Dubois to travel with someone.*

'There is a convoy of Bedouins accompanying us for protection,' the trader explained. 'The men of the Ruwallah tribe. They have pitched their tents not far from here. If you'd like, you can ask them.'

It was not as hard as Evelyn feared to find the cave that housed the current encampment of the Ruwallah tribe. They had pitched their tent in the countryside just outside of Beirut, close to the caves that would provide them protection from the elements as well as the khan would have. Talking Miss Bright into approaching it, however, proved a Herculean task.

'But these are Bedouins!' Melanie exclaimed. 'I've heard they are so fierce that even the Turkish Janissaries were afraid of them.'

'The Turkish tax collectors, more like,' Evelyn replied with a light-heartedness she did not feel. 'That, I can readily believe. But we are not trying to take their flocks – therefore, we have nothing to fear.'

'But ...'

'The Bedouins are very pragmatic people, Miss Bright,' Verney commented. 'How would it profit them to slaughter us on the spot? Now, ending up captured and held for ransom again – that is something that can happen to us, of course.'

'Why, thank you, Herr Verney,' Evelyn said sarcastically. 'You've clearly calmed her down.' She turned to Melanie, her heart full of resolve. 'You won't have to say a word,' Evelyn promised. 'I will do the talking.'

For a second, she was afraid Melanie might remind her of the results her doing the talking led to in the gambling den – remind her of her abject failure.

Melanie squeezed Evelyn's gloved hand. 'I wouldn't have been able to do the same if I tried. Remember, I don't speak their tongue.'

'I remember. I also remember that I've promised to teach it to you.'

'You do?' Melanie asked, and it occurred to Evelyn that she might not have been noticed or had promises to her remembered very often in this life.

'Of course.'

'I wish I had a token to give to you as my blessing.'

'What, as if I were a knight riding into a tourney? There is no need.' To be honest, deep inside Evelyn felt she would have been rather grateful for that right now. 'Although, you can give me a chaste kiss.' Without waiting, she got down on her knees and closed her eyes as though the mischief could expunge the nervousness that gripped her.

For a second, there was a hesitation. Then Evelyn felt the cool and silky touch of Miss Bright's lips on her forehead.

'Well,' Evelyn whispered, looking up, 'now I will surely be protected.'

'You will be.' Verney coughed. 'But mostly with my gun.'

Evelyn pushed through a narrow opening of the cave and was grected with biblical darkness and the bleating of cattle.

A score of sheep was standing placidly along one wall, munching chopped straw from their rock-hewn mangers. Along the parallel wall, plain quilts were spread on the ground for sleeping. She picked her way carefully into a low-ceilinged passage to the second chamber. She could see the red light pulsing from within.

Evelyn lowered her head and bent almost in half to squeeze through into the second chamber. Once inside, she straightened to her full height and met the gazes of dozens of men sitting around the fire.

The fire was painting the walls of the cave with orange flickers, making the recesses even deeper and darker. The shadowy figures around the fire were all alive with colour and details. She spotted the man who must be the sheikh of this tribe. There was no visible elevation in his seat – not even a pillow – but he was surrounded by an air of deference. His boots were of costly red leather, and his cloak was covered with stripes.

'Esteemed Sheikh Nasir of the Belka,' Evelyn called out, 'my greetings to you.'

There was a moment of crystal silence, with dozens of gazes turned to her, that made her question the choice of her words.

The richly dressed man by the fire nodded. 'My greetings to you, traveller. What is your name and the name of your father?'

'Evelyn, esteemed sheikh. My father's name is … was … Gerald.'

'What do you seek among the Ruwallah, Evelyn bint Gerald?'

There was a sense of an almost religious ceremony in this plea for hospitality, a feeling deep in Evelyn's bones.

'I seek friendship, esteemed Sheikh.'

'You shall have it.'

'And my companions?'

'Your companions shall have a place by our fire, too,' he declared.

Carefully, Evelyn took her place within the politely parted circle around the roaring flame, amazed by the ease with which this had been accomplished and wondering about a catch – or a trap.

'I am also seeking information, Sheikh Nasir of the Ruwallah,' she said, looking at the desert potentate through the shivering curtain of flame. 'Do you know anything about a Frank by the name of Vincent Dubois?'

:It was as if a tide of sighs had rolled through the gathering. The name was clearly familiar to them. However, the sheikh decided to profess otherwise. 'This man is not my acquaintance, Evelyn bint Gerald. Nor is he known to any of my friends and allies.'

'He is a French agent whose legacy I am seeking.'

'The Ruwallah want no part of the wars beyond the desert.'

'I understand, and I have no desire to enmesh the Ruwallah in them. But it is in the desert that he spent the last years of his life, and it is in the desert that his papers are most likely buried. I know no one else who could know about him as much as a man of your grandeur would.' She flattered him, feeling herself once again at one of the dinner parties in her uncle's London house.

'Do you know the surest way to a gruesome death, Evelyn bint Gerald?' the sheikh asked.

'I hope you are not threatening me?'

'Far be it from me to threaten a guest under my roof! I'm only asking. Do you know the surest way to a gruesome death?'

'I know several.'

'The surest way for a humble man to die is to get caught in the fight between two giants. The Ottomans are one such giants. The French another.'

Evelyn couldn't resist the impulse to look farther into the depths of the cave, beyond the illuminated circle. In the shadows, she could now make out the silhouettes of women tending a much smaller fire, and cooking. The wet, white smoke made her think of rice. They were absorbed in their task and did not meet her gaze. Beyond them, farther still, there was another gateway, a tunnel into the rock; and beyond it, no doubt, another and another and another. A whole world to bury secrets in.

'There might be a reward in there for the Ruwallah,' Evelyn promised.

'We need no golden coins or stone houses. The rewards in which your people trade do not interest me.'

'How about a freedom from the Ottoman tax collectors, then?'

'The sultan is not going to leave us alone.'

'He will if his friends press down on him. My country is a valuable ally of the Sublime Porte. I happen to know a few men who could drop a whisper into Sultan Selim's ear.' She thought about Lord Howick and wondered if he was going to mind fulfilling such a promise given on his behalf.

Then Evelyn straightened her back. Now was not the time to show wavering or fear. Besides, he was the one who pushed her into this mission; it would only be right if he did his part.

'Do you swear on your honour and your blood that you are going to do this for us, Evelyn bint Gerald?'

'I swear on my honour and my blood.'

'Then know this: the man you seek was not a great friend of the Ruwallah, but he rode with us and feasted with us when our pathways crossed in the desert. The last we've heard of him before his death, he was riding towards Aleppo with the Anazeh.'

'Aleppo' Evelyn did her best not to show her disappointment. She was sure the paper treasure of Vincent Dubois was lying somewhere in the desert, somewhere where she could find it with the help of these masters of the wilderness. But a city could become just as much a wilderness and one much easier to disappear in.

'Aleppo.' Sheikh Nasir nodded. 'Our route is stretching there again. We are to sell our carpets and our flocks and buy the treasures of the cities for our warriors and our ladies. You can come with us if you so desire.'

'I desire so very much.' Evelyn added, recalling the stature of the potentate she was speaking with – at least, the evident stature that existed in his own eyes. 'And I thank you for your hospitality, Sheikh Nasir of the Ruwallah.'

'Let it never be said that true courtesy has departed from the world,' the middle-aged man said approvingly. 'We have not many tents; you would have to share with your lady companion. It would not be right for a woman's honour to be sleeping in the same tent as a man not her brother.'

His view on the matter seemed to coincide perfectly with that of the proprietresses of Almack's. She nodded almost automatically before the thought had truly penetrated her mind. When it did, she bristled. This was how it was going to be? She had kept to a solitary room for the earlier part of their journey. Now she was going to suffer a foreign breath, a foreign warmth, a foreign touch –

But it was either that or sleep beneath the stars. Therefore, she gave him the sweetest of her ton smiles as though this suggestion – this direction, if she was being honest – brought her nothing but joy.

Out of the corner of her eye, she saw Melanie Bright looking like a deer pursued by hunters. The young miss apparently did not relish the thought of sharing the tent with her either.

'We are killing no sheep tonight,' Sheikh Nasir continued, 'but we have some beans, and we are frying Yemeni coffee. Gablan,' he addressed a youth sitting to the right side of him – judging by the resemblance, his son, 'pour four dishes of coffee for our guests.'

Evelyn expected the young man to bristle at what was plainly a servant's job; however, he performed the task without so much as a sigh or a look. Soon, all four travellers had a cup of steaming coffee in their hands.

The vessel in her hand was fire-hot. Evelyn did her best to hold it with her fingertips only.

'Drink up,' Sheikh Nasir encouraged her. 'It is the finest. I never serve my people dregs.'

'I believe you, esteemed Sheikh, but...'

'Or, perhaps, you have been accustomed to something finer in your homeland?' He raised his eyebrows. A few men turned towards her, their eyes gleaming as brightly as the swords at their sashes.

Evelyn took a vigorous sip. The bitter coffee scalded her mouth, and she bent almost to the floor in a fit of uncontrollable coughing. She heard good-natured laughs. Several pairs of hands slapped her back. The circle around her grew tighter.

'A double health to you, Sheikh Nasir of the Ruwallah,' she said, looking up. 'May you live long.'

Chapter 8

Later, Evelyn wanted to say she had felt it all along – that, ever since the day broke, she could feel the unsettled strangeness of the situation on her skin, that she heard the murmurs of the conspiracy just out of the range of her hearing. But, in truth, she had to confess to herself that she knew nothing, being as blind as a stunned calf at the Smithfield Market. She knew nothing until, in the depth of the night, she heard the stomping of hooves, the neighing of horses, and the voices of the warriors calling into the darkness.

'What is the meaning of this?' she demanded, all but crawling out of the tent. Her clothes were crumpled after half a night's sleep, and her hair was a veritable crow's nest, but there was nothing she cared about less in the predatory light of the torches.

'Ah, my lady.' Sheikh Nasir, tall even among his warlike entourage and lit brightly in the firelight wheeled his mare about. 'We are riding out for a raid.'

'With whom?' Evelyn asked not without some suspicion.

'You are a curious woman. Does your land not have a proverb about curiosity causing the death of a feline?'

'Perhaps, we could help,' Evelyn offered innocently. 'I am far from being a fainting flower, and my steed is true.' As true as a steed bought in the bazaar of Beirut could be, of course. The same could be said of their weapons, the subpar leavings of the Napoleonic campaign in Egypt that washed up in the Eastern markets several years after the invasion. Still, she felt more comfortable knowing her companions – even the mild-mannered Melanie – were armed adequately.

'We do not require your help,' Sheikh Nasir replied curtly, his earlier courtesy forgotten. 'You are to stay where you are.'

'But—'

'Sleep well, Evelyn bint Gerald.' Sheikh Nasir turned away. 'It is going to be a long day tomorrow.' He trotted in the direction away from the tents, away from the warm and fluttering flame of safety in the wilderness surrounding them, and his brothers-in-arms followed him in a stream of firelight glinting on metal. It was as though they were iron blood flowing in the veins of the tribe, and now they were leaving it.

Leaving it – and their guests – open to any invasion from without.

Evelyn didn't stand watching them for long. As soon as the last Bedouin was out of her sight, she got back into the tent and shook Melanie's shoulder urgently. 'Miss Bright. Melanie. Wake up.'

'What?' the younger woman murmured sleepily. In the dark, Evelyn could see the softness of her curls falling upon her Cupid-like cheek, the Fragonard fairness that even the weeks of arduous travel could not dust. 'Is it morning already?'

'It's worse. Sheikh Nasir is gone.'

'Gone?' Melanie was up in an instant. 'What do you mean, gone?'

'He and all his warriors have ridden out God knows where. He said it's for a raid but did not say upon whom.' Which is strange, her pragmatic, somewhat cynical side noted. It would have been an easy lie to a foreigner unfamiliar with the intricacies of the desert politics and would have, perhaps, won them their guests' complacency.

Unless he didn't need their complacency. Unless he was sure that, by the time they came back in the morning, their guests were going to be dealt with.

'This is preposterous.' Melanie gave her verdict upon hearing the urgent summary of events.

'Do you think he would not have led us intentionally into a trap?'

'No. I think he would not have sacrificed the women and children of their own tribe to whatever enemies lurk in these plains only for the sake of harming us.'

Harming. What a charming habit of understatement Melanie has. Harming instead of killing.

'Perhaps.' Evelyn couldn't help but concede to some of her reasoning. 'Perhaps, his feud with the Ottoman government might mean more. Besides, the wars of the Bedouins are rarely bloody; one usually needs to fear plunder and shame, not murder.'

'Unless one is us?'

'Unless one is us.'

Somewhere, by the more sumptuous tents close to the centre of the camp, lambs tied up for the future slaughter were bleating.

'Even if Nasir was telling the truth,' Evelyn continued, 'even if they have truly departed without any ill intent, it doesn't mean no one is going to fall upon our camp without their design. We would do well to arm ourselves.'

'Arm ourselves!' Melanie jumped up, flinging the quilted coverlet to the side. 'I – you cannot mean. I—'

Evelyn put her hands upon Melanie's shoulders firmly and looked into her eyes. *Such fair eyes. Blue like forget-me-nots.* 'I would never force you to take part,' she said. 'I would never fling your life away. Not because we are friends but because I am a human being with a beating heart. If you would like to, you can stay in the tent. I would be outside and do my best to protect you.'

It was as if Melanie's flesh turned to warm wax beneath her fingers, by the way the fair-haired lady looked at her.

'I won't force you to do that either,' Melanie whispered. 'I ... I know how to hold a sabre, thanks to you, now. I will stand by your side.'

'You don't have to.'

'But I want to. Let no one say that Melanie Bright has not a whit of bravery in her bones.'

'There are different kinds of bravery,' Evelyn said, to her own slight surprise. 'Not all of them have something to do with holding weapons.'

Gently, Melanie cupped her cheek with one hand. 'I cannot huddle here while my friends are standing their ground for me. I have been raised to be brave and capable even if I failed along the way sometimes. I know that there are different kinds of bravery, of courage. I have always been taught the ladylike kind of courage – the quiet, Christian perseverance sort of courage. I used to think it's preposterous for a woman to display the other sort, but ...'

'But?'

'But, had we followed my precepts, we would have been dead in that gaming hell. I am no swordswoman, no Scythian Amazon, and I will never be. But there is a place and time for different sorts of bravery. I know which one I am choosing now. Besides ...'

'Nobody will ever know what happens in the East if we choose not to tell them.' Evelyn couldn't help but allow herself a slight smile.

'Precisely,' Melanie replied with palpable relief in her voice.

It did not take long for them to saddle their horses nor to rouse Dr Wharton or convince him of the peril of the situation. When Evelyn asked about Verney, the physician merely shook his head. 'He rode out with the tribe. I understood that there was some prior agreement about taking part in a raid. I didn't think much of it – he used to be a warrior of the first water, after all, and it stands that he wouldn't want to miss the action now.'

'Rode out with the tribe?' Evelyn's skin grew cold, and her mind grew heated. 'Prior agreement. Heavens, we have all been fools.'

'It might not mean anything.' Melanie squeezed her arm. 'It might still be a genuine raid and him an adventurer hungering for excitement.'

'It might be,' Evelyn replied drily. 'But, in the event that it's not, I would ask you all to get on your horses and take your positions by the entrance to the camp.'

They obeyed her without a word.

It seemed like a bad joke – a doctor, a debutante, and a hoyden whose last fencing lesson with a true master had been years ago. The fairy tale number of three. The jester's number of three.

The cold wind of the night was nipping at Evelyn's skin, and she drew her waistcoat tighter around herself. She couldn't resist the temptation to look back. Her eyes met Melanie's face, faint and translucent in the moonlight. *I should have insisted for her not to come. I should have tied her up with her own sash.*

She couldn't understand such fretting protectiveness where there had been none. Why would she think this way of Miss Bright – of Melanie – and not, say, of Wharton? Evelyn reasoned it was because Wharton was a man and stronger while Melanie's only fighting skills had just been picked up in the last weeks.

The camp was still around them, as though unpeopled in truth. They did not have to wait for long. Evelyn heard them before she saw them: a whole cavalcade of horses' hooves. The first figures she sighted over the crest of surrounding hills looked like night spirits instead of men of flesh and blood, their white camelhair abbas bright and pale.

Evelyn did not waste time shaping words to describe the deadly majesty of the moonlight and the firelight glinting on their sabres. Instead, she raised her weapon and charged forth.

These could not be Nasir's men, for no raid took a mere couple of hours to enact. These men were of a far greater number than even his avalanche of warriors – the size of a formidable cavalry unit.

The size of a formidable cavalry unit, and they were bearing down on them.

Evelyn did not give her friends a sign to follow. She would not be responsible for their deaths. If there was the glory and gore to find here, she was going to find them on her own.

The ride towards the outpouring of warriors was as fast as wind, but it felt like it took decades, the air slow as honey. Evelyn felt no fear, just as she had felt no fear when talking to the French agent and imagining the perilous mission at the court of Bonaparte. Her arm, holding the sabre aloft, knew no tiredness.

Is this how true soldiers feel the seconds before the attack? Moments of time made full as a brimming cup with every feeling sharp as a blade. Riding to meet a certain death, she felt more alive than ever before. More, perhaps, than even when—

No. There were some blasphemies she was not going to allow herself to commit. There was only one chance, one very faint chance, that her madcap plan was going to succeed, and even that chance was slipping out of her fingers now.

Still, she had to try. Not so much for herself as for those behind her.

'I challenge thee to a single combat!' she cried out in her bookish Arabic pointing her sabre at the man at the head of the cavalcade. 'If your honour is true, the victory is going to be yours.'

Heavenly dove, the man stopped in his tracks.

'Clash with me if your bravery is not that of a dog,' Evelyn taunted, feeling her life leaving her veins, like a golden elixir dripping out, with every word. 'Clash with me.'

'Your words are bold.' One of the chieftain's companions raised his voice. 'Let us see your deeds, too, Frank.'

Her gambit worked. Heavenly dove, it worked. She was not going to make a habit of calling out the honour and manhood of Bedouin chieftains, of course. That was a sure way to an early grave. Provided she was going to survive this fight.

The horsemen stopped, clustering around them. In the ensuing circle, the leader raised his sword. So did Evelyn. The dance of steel commenced. Evelyn ducked and dived, evading the deadly swish of the sabre where her head just been. She wished, for a second, that she had Melanie's aptitude for nimble movements and could avoid stabs and slashes just as easily. Since she did not have it, she put her eggs in one basket, and the name of that basket was attack.

Stance. Lunge. Retreat. Stance. Lunge. Retreat. There was nothing apart from it, nothing in the present or the future. The world had shrunk to the point of a steel blade. Maybe this was how she was supposed to live, Evelyn realized with a shocking recognition. *Maybe this is the ultimate truth.*

Her opponent was a skilled swordsman and gave her no moment of respite. Even after a particularly crafty, lightning-fast lunge, Evelyn managed only to slice the cloth protecting his nose and mouth. The pieces of cotton fluttered to the ground slowly.

Not a single man spoke as Evelyn looked into the face of Sheikh Nasir. 'You are not going to get away with this,' she whispered, out of breath. 'The desert is going to resound with your tale of the breaking of the guest-right.'

'You were the one who raised the weapon against me, Frank. The Fid'eh are not going to save you from the rightful death.'

'The Fid'eh? Who are the Fid'eh?'

'Do not pretend ignorance. Your plan to lead us into a trap has been foiled.'

Her sabre in the outside guard, Evelyn straightened to her full height. 'I know that our faiths are different, Sheikh Nasir; I know that your people think mine to be erroneous. But we respect the same prophets, and I can swear by the name of the man from Galilee you hold as sacred as we do that I had no evil intentions when asking you to take me to Aleppo.'

Something shifted in the night air. Sheikh Nasir did not allow her a step outside their circle; however, he lowered his sword. 'You have a silver tongue, Evelyn bint Gerald. But a silver tongue does not always speak the truth.'

'You are a wise man since you know it. Tell me how I might prove my words, and I am going to do it.'

'I have been told by a man I consider a friend and a brother that you were a spy for the Ottoman government that has long desired to humble the Ruwallah and that you have warned the Fid'eh, one of the tribes of the Anazeh, that we are going to be travelling this route to Aleppo.'

'Joseph Verney.' Something stung in her chest. The dark-haired guide had not been her friend or her brother, and yet, he had been a man she trusted. One of the few men she trusted in this new life of hers.

She should not have. She should have kept her heart and mind guarded and aloof, just as she had resolved after what happened in Egypt.

'Joseph Verney.' Sheikh Nasir nodded. 'He had often shared bread and mutton with me and the men under my rule years ago. I had no reason to disbelieve him when he told me about travelling with you to keep an eye on your doings.'

'He was travelling with me because I hired him and paid him,' Evelyn said heavily. 'I take it that it had all been a sham? He was no knight of Malta?'

'No, he really did belong to the fighting men who once defied the great Suleiman on that rocky island of theirs. Then he came to Egypt.'

'How—' Something hit Evelyn. She understood. 'Of course. Bonaparte has turned the knights of Malta out of their house and home ... except for thirty-four men. The thirty-four men he press-ganged into accompanying his expedition to Egypt, all those years ago. Verney must have been one of them. This is where the French got him.'

How could the people at home, people whose very professions were intrigues in the dark, not have known this about him? On the other hand, even such people tended to see what they were prepared to see. Everyone knew about Bonaparte's ignominious treatment of the ancient knightly order.

Sheikh Nasir looked at her now with something that most of all resembled pity. Pity for the poor, easily deceived lady. This was what she had come to.

'Find Verney and bring him to me,' he ordered one of his companions.

Without a sound, the man disappeared through the ranks. There were shouts and unceremonious scuffles, the sheikh's inner circle cutting through the mass like a scythe.

'Who are your other warriors?' Evelyn couldn't help but ask. 'The number of your men who left for the supposed raid was much smaller.' When she translated her words into Arabic in her head, she didn't translate supposed. It was never done to push his own lie into a powerful sheikh's face, even if the deception in question had already been uncovered.

'These are our allies.' Sheikh Nasir straightened his back, looking more than ever like an Old Testament patriarch beneath the starry sky. 'The Ruwallah of the sands and the plain. We were preparing for a reckoning with the Anazeh. As it is, we would be honoured to serve as your escort to Aleppo. You are our guest, and you have suffered because of my ally's deception. I would not have deserved this mantle if I left injustices and slights unanswered.' There was a steely quality to his tone, and Evelyn found herself pitying Joseph Verney.

'My Sheikh.' An out-of-breath man raced up the sheik. 'He is not here.'

'What do you mean, he is not here?'

'He must have slipped away during our ride for the camp. There are a lot of men with us now; far more than a raid would have merited. It must've made it easier to lose him,' the Bedouin reasoned.

'Son of a jackal. No matter. Our world is only vast to the Ottoman officials in their houses of stone. It's impossible to disappear for long from those who truly know the world of the desert and the wild. Let it be known' – Sheikh Nasir's voice grew booming, as if he were addressing the whole of his army – 'that, from this night onwards, Joseph Verney is not our brother but our blood foe. Let the skies be as hot iron to his head, let him find no succour in the storm, and let no vengeance be wrecked upon those who spilled his blood.'

Which is all very well, Evelyn thought, the bitter, distant quality to her mind back again, *but vengeance can wait. Aleppo cannot.*

'You are utterly insane,' Melanie exclaimed once Evelyn staggered back through the ranks of the Ruwallah. 'What on earth made you charge them like a Fury?'

'Fine words for a debutante.' Evelyn couldn't help but tease her. 'Besides, the Furies charged no armies. They pursued matricides and oath breakers. You are confusing them with the Valkyries.'

'Miss Bright is not wrong,' Wharton interjected. 'You could have found your death there and such a death that no physician's skill could have sewn you back together.'

'Thank you for the wonderful imagery for the night, Dr Wharton. I knew what I was doing.'

'Did you?' the man enquired. 'I have rarely treated patients with ailments of the mind, but to me, it looked less like bravery and more like a lack of desire to live.'

For a second, blood seemed to have left Evelyn's face. How – did he know that she – was he right?

No, of course not.

To her eternal gratitude, Melanie came to her help. 'You are being foolish, Dr Wharton. Lady Evelyn has more life in her than me and you put together. She would never want to willingly bleed it all away. She was being recklessly gallant, that is all.' She turned to Evelyn. 'And she must promise never to be so again.'

'Well, I don't think we can expect a united force of Bedouins to charge us again in the future.' Evelyn tried to avoid making a promise.

Melanie met her with a set expression and a pair of raised eyebrows that would not have disgraced a society matron.

'Very well.' Evelyn sighed. 'I promise … promise not to throw myself into a battle with terrible odds, sabre aloft, ever again.'

'This is rather specific,' Wharton said. 'Miss Bright, I suspect my employer is trying to get out of the obligations.'

Irritation rose up within Evelyn's heart. What right did these two have to question her actions and unravel her motives? One was her employee and the other a companion thrust upon her by her uncle.

She looked at Melanie's sabre, still resting peacefully in the sash. She should not have allowed the girl to get out of the tent. Melanie would have been slaughtered if not for Evelyn's desperate throw of the dice. Was it so terrible of Evelyn to be expecting gratitude instead of interrogation?

'It doesn't matter,' Evelyn said curtly. 'What matters is that we get to Aleppo and follow Dubois's footsteps as quickly as possible. Before Verney does.'

'That scoundrel,' Wharton muttered. 'I should have guessed him to be such.'

'How?' Evelyn turned to him. 'His backstory had been perfectly plausible; he was competent and courteous and did his part. Not all villains wear the mark of Cain, Dr Wharton. Some wear pleasant smiles instead.'

'Thank you for the wise lecture, Lady Evelyn,' he replied with mutiny lurking in the spaces between his words.

'How are we going to know where to go in Aleppo?' Melanie asked reasonably. 'Dubois could have stayed anywhere.'

'Not anywhere.' Evelyn shook her head. 'Aleppo is a city quite hostile to Christians in general and foreigners in particular. There is a reason why few of our merchants can be found there despite the splendid cotton of Acre. There are not many households that could have accepted him.'

'We won't be able to comb through them all.'

'It didn't have to be a household,' Wharton said pensively. 'It could have been a monastery.'

'Is there one?' Melanie asked with some disbelief.

'Of course. A community of Maronite monks. I haven't been there myself, but I've heard it's still standing, even if the church is forbidden to ring its bells.'

'I've read that Maronite monasteries did not allow female visitors.'

'That's just the Mar Antonius, the house near Ehden. They are indeed so devoted in their enforcement of the rule that they even have their hens cooped up so that the female birds do not stray into the sacred precincts. The friars of Aleppo are a great deal less strict than that.'

"Besides, the locals' dislike of the foreigners means that we would do well to continue wearing Turkish dress while there,' Evelyn added. 'I am sure we can procure some at the bazaar.'

Which would mean, in turn, that she would be able to gaze at Melanie Bright's well-shaped legs within the wide folds of the Ottoman garb for the days to come.

Chapter 9

'This place seems ... a little deserted,' Melanie said when they stepped beneath the great stone folds of the Maronite monastery of Aleppo. It felt queer to feel the cloth of her old travel dress around her instead of the harsh white cotton of the Turkish garb.

'It is not for long,' she said to herself. Now that they were in possession of funds again, they would be able to procure local clothing in no time at all.

Wait. Did she really have to soothe herself that the return to ordinary, modest manner of dress was not for long? What had this journey done to her?

Nothing, Melanie reasoned, *but convinced me that some situations call for a European dress and others for a Turkish shirt, just as one would not wear a ballgown for a morning bout of riding. Nothing but that. Nothing at all.*

It felt even stranger to see Evelyn changing into her own gown in the enclosed murk of their tent. Melanie did not want to admit it, but she found herself watching her and painting pictures in her mind with her words. How would she have described her older companion's body had she been called to do it for some reason?

Her carriage, iron-straight – except that sounded silly; iron could be moulded into whatever shape one wished, provided it was hot enough.

This iron was cold, then.

Her skin, grown rugged and – oh, the scandal – tanned under the merciless Lebanese sun that covered Melanie's face with unseemly red splotches. Instead of looking vulgar, the golden-brown tint set Evelyn's raven locks off.

Her hair, freed from the prudent prison of the pins and hanging down to her waist, dark like the depths of the storm-lashed sea.

Her breasts, ripe and firm as pomegranates, the heavy nipples peeking slightly through the shift.

Melanie imagined Evelyn's breasts were firm, but she would have o touch them to know.

And she couldn't touch them, much as the notion robbed her of breath.

Melanie had never had such wanton thoughts about the beaux who courted her half-heartedly during her first season, years ago. She thought of them as sweet companions, good friends, possible providers of her future, and marks of her honour as a debutante – but never carnal objects of desire.

Evelyn never did anything half-heartedly. Had she been able to court her the way she was able to waltz with her, she would have swept her off her feet.

Melanie remembered their last evening with the Ruwallah, the evening of a great feast with a slaughtered lamb. She was not vain enough to imagine the reason for the magnificent dinner had anything to do with their guests; it was merely a celebration of a felicitous arrival in Aleppo, where they could sell the wool and the carpets woven by their women and buy medicines, armaments and Turkish cigarettes, as well as hear the recent news from the world beyond the deserts.

The mutton was dripping with fat, and although the Ruwallah ate with great decorum, there was no mistaking their hunger. Melanie now shared it. After weeks of traveling the wilds of Lebanon, subsisting upon nothing but rice and ewe's milk, she found herself shivering with eagerness when confronted with meat. She barely restrained herself from biting off a large chunk of the mutton and the flatbread upon which her portion was placed.

But that would have been deeply unladylike, and while her hands shook from hunger, Melanie prevailed. She held the mutton and flatbread with her right hand and contented herself with delicate bites.

'How Seneca-like of you,' Evelyn, seated next to her, commented.

'What?'

'Seneca. The Roman Stoic philosopher. He wrote a lot about temperance and never allowing oneself to be ruled by one's body.' Evelyn's lips glistened with the mutton fat, and her sharp teeth flashed in the firelight. The flames reflected in her dark eyes, making them, for a second, almost golden.

'These seem like good precepts to found one's life upon.'

'Perhaps. But we shouldn't forget ...' Evelyn leaned down and whispered into her ear, 'Seneca got on extremely well with Emperor Nero.'

For a mad second, Melanie wished the walls of Aleppo would recede in front of their eyes tomorrow or something equally impossible would happen t to prevent them from leaving the Ruwallah. That way, they could remain frozen forever in this fever dream of a journey, like flies in amber, riding forever through the wilderness, their robes white, steel sabres in their sashes.

But that was not to be. The world had its own laws, Melanie reminded herself, and one tried to ignore them and live in a little bubble at one's own peril – her mother was proof.

Now, she was as close to back to normal as was possible. She wore a good English gown, and she walked through the corridors of a Christian monastery and conversed with her friends in the language of her childhood.

As it should be. As it should have always been.

The starry nights above desolate plains, the coldness of metal in her hands and the memory of sparring – those meant little.

She was not disappointed at the thought. Not in the very least.

'Plenty of Maronites are migrating to the lands of the Druze, where they would be free of persecution,' Dr Wharton said. 'The monasteries are dying like a man being bled.'

'I would have never thought you to have such a poetic tongue,' Evelyn noted, looking around with interest.

'The Mariamites are a dutiful people.' Wharton bristled, as he always tended to do at her teasing, his fair skin blushing slightly. 'They deserve help, not mockery.'

'Mariamites?' Melanie asked. 'I thought you told us they were pronounced as Maronites.'

'They are. The Mariamites are a monastic order within the Maronite Church. *Ordo Maronita Beatae Mariae Virginis.* They are dedicated to serving the queen of Heaven with their prayers and their works.'

'So, they are something like Catholics?'

'In a way, they *are* Catholics. They acknowledge the supremacy of the pope.' There was no mistaking the slight satisfaction in Wharton's voice.

'So did we before the whole Anne Boleyn business.' Evelyn shrugged. 'There is no need to look so smug.'

'I would never dare, Lady Evelyn,' he demurred unconvincingly. 'Besides, in practice they usually look towards the patriarch of Antioch.'

Their conversation was interrupted by the arrival of a young altar server, his robe so white one could, paradoxically, almost take him for a Bedouin. 'The abbot is going to see you now.' He inclined his head in a respectful bow. 'I beg your forgiveness for the long wait, but we are a busy order.'

'I know you are,' Evelyn replied in her pure Arabic despite having known – as far as Melanie was concerned – no such thing until very recently. 'We would be glad to convey your abbot our admiration in person'.

The altar server glowed with pleasure as he conducted them to the heavy door.

The office beyond was furnished sparsely. Moreover, to Melanie's surprise, the spiritual leader was sitting on the floor, his legs criss-crossed in Arab style, his writing deftly balanced on his knee.

He got up with a sprightliness belying his age. 'It is a great pleasure to greet fellow Christians here,' he proclaimed. 'I was left to understand from your note, Lady Evelyn, that you are asking for shelter for yourself and your companions? You shall have it.'

'You are a generous man, Right Reverend,' Evelyn said as courteously as if they were conversing in a ballroom. 'I find myself in need, that is true. However, I also hoped you would satisfy my curiosity.'

'About the ways of our order?'

'I am afraid not, though I am sure it is a riveting topic. I have heard about a man, a Frenchman, who sought shelter in this very monastery a few months ago.'

Internally, Melanie winced. She would not have conducted this conversation this way. She would have postponed the crucial question until the quiet monastic supper, having softened the abbot with small talk and the rare news from Europe.

'I know about the man you seek.'

'You do?' Evelyn exclaimed, visibly unable to stop herself. 'Oh, I must confess, I didn't dare to pray for such good fortune. His name was Vincent Dubois, wasn't it?' Her face was burning with pink joy, as though she were a maiden receiving a marriage proposal in her very first season.

'That was indeed his name. He sought refuge with us when he was ill with the vomiting sickness. Our brothers nursed him back to health.'

'Vomiting sickness?' Dr Wharton asked, growing slightly paler. 'Do you mean, by any chance, the Asiatic cholera?'

'I do, although we do not call it Asiatic.' A slight smile touched the corners of the abbot's mouth.

'It was kind of you to help a man in need,' Evelyn said, her face schooled into careful politeness. 'But Vincent Dubois has been a carrier of dangerous secrets.'

'I should have guessed you were seeking the secrets in question. But, whatever he imparted to us, it is going to be buried behind the walls of this keep. The brothers of the Virgin are no spies.'

'I understand, but the papers he carried are of the utmost importance ...'

'To your government, perhaps. Our order serves no government but that of the kingdom of Heaven.'

'You have already admitted to having known Dubois,' Evelyn pointed out. 'Why say one and withhold the other?'

'Lying is a sin. Silence is not. Indeed, in some circumstances, it can be called the utmost virtue'.

'I know that your order is struggling. Let me make a donation—'

'It is not struggling so hard as to accept bribery for political services.'

'It is not simply the matter of political services. You are a Christian in the Ottoman Empire. You know what it is like to be besieged by enemy forces.'

'With all due respect, our situation and that of your native island are not the same.'

'They sound very similar to me.' To Melanie's astonishment, soft, silken pleading crept into Evelyn's voice, something she had not heard before. 'As I said, it is not simply the matter of politics. My country has been at war ever since the days of the revolution in France. The sons who were newborns when their fathers died in that first war grew up to die in Spain in the second. My country is starving, its trade stifled, its taxes unbearable. It is not for myself that I am asking you; it is for every woman of my land who had to read a letter informing her of her father's death as a girl, a husband's death as a lady and a son's death as a matron. If whatever Dubois carried had any chance to shift the balance of the war and help bring it to the close, I need to have it, and not for my own sake.'

'To shift the balance of the war in favour of your own government, of course.'

'Of course,' Evelyn admitted, unflinching. 'I love my country, for all its follies and foibles. You have dedicated your life to good works, Right Reverend. This could be your best works of all – a deed to save countless lives.'

Dr Wharton directed his gaze at his lady employer, his eyes full of dismay.

The abbot sighed. 'You certainly have a convincing argument. However, I cannot give you that which I do not possess. Vincent Dubois left us nothing but his sincere gratitude and a string of cryptic words.'

'A string of cryptic words?' Evelyn asked, excitement seeping through her voice like hot lava through cracks. 'Perhaps, we could decipher them.'

'He said that, should his countryman come upon our abode and enquire about him, we relay to him that that which he is seeking shall be buried in a place praised for its onions, where Joseph drew his water.'

'A place praised for its onions ...' Evelyn chewed on her lower lip, deep in thought, and Melanie couldn't help but notice the spot came out of it looking ripe and red, like the heart of a rose. 'Praised by whom?'

'He declined to elaborate, I am afraid.'

'By some author, perhaps?' Melanie ventured. 'He must have thought his successor in service is going to interpret the riddle easily. He would not have hoped for it if they didn't have some common reference.'

'It might be the New Testament or else one of the writings of Christian desert fathers. Not to mention that a Catholic Frenchman would have studied the lives of saints as a child.' Evelyn turned again to the abbot of the Mariamite monastery. 'Right Reverend, do you happen to have a library here?'

'Of course.' The old man seemed to be slightly affronted by her question despite preserving his fulsome dignity in the answer. 'We have all the books you have mentioned in the most exquisite editions, not to mention works on history and medicine our brothers bring from Italy.'

'Your brothers travel to Italy?' Melanie asked, working hard to conceal her surprise.

'To study, yes. Although I understand,' the abbot said, his forgiveness suggesting offense, 'why you might think that our world is bordered by the sea on one side and the desert on the other.'

'Did you speak the truth, Lady Evelyn?' Wharton asked as they were riffling through yet another bookshelf.

'When in particular?' There being, in the Arab fashion, no chairs or desks, Evelyn was sitting on the floor, in the same position as she had during the last feast of the Ruwallah, and scanning the pages of the book opened on her knee for a single word. Onions.

'When you told the Right Reverend about your motives.'

'Well, I do care for the lives of my countrymen.'

'I have no doubt you do.' His gaze buried itself in her forehead. 'But is that truly why you want to reach Dubois's papers so much?'

'I want to reach Dubois's papers because that is my task.'

'Why have you accepted this task?'

'Because I don't like the thought of being charged for high treason.'

'Was that the only reason?'

'It was a necessary one. Why are you asking all this, Wharton?'

'Because I don't like the notion of lying to a man of God.' He turned away to the shelf, his cheeks burning.

'Heavenly dove! How did you survive all these years?'

'I have learnt the lesson of retaining my principles without voicing them to dangerous people. Besides, these years have not been all that numerous,' he added..

'Wharton, we have a mission to accomplish. Saying the things that are not even lies in their entirety to a man who would never be harmed by them is the least thing I would do to succeed.'

'The most thing being charging a horde of Bedouins alone?'

'No,' Evelyn replied, and Melanie's insides twisted and turned cold. 'Not even close.' She leaned over the pages and began reading again. 'Melanie! Wharton! Look here!'

They huddled around her, the argument buried in shallow waters.

'*The country of the Ascalonitae is a good onion-market, though the town is small*,' Evelyn read aloud and held the book up triumphantly. 'Strabo, *Geography*. Our Frenchman was a well-educated chap.'

'Either this or we have missed something in the other books,' Melanie commented calmly even though her heart was thumping with excitement. Finally, after dark and hungry hours in this library, beneath the crumbling gaze of a Byzantine Madonna on the ceiling, they had found something that might – just might – lead them to what they needed to find.

Unless, of course, Verney got there first.

'Now we just need to find out where is this Ascalonitae,' Evelyn concluded.

'I think I know it,' Wharton interjected. 'I've treated an antiquarian once who was planning to visit the ruins. The place is called Ascalon now.'

'Do you know how to get there? Is it far from here?' she asked avidly.

'I don't know, but we will surely be able to find a guide here. Hopefully, we are going to be more fortunate this time than we had been with our first guide,' He clearly couldn't quite resist a pinch of irony.

'A guide and supplies,' Evelyn stated as though declaring war. 'We are going to find these on the morrow. We are to rise with the sun.' Her gaze circled the room, stopping on Melanie as though the tall woman had been suspecting her in particular of morning slothfulness. 'I am going to beat Verney to these documents if this is the last thing I do on this earth.'

Melanie had always imagined an Eastern bazaar to be a place of exotic treasures. It felt almost strange now to be shopping there for coffee, rice, fuel, and malted wheat, all in preparation for the expedition ahead.

Dr Wharton went off in search of a guide and the workers they were most likely going to need once they neared the antique site. Evelyn, in turn, volunteered to arrange the delivery of goods already purchased to the monastery storehouse to be held there until the time came.

If Evelyn had her way, clearly, the time would come tomorrow.

Melanie gazed around her, striding through the tightly thronged world of barbers and tinners, saddlers and locksmiths, and mercers and even sellers of sweetmeats. With only the mildest rebuke to herself, she bought a dumpling of minced meat and felt her blood surge in response to the filling spiced delicacy.

She wanted to get off the bazaar pathway, find a secluded corner, and enjoy the snack quietly and seemly. But there were no secluded corners. Each square centimetre of the market was covered with the teeming humanity, the bright silk shirts of swaggering youths flashing next to the pale veils of wealthy housewives while beggars pleaded by the ancient walls.

Something else had seized Melanie in its grasp. Not the realization that she was alone and unchaperoned in the centre of the universe that no one from her own world would have considered civilized, but something far more primal.

Namely, hunger.

It might have been a belated response to the weeks of travelling with the Ruwallah with the thin meals and great exertions. Or, perhaps, it was the much more distant memory of her family dinners after the great divide with their staid silence and quiet clink of cutlery and glares if she dared to hold the fork too close to its teeth.

Whatever the reason, Melanie devoured the dumpling as if she had spent months in prison without so much as a crumb between her teeth and then bought another.

The sun was beaming overhead, saturating her skin with its warmth. The fresh meat was melting on her tongue, the spices scalding her throat in an undeniably pleasant way. The cotton and silk, newly purchased – the same those swaggering youths were wearing – were cool against her limbs.

Something shifted within her, something Melanie, the rational being, could not quite express but had nonetheless felt. It was an impulsive decision – the kind she had never allowed herself before.

There is enough time until our agreed meeting.. Most supplies have already been purchased and sent away. There is going to be no harm if I explore the other parts of the bazaar.

And she set off, unaccompanied, her hand firmly on her purse, into the pulsing centre of the main bazaar of Aleppo. The noise around her became as a rushing river, and a whole crowd of people – some in elegant and pale Turkish garb, some in colourful Levantine clothes, and a few in the restrained waistcoats of a European – thronged the street.

This section of the bazaar was clearly dedicated to vessels of copper. Beneath the blazing sun, the surfaces of the bowls, incense burners, and ingenious carafes wrought in the shapes of falcons and eagles shone brightly like beaten gold. The shining was painful to the eye, and Melanie barely resisted the impulse to close hers.

Some merchandise in the stalls surprised her with its proximity to the world she knew. There was cloth from Languedoc and Lyons laces as well as cochineal from Cadiz and West Indian coffee. These must have been transported here from Europe via the entrepots of Alexandretta and Latakia.

But there were also dates and sugar, carpets manufactured in Persia and burning with designs of red and blue, and silk stuffs of Aleppo itself, water-like in the sun. There were shawls and muslins from India, so colourful that Melanie wished to wrap one around her shoulders despite the blazing sun. There was copper from Egypt, shining like burnished gold in the morning light, and redwood coffers from the holy city of Mecca.

Countless cries were clamouring for her attention:

'Lady, look at my wares! Cottons from Acre. All the women of your land adore them!'

'You've never seen such perfumes, lady. They'd make you fragrant as the Queen of Sheba!'

'Silk from Saide, lady! From the very mulberry trees of the Druze!'

Melanie shivered in the open sun at the last cry and dived close to a mercer's stall. There shouldn't be so many seductions here, she decided, for the simple reason that she had never liked jewellery.

At first, she didn't even notice the proprietor, an old man, looking as though his skin was made of paper, as he emerged from the gold-glittering darkness without so much as a noise.

'I see you are interested in my humble goods, lady,' he said, giving her a deep, old-fashioned bow.

'Guilty as charged.' Melanie smiled, deciding this was one of those circumstances where a fib was forgivable.

'Perhaps, you would like a pair of earrings? Your husband would never begrudge you the purchase once he saw how you look in them.'

Melanie's Arabic was as imperfect as her sabre-fencing. However, it was enough to be able to say: 'I have no husband.' A year ago, this sentence would have been uttered with tragic resignation to the cruel fate that left her reputation in tatters and deprived her of the means to acquire a spouse. Now ... now she was merely stating a fact.

The proprietor clicked his tongue. 'Such a shame! Such a fair young woman, and no husband. Have no fear, lady, you would be sure to catch one once you wear my earrings to the mass.'

Melanie decided not to dive into the differences between Christian denominations and explain that she belonged to the kind of church that hosted no masses. She opened her mouth to thank him politely as a prelude for leaving when the sun struck the gleaming edges of the stall and caught upon the most intricate thing Melanie had ever seen.

Caught upon the most intricate thing Melanie has ever seen.

It was a locket bound in gold and glass, the links on the chain resembling leaves. *Leaves of autumn, perhaps. Beauty frozen forever into one gilded form.* 'How lovely,' she whispered, leaning towards the locket.

'Ah.' The stall owner beamed. 'This thing came with a caravan from Baghdad merely last morning. You are a fortunate lady to espy it so quickly.'

Why was she so captivated? With her pale skin and fair hair, it was going to look hideous upon her neck – something turning an angel into a Cyprian and not one with the best taste in Covent Garden either.

But what if she put it on a different neck altogether? A neck tanned into olive. A neck framed by raven locks. She imagined the golden chain snaking slowly between Evelyn's full breasts. She imagined tracing the path of the jewel with her fingers and with her mouth.

Something clenched sweetly in her, something she could not quite put a name to. Shoving the sensation forcibly away from her mind, Melanie asked, 'How much does it cost?'

'One hundred and seventy piastres.'

Melanie's breath caught. This was more than she could afford, more than she even had in her purse after all the necessary purchases of the morning. 'You must be joking!' she exclaimed before she could stop herself.

'I never joke on business, lady. Only in a coffee house afterwards.'

'Still, it's – it's an outrageous price!'

'Ah, very well. One hundred and sixty-five.'

Melanie stared at him dumbfounded. Did he actually expect her to bargain with him?

Perhaps her grandmothers had shopped this way, but not her and not her mother either. In the life she once inhabited – in the life she was going to, of course, return to one day – a price was a price, and that was that.

But, if this order of things was going to allow her to afford the thing she craved... 'One hundred and sixty-five for this bauble? No, no, there is no way you are serious.'

'I swear by my poor mother's virtue, I am!'

'I suspect your mother's virtue is now guarded by angels. One hundred and forty, and no more.'

'Mistress, you are breaking my heart! One hundred and sixty.'

'I have seen better jewellery on the beggar-women of Constantinople!' Melanie, who had never been to Constantinople, exclaimed.

'Pah! That's Constantinople. They are all guzzling our produce there. No surprise that their beggar-women are dressing better than my poor mother.'

'Let me be cursed if your poor mother is now dressed in anything but wood. One hundred and forty, as I said.'

'Oh, the Merciful and the Compassionate, you are being unreasonable! See how precious the stones are—'

'It's glass.'

'See how the sun is playing upon the golden chain!'

'Does that mean that the locket is going to diminish in value on a gloomy day?' Melanie asked. She was rather enjoying the wickedness of the faint spirit of a verbal brawl.

But that was not the reason why she bargained for the bauble so hard.

Was it truly the desire to please her travelling companion?

She thought back to the ballroom, to Lady Evelyn's back turned to her, to her derisive comments during the madcap dance...

The madcap dance that Evelyn didn't have to invite her for. The madcap dance that soothed Melanie's heart and saved her evening.

She thought back to the hexagonal room, the light of the dawn glittering upon the points of blades, and Evelyn's warm hands correcting her posture and the position of her pliant limbs.

She thought back to the last morning with the Ruwallah and Evelyn's dark locks falling freely on her shoulders, as if she were a girl whose hair had not been put up yet.

The proprietor of the stall threw his hands up. 'Ah, lady, you are carving me without a knife! One hundred and forty-five, and not a piastre more. Mind you, I am consigning myself to starvation for your sake.'

'I appreciate your sacrifice,' Melanie said with all the gravity she could muster and untied the strings of her purse.

Melanie deftly circumvented a large vase standing by the entrance to a workshop and, following the earlier instructions, dived through the curtain to the workshop beyond.

It turned out not to be a workshop at all. It was, peculiarly, a kind of coffee house where people were sitting in pairs, drinking the bitter Yemeni beverage, and, judging by their lowered tones, discussing business.

Evelyn was waiting for her in that impromptu coffee house attached to a stall. Three small cups of coffee were already standing by her feet along with a vessel with hot water, but Wharton was nowhere to be seen.

'Evelyn, I have bought you—' Melanie froze.

Across Evelyn's knees lay the most beautiful sabre Melanie had ever seen. Not that she had seen much, of course, but this weapon, with its razor-thin blade and heavy, silvered hilt decorated with forms of stars and circles, looked like the pure idea of a sword. The kind of sword one always imagined when reading storybooks. The kind of sword one saw extracted from its sheath by Homeric heroes, if the illustrations were any good. The kind of sword Melanie sensed would cost a fortune.

'What is this?' she said, sitting down carefully, as though her breath could stain it.

'A Damascene blade. The Arabs call it tahane, which means tempered. There were other swords – the black steel of Khorasan, the pale blades tempered in India – but none of them seemed good enough for you,' Evelyn whispered.

Melanie's heart skipped a beat as she touched the mirror-like steel. 'It is sublime. So beautiful.'

'It is also swift and deadly and pure. All the qualities I thought would be perfect for you.' A lock of black hair slipped out of the kerchief prudently covering Evelyn's head and was now clinging to her temple like the lingering touch of a lover.

'Do you think me deadly, then?' Melanie's fingers were itching to produce her own gift, and yet she couldn't quite stop looking at the wonderful blade. Slowly, carefully, she took it from where it rested and held it up in her hand. It was lighter than the cheap, battered swords they'd bought in Beirut. It also looked so sharp Melanie was seized with a mischievous desire to test it on something, anything – a bolt of cloth, if it might be.

'I think you are capable of being so.' Evelyn smiled, her ripe-red lips parting. 'I see you have no quarrel with the other adjectives. I am glad.'

'I have bought something for you, too.' Putting the sword down, Melanie reached into her purse and produced the locket. 'Let – let me put it on your neck.'

In her old life, she would not have been so presumptuous even with a friend. But here, now, there were few onlookers and few formalities to regard apart from the common courtesies of the bazaar. Besides, Evelyn did not raise her eyebrows or in any way indicate surprise or dismay. She inclined her head and bunched the lower part of her kerchief up.

Melanie's breath caught at the sight of the dark hair bared by the movement, glued to her neck, the sunlit sweat gleaming on it. Kneeling beside her companion, she slipped the locket up her chest and united the chains around her neck.

The desire to touch the tender, golden-tanned skin –or to place a lingering kiss upon it became almost impossible to resist. 'It is lovely on you,' Melanie murmured, leaning closer. 'You are lovely.'

'Lady Evelyn! Miss Bright!'

Both women turned to the cloth marking the entrance to the coffee house, Melanie's body aching from curdled heat. Dr Wharton stood in the improvised doorway, and his face was florid as if he had been drinking or running.

'What happened, Wharton?' Evelyn asked, and Melanie thought for a second she could hear displeasure in her voice.

'The worst possible thing.' The doctor not so much sat as fell down, gulping air down like a man dying in the desert would gulp down water. 'The Ottomans. They have changed sides.'

'What?' the women asked in unison, looking at him righting himself.

'The Sublime Porte is now officially fighting on the side of the French Empire,' Wharton said grimly as if it could render the news somehow less shocking. 'Bonaparte promised to help him suppress the rebellion in Serbia, and Sultan Selim caved in. He opened the Dardanelles to the French warships. *Exclusively* to the French warships.'

'What would that mean for us?' Melanie asked, reeling as though she had been hit by something heavy.

'That would mean we have to pack up and get out of the Ottoman territories as fast as we can.'

'No,' Evelyn said decisively. 'I am not giving up so easily.'

'Easily? I don't see anything easy in this. You have done everything you can, Lady Evelyn. No one would be able to fault you if Verney prevails in this one.' Wharton wiped a hand across his brow.

'We don't know what is in the papers. It might be that, if he prevails in this, he is going to prevail in everything. Besides, *I* would be able to fault myself. It is more than enough.'

'What about Miss Bright? She is a woman of her own. She has no mission. What about her safety?'

'What about Miss Bright indeed,' Evelyn echoed and turned to Melanie. 'What about Miss Bright?' she asked, looking into Melanie's eyes. 'If Miss Bright would like it, I can find her the best guide to Beirut in this city.'

'I have rejected your offer to leave you once.' Melanie coughed. 'I am going to do it again.'

'You didn't comprehend the extent of the danger when you agreed to accompany me to Lebanon. Neither have I. I thought the worst I would have to contend with would be the danger of shipwrecks by the Syrian coast.'

'I have never been the kind of woman to leave endeavours easily,' Melanie said. 'Even if my endeavours have always been much more modest than yours. I would not forgive myself if I betray my principles now.'

Chapter 10

If Evelyn was asked to describe Ascalon in two words only, she would have said glorious desolation.

The city that was noted by Strabo, praised by William of Tyre, possessed by Prolemy Lagos and respected by Herod the Great now was a heap of ruins, whitened by the sun. A few crumbling walls ran in parallel to the lush seashore, the wine-dark sea churning below the cliffs. In what must have once been the centre of the city, eight columns were standing, rising upon the pedestals, in the chief temple. A chasm, with the remains of ramps leading down to it, gaped in the middle of the site. Broken stones and fragments of marble ornaments were strewn upon the ground like so much rubbish – stones that remembered the antique monarchs of the East and the ambitions of Richard the Lionheart.

'This spot looks freshly churned up.' Melanie's voice caught slightly with fear.

It might mean that Verney had been there first.

'It's them people of the Pasha of Saide,' one of the hired workers explained grimly. 'Pasha of Acre, more like, for all the time he wastes there. He gets porphyry here for his seraglio and marble for his baths.' Unceremoniously, he spat upon the ground, as if having mentioned the devil.

Melanie's shoulders visibly relaxed. Evelyn was not sure this was good news. After all, the men of the Ottoman government, on whatever level, would be as interested in the papers of the French agent as they were.

Evelyn circled the site with her gaze. When she first heard about this spot, she imagined something like Baalbek – a small spot of ancient ruins where one could conceivably bury a paper treasure. But this was indeed a city, wide and broad, a place where avenues had once run between the places of worship, the places of learning, and the places of public debate.

How was she to know where to dig?

The workers, Wharton, and Melanie were all looking at her with expectation. She was the woman on a mission, the leader of this expedition. She had to say something.

'I think ...' Evelyn coughed, buying herself time. 'I think we should dig along the western wall. It seems a convenient spot to me for burial.'

She breathed out slowly at observing the resulting movement. This was not the first time in her life she saw people obeying her orders; she had managed her uncle's gargantuan household, after all. Back then, her authority derived from the drop of his blood in her veins; she had been nothing but a vessel carrying out his will. Here, she was a lady of authority in her own right. *Evelyn bint Gerald.*

Yes, her inner voice whispered, *for a minute. Because you are paying them. For no other reason.*

Doesn't matter. Evelyn clutched her hands into fists. *I am going to prevail. I am going to uncover these papers, and I am going to outrun Joseph Verney.*

If he did not outrun her.

The lush stillness of the surroundings was bathed in the golden light. It was a deceptive calm. The kind of calm that stranded ships in the middle of the ocean and bled moisture and strength out of the crew's bodies.

Hours passed by, signified by nothing more than the movement of the sun in the glaring heavens. Evelyn was walking up and down the wall, distributing water to the tired workers, giving directions, and cheering people up in her Arabic when she heard a triumphant cry.

Her mind instantly compressed into a dot of determined, blinding light, and Evelyn ran, her shirt flapping, to the source of the sound. 'Have you found something?' she asked breathlessly.

Without a further word, the worker pointed to a shallow trench. Among the mossy stones lay a few scattered human bones. The disappointment was physical. She felt like a starving hermit who had the last piece of bread snatched from him just when he was getting ready to pierce it with his teeth.

'It's ...' Evelyn's voice shook.

'It was probably some poor victim of robbers. There is nothing to fear,' Melanie said, her voice soothing and matter-of-fact.

Nothing to fear indeed, Evelyn thought, looking around into the green-and-white stillness. *Nothing to fear apart from Verney finding us.*

Nothing to fear apart from the most abject failure.

Melanie was not sure why sleep evaded her. It might have been the unquiet nature of even the quietest new place, where even the air itself seemed to have new and peculiar strains. It might have been the freshness of the night that crawled even beneath the coverlet, even between the tangle of warm limbs.

It might have been fear.

Every noise seemed to her the rattle of hooves, heralding the coming of their enemy.

Or, perhaps, the enemy had already been here. Perhaps, we are digging for naught.

After tossing and turning too many times, Melanie wrapped her shoulders in an Indian shawl – one that would have cost a small fortune back home and was sold for a pittance in the bazaar of Aleppo – and stepped outside the tent.

Once again, the night sky shocked her with its icy brightness. So many stars, and she didn't even know the names of most constellations. She wondered if the Bedouins had their own names for them. She wondered if she would ever have a chance to learn that.

Beneath the sunless skies, the ancient city was standing still, majestic in its ruination. The columns in the destroyed temple looked silver-bright in the moonlight. The enigmatic chasm was gaping just as black.

Curious, Melanie walked closer to it, watching her steps. In the back of her mind, a nightmarish sequence of stumbling and slipping down into the darkness was already unfolding.

Melanie wondered what the pit was for. How did the people who, if one believed Evelyn, worshipped the goddess who demanded castration of her priests and licentiousness of her women, use it? Was it a place of sacrifice before the coming of the strict Roman order?

The ramps leading down to the chasm were enormous. She could easily imagine chariots of kings rolling down into a stygian darkness, never to be seen or heard from again, apart from the prayers of their people who turned the sacrificed dead into talismans.

You have too vivid an imagination. Melanie rebuked herself out of habit. *This spot most likely had a practical aim.*

What kind of practical aim could such a thing have?

Not one to disregard questions easily, she peered down into the depths, wondering if she might have ever seen anything like it at home. Grain storage, maybe? Suddenly, it hit Melanie that she had indeed seen something like it at home. *Oh God, that explains everything.*

Unheeding of the rules of politeness, she ran back into the tent and shook Evelyn's shoulders. To her credit, the dark-haired woman sat up immediately, like a soldier standing to attention.

'What is that?' she demanded, only the barest trace of sleepiness in her voice. 'An attack?'

Melanie shook her head. 'I know what Dubois's directions meant,' she whispered urgently, as if their rival could hear them across the night-clad plains that separated them. 'The place where Joseph drew his water. I've seen it.'

'What do you mean, you've seen it?'

'On an engraving back home. In a book about Egypt. There was this chapter about the Citadel of Cairo. There is this construction – Saladin built it to provision his cavalry, but they are calling it St. Joseph's Well. There are ramps leading down to it so that horsemen could approach it on their steeds and draw water easily. That is why it looked so strange, not like a normal well at all. Dubois had been in Egypt, hadn't he? I remember you told me.' Melanie finally stopped, catching her breath, and stilled herself, rapt in attention for what would come.

It was not simply Evelyn's praise that she sought or even the approval of a learnt companion. What she sought was nothing less than vindication. All her life, she thought her passion for stories about traveling was nothing but an embarrassing hobby, something her family could tolerate while she was still unmarried but something she would have no time for once she was wedded, once the duties of the household and motherhood grew upon her like moss upon stone.

Yet here, now, if she was right, –her useless, inane passion could bring them victory. Which meant that it was not useless. It was the opposite of useless and had been all along. If only her friend agreed.

'Melanie, you are brilliant,' Evelyn exclaimed and buried her face in Melanie's neck. Melanie froze – not out of fear or displeasure at the touch but out of the unwillingness to ruin it. This moment felt so perfect with Evelyn's body, still warm from sleep, pressing into hers, and her lips, even though they were still, against her neck.

Melanie embraced her in turn and stroked slowly down her back. Evelyn didn't move or shift away. *What would Evelyn do if I turn my face a little and kiss her?* An unexpected feeling of cold assaulted her body when the dark-haired woman moved away.

'You are a blessing from God,' Evelyn murmured and kissed her on the cheek.

It is a truth universally acknowledged that no titled lady, be she a daughter of an English earl or an Eastern emir, should lower herself to manual labour. If she had people who could do that for her, she should let them while she stayed under the cool roof of her tent.

Evelyn's hands shook with the impatience for victory that seemed to elude her forever yesterday. She also felt invigorated after her conversation with Melanie in the night. Therefore, she asked one of the labourers to lend her a shovel, fixed her kerchief, and strode out where the morning sun was the brightest.

They were digging near the nameless well that the mind of Vincent Dubois might have connected with the well of Saladin and St. Joseph. The physical effort felt unexpectedly good despite the beads of sweat ripening on the back of her neck and the feeling of strain in her wrists and forearms that came soon enough after Evelyn started digging. She was doing something. She was not standing still. Yes, her back was aching and would most likely ache all the more tomorrow morning, but it was aching from the honest steps she took to achieve her goal.

It was a good ache. At least for her. Evelyn didn't think Melanie would share her feelings on the subject.

'You don't have to do it,' she called out, seeing Melanie cast her glance around for another shovel.

'I want to join you.'

Evelyn did not protest but made a point of keeping an eye on her companion, turning around whenever the sound of strained breathing coming from her digging spot became too tortured and loud.

'You are not used to that,' Evelyn commented.

'No more than you are,' Melanie retorted, the fire in her voice unexpected. 'And no less.'

'Still, you must be thirsty.'

'Not really.'

'You are not a good liar, Melanie Bright. If you want to train to become one, you should not practise your exercises on me.' Evelyn laid down her shovel and took a flask of water from her saddlebag.

'It's nothing,' Melanie protested. 'I really am—'

'You don't need to play a Spartan boy to impress me,' Evelyn said in a tone she hoped was soft. 'I am grateful for what you did last night.'

If some English-speaking stranger were among their company, they might have misconstrued that last phrase quite seriously.

Amused by her thought, Evelyn touched Melanie's cheek, tipped her chin up, and felt no resistance. 'Drink,' Evelyn commanded, putting the flask to her lips.

To her relief, Melanie took a few sips even while looking up into her eyes with some residual mutiny.

'Good girl,' Evelyn teased, and saw her friend's cheek light up slightly. Most likely because of the heating sun.

Evelyn had called her a Spartan boy as a mere metaphor, but there really was something boyish in Melanie's appearance right now. Her garb was that of an Ottoman youth with wide breeches and long flowing shirt. Her fair hair was curling slightly from the heat and the damp of the seashore, and a few golden threads could be seen glinting where the kerchief couldn't catch them.

Melanie had lost weight, too, over the time of their travels, making her look like an unusually graceful and slender urchin rather than the soft-cheeked nymph she was before. But even through the large shirt, Evelyn could see the slight outlines of her breasts.

Evelyn didn't even want to know how she herself looked now. Frightful, probably – a termagant with a shovel. 'Melanie …' She stepped closer. She was not sure what it was she intended to say – an enquiry about her health? An apology for dragging her through half of the East?

'Something here! Come and see, lady!' one of the workers shouted, preventing Evelyn from saying anything more to Melanie.

With a strange mix of irritation and relief, Evelyn ran to where the man was standing. He was pointing at something pale grey peeking out from the earth.

'My shovel struck,' he said excitedly. 'There's something here, lady. By my brother's guts, there is!'

'Right.' Evelyn rolled up her sleeves. 'Then let's see what it is.'

Removing no less than six feet of rubbish and mould covering the rest of the strange find took most of the afternoon, and the sky was already growing dim and tender when the group stepped back and realized what they had unearthed.

'How beautiful,' Melanie said disbelievingly. It must have felt as peculiar to her as it did to Evelyn to find something so pristine and whole in this desolate place.

Well, for the given value of pristine and whole. The statue, after all, did spend centuries under the earth, and it did lack a head. At any other time, Evelyn's heart would have beaten faster at the sight of such antiquity. Her gaze was drawn to the little pale rope snaking around the statue's ankle that didn't look ancient at all.

'I will give you all the double of what I've promised,' she said, the value of coins diminished to nothingness in the light of the impeding triumph, 'if we work through the evening. I will be digging alongside you every second of the way.'

'So will I.' Melanie raised her voice in her heavily accented Arabic. 'So will I!'

By now, Evelyn knew her too well to try to dissuade her. The moon had risen, bathing the ruins in a pale silver glow, when the company finally removed the soil from around the figure. Unable to wait, Evelyn fell to her knees by its side and dug up the object tied to the statue's ankle with her bare hands.

'Here it is,' she whispered, raising the small leather satchel up as if it were the head of a fallen enemy. Through the material, she could feel the unambiguous rustling of tightly packed paper. 'Here it is.'

'Lady Evelyn.' Dr Wharton's voice came from above. 'What are we to do with the statue?'

Like Melanie, like them all, he looked exhausted yet determined, his forehead glistening with well-earned sweat and his palms darkened with soil.

'It belongs in a museum,' Melanie said, looking down.

For the first time in the last few hours, Evelyn turned her gaze towards the giant marble figure. It was majestic even despite its decapitated state: the shoulders of the unknown man were decorated with the thunderbolt of Jupiter or Zeus and the chest with Medusa's head. Evelyn wondered who he was. Who was he supposed to represent? Perseus, the legendary vanquisher of the woman-monster? Zeus himself?

Or, perhaps, some deified king, one of the fiery successors of Alexander the Great?

Evelyn imagined the reactions in London to this statue that could have been erected before Rome came into its iron might. She imagined the crowds on the Southampton docks awaiting the arrival of the ship bearing the precious cargo, the papers and the gossips alike proclaiming her at least an equal to Lord Elgin with his marbles.

Fame. Glory. Power. Everything she ever wanted – and she wouldn't even have to die for it.

Evelyn looked up from the pit and saw the lithe figure of Melanie Bright hovering by the edge, and she knew her plan was impossible. 'We won't be able to transport the statue back to the coast without the Ottoman authorities noticing,' Evelyn said, touching the dirty marble that remembered the reign of pagan gods. 'If they do …'

'We are not safe here anymore.' Melanie nodded sagely. 'Not with the Porte changing sides.'

No, Evelyn thought, *you are not safe here anymore. My uncle can strong-arm the foreign office into bearing diplomatic pressure upon the Ottomans, should I be captured; Wharton can claim ignorance and being nothing but my paid employee. But there is no refuge Melanie Bright can take.*

'Precisely,' she said aloud instead.

'What are we going to do, Lady Evelyn?' Wharton asked.

Evelyn closed her eyes as if trying to imprint the vision in marble on the inner side of her eyelids. She opened her eyes and said, 'We are going to take what we have come for and bury the statue back.'

'The Pasha of Saide might break it as a heathen idol if he ever unearths it during his excavations for stone.' Wharton's face was indignant.

'Yes.' Evelyn forced coldness into her tone. 'He might.'

She couldn't remember how she made it out of the pit and into the tent again, the satchel clutched to her chest. Her head was throbbing as though the heat and the exertion of the bygone day, kept at bay by her avid excitement, had now 'fell upon her like a boulder.

She did not weep. She rarely wept those days. She rarely wept even before. But there was a savage pain coursing through her mind, a pain that could not find an exit.

'I know why you did this.' Melanie's mellow voice came from behind Evelyn.

Sharply, Evelyn rolled to the other side and saw Melanie standing in the entrance to the tent, framed by the starlit sky.

'I hope so,' Evelyn said tersely, 'since I've spelled the reasons out down there.' She almost hoped Melanie was going to cringe and go away, hurt by her tone; however, the fair-haired sylph, the boyish beauty, stood her ground.

'I mean, for whose sake,' Melanie replied calmly and sat down beside her.

Almost against her own will, Evelyn looked up into her eyes. Such dear, sea-blue eyes. The panic came almost before the thought. The panic that could only express itself in a silent, mind-melting scream of *No, no, no, no, no.*

Evelyn had fallen in love before and with much less vulnerable a creature than Melanie Bright – with someone who could marry her honourably, at that. It ended in tragedy. She could only imagine – and shudder to imagine – just how bad an end this kind of affair could come to.

Bold of you to assume it even has a chance of taking place, her inner voice whispered. *Just look at her – a debutante through and through. You know her dreams. You uncle told you. A handsome diplomat to sweep her off her feet and carry her, bridal style, into a life in foreign climes. Not a wounded heiress to hide with in the dark.*

'You do?' Evelyn's voice should not be catching so.

'Of course.' Melanie nodded, looking into her eyes. 'For us. Me and Dr Wharton. You are a good leader and a true –

mother to your men, I suppose.' She smiled slightly. 'I am sorry for having misjudged you.'

Evelyn drew a breath of relief. Melanie didn't know. And what she didn't know could not hurt her. 'Misjudged me?'

'When we'd just met, I thought you a wild and spoilt heiress. I didn't know about your true qualities then, not about your past.'

You don't know about my past even now. Not the whole of it. 'Don't put me on a shining pedestal now. How do you know my decision had nothing to do with my own preservation?'

'I saw you charge that cavalcade of Bedouins. I know you don't give a pig's foot about your own preservation. I agree with Dr Wharton, by the way,' Melanie added. 'That cannot be healthy. Definitely not for a young woman.'

Cannot be healthy. Evelyn barely kept a rueful smile off her lips. She could well imagine Melanie two decades later, dispensing household cures to her cosy horde of children.

'Dr Wharton worries about me overmuch. As do you.'

It was a strange feeling to be fussed about so. Strange and dangerously pleasant, like a warmth that was a little too much, barely a breath away from burning.

And apt to be snatched away at any moment.

'Call him here, if you don't mind.' Evelyn changed the subject. 'Let us see our Holy Grail.'

Melanie rose from the floor of the tent with what looked like a strange air of disappointment.

Minutes later, all three were sitting in a circle as though the leather vessel were an artifact required for some occult ritual that could only be enacted in a rule of three.

'The moment of truth,' Evelyn said drily and opened the bag. Whole batches of paper fell out of it, scattering on the floor. 'That could have been done better,' she admitted, gathering the sheets closest to her. 'It's a great fortune all of us know French.'

'Unless the thing is written in code,' Melanie said.

'How do you know about such matters?'

'I've kept my eyes open this past month.' She shifted uncomfortably. 'And also read a lot of novels back home.'

'There are a few maps here,' Wharton said, gazing at the bounty of secrets in his hands.

'With markings of our Egyptian positions, no doubt,' Evelyn muttered, reading the first page of notes.

For ten minutes or so, silence and concentrated work reigned in the tent. Evelyn emitted a very unladylike whistle. 'Heavenly dove!' she exclaimed. 'No wonder our government was in such a hurry to get these papers.'

'Why?' her companions asked in unison.

'What is there?' Wharton added, ever the more impatient one.

'Vincent Dubois had been tasked by his master to map and explore the desert heartland between Syria and Persia.' Unable to resist a little theatricality, Evelyn paused. 'In order to find a secure overland route towards India.'

The two exchanged telling glances. She did not need to explain to them what a catastrophe such a discovery would be for Britain.

'Does it look like he was any close to success?' Melanie asked pragmatically.

'It does. He mapped out a veritable net of the alliance connecting the desert tribes. If the French could broker peace by, say, the Anazeh and the Ruwallah...' Evelyn did not need to finish her thought.

Melanie swallowed, and Evelyn couldn't help but gaze at her throat moving through the little opening in her shirt, baring the tender, pearly skin and its faint movement.

'They won't find the way now,' Melanie said. 'We have the papers. We have bested Verney.'

We have bested Verney. Those four words felt like glorious fireworks exploding inside her head, the fireworks that no pleasure garden at midnight could have competed for. It felt like triumph igniting the blood in her veins.

It felt like life.

Evelyn imagined Lord Howick shaking her hand. *I say, Lady Evelyn, I have somewhat misjudged you in the beginning. I can tell you without prevarications that you have saved the Empire.*

'Evelyn!' Melanie's voice broke through her daydreaming. 'You are smiling!'

She turned her gaze to Melanie and saw her grinning in amazement before clutching her in a sudden embrace.

'We have done it,' Evelyn whispered against her neck that smelled of fresh sweat and linen, and for a second, everything in the world seemed perfect and possible as though the planets aligned. 'We have done it. Now the only thing left to us is getting to Beirut and finding a boat willing to take us back.' Such a small thing after everything they'd been through.

Such a small thing – perfect and possible.

Chapter 11

As she made her way through the narrow alleyways that were supposed to lead to her destination, Melanie decided she definitely liked Damascus.

Never, in the West or in the East, had she seen a city so brimming with water, be it in the form of canals, or gushing fountains adorning every courtyard, or even the high, cold waters of the Barrada River. Never had she seen a city so breathing with peaches, so abundant in fruit trees.

And never had she tasted so many sweetmeat cakes of roses and apricots.

Even though she understood the need to get out of the country, Melanie was almost disappointed they were staying in the great city from whence her new sabre hailed only for a couple of days to resupply.

It was a shame. She knew, by Mary Montagu's example, that, if she hoped to write colourful and edifying letters about her sojourn in Syria and Lebanon, she had to penetrate the very marrow of the place, not skim the cream off the surface.

She was now carrying in her bag two letters composed yesterday afternoon. One was supposed to soothe her father and tell him of the wonders she had seen in the countries that the Germans called the lands of the morning.

The other was destined for her mother.

Melanie halted putting pen to paper multiple times when it came to this one. At first, she held herself back by reminding herself of the ban on the correspondence with her and of the imminent punishment – or, worse yet, paternal disappointment – that was sure to descend upon her if she broke this covenant. Then a light, mischievous voice crept into her mind, telling her that her father was never going to know. Not of this one letter. One letter couldn't do any harm.

When the fresh sheet of paper was procured from their host's possession, Melanie realized she didn't even know where to start. How did one approach a mother one hadn't seen or spoken to for more than a year, one she was not supposed to speak to still?

One that she betrayed?

The first brush with this word was almost accidental, but it lingered and grew.

Betrayed.

Was that the notion she, Melanie, should apply here? Is that what happened?

What else could have happened, you milksop? Your mother never had a harsh word for you, and you fled from her as if she were a leper the second they turned on her. All because you wanted a pristine reputation and a handsome bridegroom. In the end, you got neither. Well, traitors always get the reward they deserve.

Something wedged itself in her throat. Tears were ripening in her eyes.

I have to prove I am no milksop. Not anymore.

I am stronger than this.

With this resolution, Melanie took the pen up once again, and wrote down two lines:

Dear Mother,

I hope you will find it within your heart to forgive me.

The first paragraph was excruciating as if she were weaving it out of her own sinew and bones.

The words did not flow easily. Nonetheless, Melanie managed to set out the whole tale, starting with her father accepting Sir Owen's offer on her behalf and ending with the circumstances of her arrival in Damascus. Not being a fool, Melanie concealed the reason of her friend's sojourn into Lebanon, knowing how easily a letter can be misplaced.

She knew she would never receive an answer. She was never going to come back to this address in Damascus, after all, and, should mother direct a letter to her home, it is going to end up in the fireplace before Melanie could have a chance to read it.

This would be her first and only chance. The one and only scream into the void.

Now, Melanie could only hope against hope that, in the absence of a regular postal system in Syria, the merchant caravan she had been told about by their Armenian host was going to be a reliable carrier.

The dark alleys finally led her to a high caravanserai, its walls high. Now, the place was crumbling, the glory days of the caliphs long past. Melanie let out a breath of relief when she sped into the courtyard and saw a crowd of men and horses standing around a veritable army of carts. She wasn't late.

I am rather lucky when it comes to caravans, am I not?

'Forgive me,' she addressed the man in a silk shirt, evidently the leader of the caravan. 'I have heard you are going to the port of Latakia?'

'That is true,' the merchant nodded, his speech slow and solid. 'We are carrying the goods for Malta and Cyprus.'

That was even better than Melanie had hoped it to be.

'Then you would sell them to one of the Frankish merchant ships?' She asked.

'God willing, yes. The times aren't good for trade, of course, but pearls of Bahrain and shawls of Malabar, not to mention the coffee from Yemen, usually find their buyers.'

'I hope they would,' Melanie replied politely. 'Would you mention passing two letters from me to the captain? They are both addressed to my family in England. From Malta, the way from them should be easy.'

The trader stroked his short bead.

'You are from Evelyn bint Gerald's household, aren't you?'

'I am. How did you guess?'

'Not so many Franks in the city now. Even less newcomers. Besides, we've seen your doctor. He took a look at my leg, may God protect him.'

'Dr Wharton?' Melanie asked with surprise. 'He told us nothing about such a visit.'

'He came with a letter for England, too. You should have left yours with him,' the merchant chided her a bit. 'Not run around the city yourself. Not when there is this vomiting sickness around. Thank God we are getting out for a good long while.'

'He left a letter with you?' Melanie frowned. 'But for whom? He said he has no family left in England.'

'Strange indeed,' Evelyn said upon hearing Melanie's tale about her letters. Her knuckles grew whiter as she held her cup tighter.

'Perhaps, he was closer with some of his patients than he led you to believe,' Melanie suggested, not wishing to listen to the disquieting feeling within her soul.

'Why would he omit such an innocent thing? Why would he lie to us about his visit to the merchant? Why would he leave us to find the man's name out from our host, if he had no reason to conceal his own visit to him?'

Melanie had no answers to these questions, and she didn't want to credit the answers that the slithering, low layers of her mind were whispering to her.

'We must check his correspondence,. Evelyn decided what to do next with lightning quickness and the nonchalance of a decision to take a walk in the park.

'Evelyn, we can't!'

'We can. He is on a visit to another local patient now.' Evelyn's tone grew softer as she clearly saw the dismay in Melanie's eyes. 'Melanie, I don't like this solution any more than you do. But what if he really is concealing some subterfuge?'

'What if he is working for the French, you mean.'

'Yes.' Evelyn fixed her in place with her steady, dark gaze. 'What if he is working for the French. If he is, everything we have worked for might go up in flames.'

'If he is not, we might insult a good man.'

'I believe him to be a good man, too. But, if there is a danger, I want to leave nothing to chance.'

Never had Melanie felt herself so much like a petty thief, riffling through the scant wealth of his waistcoats and shirts, cravats and breeches. Never had she felt herself much like a prying maid when reading through the few letters she found concealed beneath the layers of personal garb.

All of them had been written from London, apart from one note from Germany, most likely from an old university friend. All of them had mostly been concerned with medical matters – a steady, lively exchange of knowledge.

Melanie's heart burnt with shame at her mistrust for her friend; of course, he must have been writing to one of his colleagues. She turned to see Evelyn crouched beside the chest of his belongings, her arms buried deep.

'I think there is something queer about the corner of this chest's bottom,' she said, looking at Melanie. 'Come here. Help me.'

Melanie sank to her knees and touched the part of the chest Evelyn indicated. Evelyn was working so close that Melanie could feel the warmth of her skin, emanating like a cloud of perfume. Except Evelyn wore no perfume but only the scent of soap and clean linen. For some reason, that was all the more intoxicating.

Banishing these thoughts with an application of will, Melanie caught the small, thread-thin space between the corner and the chest's wall and raised its bottom with the most unladylike grunt. It was easier than she thought it would be, for Evelyn was pushing alongside her, without needing to be told, as if hearing her intentions.

Both stared. Beneath the false bottom of the chest lay a scattering of carefully folded letters.

'Well,' Evelyn uttered, looking down. 'I believe we have our answer.' There was no ire in her voice. Only a strange kind of resignation.

Melanie picked up one of the letters and frowned. 'It's empty.'

'Must be invisible ink,' Evelyn said categorically. She was herself again – quick, put together, ice-cold. 'Let's light a candle.'

Melanie did so without thinking, her mind still reeling from the shock. The Armenian Christian who was so kind as to host them was not a poor man, and the candles in his house were not made of tallow but of wax – pale and tender wax, the kind that burnt in that ballroom in London all those years ago.

Evelyn tried to take the letter from Melanie's grasp, but Melanie put her fingers on her hand. 'Let me,' she said gently.

'Why?'

'I do not trust your grip right now.' Unable to withstand the temptation, she squeezed slightly. 'Your hands – they are cold and shaking.'

To her surprise, Evelyn stepped aside placidly as if accepting the chiding of a governess. Melanie doubted Evelyn accepted the chiding of a governess even as a girl. Her breath held, as if in expectation of some dark miracle, Melanie put the letter closer to the flame, the thin rivulet of smoke streaming past it.

She held it there and watched how lines the colour of burnt meat snaked across the seemingly empty paper in patches.

'I am grateful for your information regarding E.P.,' the letter read. *'I bid you to continue your good work.'*

He didn't come back until the evening cooled the air of Damascus and made it drunk with the scent of fruit trees.

All this time, Evelyn spent pacing the room, composing accusatory speeches in her head and then unravelling them like skeins of wool. Out of the corner of her eye, she could see Melanie sitting on her sofa, her hands deceptively placid upon her knees.

That did not mean that her friend – *merely friend, nothing more, not ever* – was not secretly boiling with anger. Evelyn knew her well enough by this time not to think otherwise.

Finally, she heard the footsteps of the young physician. She stood, facing the doorway of the room, clutching the now crumpled letter she barely pried from Melanie's pale fingers in her hand.

Evelyn hoped she looked like an angel of retribution. She knew, deep down, that really she was probably looking like an angry fishwife.

Wharton made barely a step inside the room and paused. He must have felt the change in the atmosphere. 'It seems I have sinned somehow,' he said, his voice light. 'Would you mind telling me my transgressions, Lady Evelyn?'

Without a word at first, she presented him with the letter and, with some satisfaction, saw the colour drain from her face.

Wharton sat down heavily next to Melanie. 'I see you have uncovered my little secret,' he noted, looking at Evelyn with only the mildest sheepishness.

'Your. Little. Secret.' Evelyn enunciated every word carefully. 'Is that what you would call a betrayal?'

'Hardly a betrayal,' he protested.

'Not for you, perhaps. You were, after all, loyally serving the interests of your masters.'

'Not just their interests.'

'Oh? So, the French are not your only employers?'

'The French?' He stared at her. 'What are you talking about, Lady Evelyn?'

'About the obvious. You have been passing the information about my movements to our enemies all this time.'

'That's absurd!'

'You must be thinking me an utter idiot.'

'No – Lady Evelyn, you don't understand! My enterprise had nothing to do with the French or our quest; nothing to do with foreign politics at all! My letters have all been for Sir Sidney Smith.'

Now it was Evelyn's turn to stare. 'The admiral? What on earth would he want from you?' You better tell me something plausible, she implied with her tone.

'It is a long story.'

'We have time,' Melanie interjected, looking at him with the polite coolness of a society lady born and bred. Which she, of course, was.

'Very well,' Wharton answered quickly. 'I take it you know about the Ottoman practice of slave trade?'

'I do,' Evelyn replied. 'Circassian girls sold into harems?'

'Not just Circassian girls – anyone captured by the Barbary pirates off the Mediterranean shores. And not necessarily into harems.' Wharton's voice was grim. 'Some are sold into a simple domestic servitude. Not that there is much difference with the degree of power their master has over them.'

'As great a degree as a respectable employer has over a scullery maid in England, in other words?'

'I beg you not to be flippant.' He bristled slightly. 'I know you are an admirer of Wilberforce. I know of your boycott of West Indian sugar. I know you are no friend to slavers, whatever their faith.'

'That I am certainly not. What does Sir Sidney want to do about it, though? And what does he want with me?'

'He had contacted me soon after your expedition became known.'

'Ah, so it became known!' *So much for the Lake District.*

'Then I realized that was my chance to make a great difference for the cause.'

'I see. However, that doesn't answer either of my questions.' Evelyn tried to keep her tone light and matter-of-fact as if it were every day that she was used and lied to by a man she considered a friend.

'Sir Sidney wanted me to get close to you, to enlist your support for his plan. Or, rather, to enlist your support in enlisting your uncle's support for his plan.'

This hurt more than it should have. She had almost forgotten, during her months in Lebanon, that, beyond these shores, she was regarded as essentially her uncle's companion and housekeeper, the vessel for his words and the planner of his political dinner parties. Expecting that someone would want her own help for its own sake was like being a well-dowered girl and expecting the men dancing around her wanted her for her own heart.

'May I ask what did this plan consist of?' Evelyn pushed the word out, not without some effort.

'Of course. It is simple and brilliant. We would enlist Emir Bashir's support and supply him with enough means to raise an army of one and a half thousand men. Given the Druze's knowledge of the land, it should be more than enough to sweep the slave-trading Barbary potentates from the face of the earth and nip the problem in the bud.'

'A thousand and a half Druze,' Evelyn repeated as though her voice could change the meaning of the words. 'All to do your bidding.'

'To collaborate with us,' Wharton corrected her.

'A very apt word. Why do you think the Druze would want such a thing?'

'They are a weak state within a state and would most likely be eager for the friendship of a great empire.'

'They already are the part of a great empire. The Ottoman one. How do you think the Sublime Porte is going to look upon us using their subjects for military purposes?'

'The Sublime Porte is too weak to enforce their rule this far to the south, not with the troubles in Serbia and Greece.'

'What will happen when the troubles are over? Are you going to just leave the Druze to reap the sultan's wrath?'

'Of course not. Should our enterprise be successful, we would support them through their later endeavours.'

'In other words, you are going to split the Ottoman Empire into a civil war.'

'Not necessarily.'

'But very likely. What on earth made Sir Sidney imagine Emir Bashir would ever agree to such a madcap scheme? He is not a fool just because he knows no quadrille or pox vaccines. He steered his people through decades of difficult rule, took back Baalbek. He did not do that by throwing himself in every alliance that presented itself.'

'He could take back much more. Sir Sidney would not hesitate to petition the government to help him.'

'He would never agree to antagonize Constantinople. By the way, which colours do you suppose these thousand and a half men are going to wear on their adventure? The Turkish ones? But they would be following no orders from the sultan.

The British ones? But that would make them outlaw rebels within their own country.'

'I would have never thought you to be so lukewarm about this enterprise, Lady Evelyn.'

'Lukewarm? I am not lukewarm. I am angry. I am angry because you pretended friendship and concern only to manipulate me into agreeing to further one of the most hare-brained schemes I have ever heard.'

'It really does sound unwise,' Melanie murmured, and it was as if her voice was the last straw shifting something in Evelyn's heart.

'I am going out,' she announced, turning on her heel. 'And I would be most grateful if you do not follow me.'

The cathedral was not hard for Melanie to find even though she had never been there. Damascus, for all its beauty, did not exactly abound in Christian cathedrals.

Melanie found Evelyn sitting in the empty pews, the dark gold of Greek Catholic mosaics unfurling over her head.

'I told you not to follow me,' Evelyn said without turning.

Melanie's heart leapt at the notion that she recognized her footsteps. 'You did.' Melanie came closer. 'But I thought it is one of those cases when I will ignore your words.'

A chuckle came from the pews. 'You are bolder than I remember. Have you so changed in a few hours?'

'Not in a few hours.' Melanie moved closer through the dim light. 'Not even in a few days.'

'How did you guess I am here?'

'Where else could you have gone to try and find peace but to the nearest church?'

'To some equivalent of Gunter's.'

'I don't think there are many in Damascus.'

'True. I miss their ices.' Finally, Evelyn turned, her dark eyes framed by shadows. 'I could have been wandering the streets. I did at first.'

'At near night? Without a companion? Even you are not as indifferent to your own life.' *Though indifferent enough.*

'I have my sabre with me. It is all the companion I need.'

'Is it?' Melanie sat down by her side, and Evelyn did not move away.

'When it comes to personal safety, yes.'

'I am starting to understand why you used to be so resentful of my company in the beginning. How long did your uncle have to coax you into accepting it?'

'A long time. Why did you come?'

'Because I was worried for you. Dr Wharton wasn't wrong when he said you have something self-destructive in your soul.'

'When did the viper say such a thing?' Evelyn raised her head sharply.

Melanie sighed. 'Just after your charge on the Ruwallah, if in different words. I don't think he was wrong in that.'

'Of course, he said that. He would have pretended concern all day long if it meant to get on my good side.'

'I don't think that was a question of pretending. If he had a cause to fight for, it doesn't mean he couldn't be genuinely worried for you.' Melanie intertwined her gloveless fingers with Evelyn's bare hand. 'As am I.'

'You, I believe. You, I have always believed. I didn't always like you, that is true, but I've always believed you.' Evelyn paused, looking around, as though seeing the dark wood and the mother-of-pearl inlaid in the frames of the icons for the first time. 'I haven't always been like this, truth be told. There has always been a certain wildness to me, but it used to be a kind of Dionysian wildness, a wildness of laughter.'

'Then what happened?' Melanie asked beseechingly, without a hope of reply.

She was a little shocked when Evelyn parted her lips.Perh aps, it had been the nervous exhaustion of the day. Perhaps, it was the blow of the earlier revelation that rattled her composition. Perhaps, it was something else entirely – something Melanie couldn't even dare to hope for.

'What happened was the most trite story in the history of the world,' Evelyn said. 'You are going to despise me if you hear how I crumbled in its face.'

'I would never despise anything about you.'

'Never? That is a bold promise. I should hold you to it. It started with a courtship, a compliment offered freely in a ballroom ...'

'A courtship?' Despite her promise, Melanie couldn't quite keep the slight disappointment out of her thoughts, if not her voice. She had imagined something magnificent and Gothic, something out of Ann Radcliffe.

'A courtship,' Evelyn nodded. 'His name was Robert Thornfield, and he was the younger son of a baronet. Uncle thought him beneath me at first, but he succumbed to my siege of pleadings eventually and allowed the betrothal to go through. It was not simply Robert's blue eyes or dashing smile that captivated me – had it been so, I would have been ensnared long ago.

'No, it was the way he ... saw me. Saw the restless energy that plagued me all my life; saw my hunger for a greater cause. He was the one who encouraged me to learn Arabic, you know; Uncle Owen merely thought it a useful hobby. I wanted Robert like a beast pursuing a prey, however much all the books of good conduct would tell you it should be the other way around – or, better yet, a different way at all with both parties exhibiting restrained manner and good sense...'

Evelyn chuckled. 'These are not qualities I have been born or raised with. Neither was he. We anticipated our marriage vows in the glasshouse straight after the engagement was announced, right amidst the fragrant orchids. Do I shock you, Melanie?'

'Not so much as you either worry or intend to. I am not stupid. I've seen newlywed couples with peculiarly early babies. What happened after?' A suspicion was already snaking its way into Melanie's mind. 'Did he break the engagement? Did he think you a wanton for succumbing to him so easily?'

'How little you know him.'

'I don't know him at all. I know the rules this world lives by, that is all.'

'You know the rules, but the universe is illuminated by exceptions. He did not leave me. Or, rather, he did, but not out of his own accord. The war called him to Cadiz.'

Melanie winced, recalling reading in the papers of the vicious naval engagements with Bonaparte's forces. She recalled, too, the dreadful long lists of the dead and the missing.

'I am sorry.'

'You don't know the ending yet. He didn't die at sea; he died of another officer's bullet. They were drinking, and the other man, who long since wanted to knock Robert down a notch, insinuated that his fiancée was little more than a lightskirt, a wild daughter of a wild father. He didn't expect for Robert to throw a glove in his face.'

Evelyn breathed out slowly. 'Or, perhaps, that was exactly what he wanted. I've learnt the details later. One of his friends wrote me a letter – it was sweet of him; he didn't have to. I was not, after all, Robert's wedded wife.'

Something cracked in her voice, and without thought, Melanie swept in to clasp her in an embrace. It was not that instinctive, joyful embrace they shared in the tent on the ruins of Ascalon; this one was a grip of someone drowning and clutching at a passing plank.

'I am so sorry,' Melanie whispered, feeling herself horribly out of her depth, her own tragedies puny. What was the calamity of a soiled reputation next to the chasm of a loss?

She remembered the well at Ascalon, the twin to St. Joseph's Well in Cairo. Was that how it felt for Evelyn? Like a dark, gaping abyss?

'You have nothing to be sorry for,' Evelyn replied, her voice stifling too much.

'I do. I shouldn't have pushed you to reveal this.'

'No, it was ... it was for the best. Some wounds need to be cleansed, I understand.' A strange, unnatural sound – half sob and half moan – escaped her breast. 'I only wish my particular wound could be left alone.'

'Have you never felt tenderness for anyone since?' Melanie enquired cautiously.

'You mean, have I ever thought of marrying someone else? No,' Evelyn shook her head decisively and sharply. 'It was ... out of question. Call me a novel reader with a mush for brains – except I've never read *Pamela* nor *Evelina* – but I cannot imagine experiencing the same kind of love again. We were as a pair of bright comets, meeting in the sky once in a millennium ... to destroy each other.'

'You didn't destroy him.'

'He would have been alive, if not for me. And if I hadn't felt such a – an actual lightskirt in that glasshouse ...'

'Do you truly regret what you have done there?'

For a while, it seemed as though Evelyn was never going to answer. She sat with her eyes closed, as if the imagery of a minute's passion, a comet's fire, was engraved upon her eyelids. 'No. Not truly. I can't imagine how I would have lived if I hadn't had even this memory of him.'

'Maybe there would never be precisely this kind of love,' Melanie conceded. 'But, maybe, there is going to be a different one. An even better one, perhaps. The kind of love of which St. Paul preached.'

'The kind that is patient? Not pompous, not inflated, not rude, and does not seek its own interests?' A rueful smile touched Evelyn's lips. Melanie watched them as though enchanted.

'Yes. Why not?'

'Because I don't believe in fairy tales, Melanie.'

'Maybe ...' Something was clogging her throat, preventing her from getting the words out. Perhaps, it was the fault of the words themselves, crowding as they were in her brain, shapeless, wild, and hoary.

One cannot express what one's own mind knew not.

'Maybe ...' Melanie continued, swallowing, 'Maybe this love already exists. Maybe it is even somewhere close.'

She was confessing to herself as much as to the dark-haired woman sitting by her side in an empty church of murky gold. It was a frightening thing to acknowledge, that something as foreign and powerful had sunk its claws into her heart and claimed it for its own.

It was frightening, and it was wonderful as the glow of the Greek saints above them.

'Melanie. Do you mean what I suspect you mean?' Evelyn's hands clasped her face.

Robbed of words by something grand and painful rising within her chest, Melanie nodded.

Evelyn's fingers moved wonderingly as though she was a blind woman revealing Melanie's features to herself for the first time, one by one. Melanie submitted to this strange examination, her heart singing and bleeding at the same time.

'You are so different from him,' Evelyn said with what was almost a gentle surprise.

'I am afraid I am,' Melanie acknowledged, unable to quite restrain a smile. 'I'll understand if you would – need time. Need years. Decades, perhaps.'

'I know you would wait decades.' Evelyn ran her thumb over Melanie's lower lip in a bolder bout of exploration. 'I know you are that kind of a woman. I am not.' She leaned closer as though closer was even possible. 'I am not.'

'Evelyn ...' Melanie murmured, clutching her hands, feeling the freezing cold of her palms between her own. Then she inclined her head and pressed her forehead tenderly against Evelyn's.

They didn't speak for a while. Through her half-closed eyes, Melanie could discern the slightly golden ends of Evelyn's eyelashes.

'I am sorry,' Evelyn said suddenly, her grip becoming painful.

'What for? For enticing an innocent maiden?' Melanie couldn't help but smile a little. 'You are forgiven.'

'No.' Evelyn shook her head, pulling away. 'For – I need—' She rushed to her feet, all but running out of the church.

Alarmed, Melanie followed. 'Evelyn? Did I say something? Evelyn!'

Evelyn did not reply. Instead, she stormed into the night, sank to her knees beside the road, and was horribly, violently sick.

Melanie had two brothers, the younger of them rather sickly. She was not a person to faint at the sight of illness. Still, she cast about for something – anything – to wipe Evelyn's lips with. Not finding it, Melanie wiped her stained mouth with her own sleeve. 'Can you stand?' She offered Evelyn her hand, easing her to her feet.

'Just barely.' Evelyn coughed, not resisting the care. 'God, I—'

'You must have eaten something. Or the coffee water had not been boiled properly.' The practical concerns had pushed the memory of the touches in the church from Melanie's mind; however, they could not erase it completely.

It was suddenly, undeniably true. Evelyn Prynne loved her. Or, at least, was capable of loving her. This thought made Melanie's feet so light that it seemed she would be able to ascend to the stars. 'Let me help you home,' she said decisively and draped her arm around Evelyn's shoulders.

The heiress nodded, unusually placid.

Luck followed them. No ruffian accosted what must have looked like two Turkish youths stumbling home from a party.

'Lady Evelyn? Are you unwell?' Dr Wharton rose in greeting, alarm in his eyes, as soon as they all but fell into the chambers allocated to them.

'You are the physician,' Evelyn snapped, her ire at the earlier revelation still burning hot in her voice. 'You have to tell me.'

'She was sick,' Melanie explained. 'It must have been the luncheon or—'

Clearly not listening to her, Wharton clasped Evelyn's hands. 'Cold and clammy,' he muttered. 'God. Do you feel any tremors, Lady Evelyn? Any shaking of the limbs?'

'A little,' Evelyn admitted, not without some reluctance. 'I've never had food poisoning before. Does that not always happen?'

'I'm afraid it is no food poisoning.' Wharton shook his head gravely. 'Lady Evelyn. I am sorry to say that, but it seems the epidemic has reached Damascus.' He put the back of his hand to her forehead. 'I'm afraid you might have the vomiting sickness, which, in Europe, is called the Asiatic cholera.'

Chapter 12

That night, Melanie remained sleepless.

It was a terrible feeling, this helplessness, this absence of anything she could do to help. Wharton called for a warm spearmint drink and camomile and camphor julep, in hope that these simply remedies could arrest the sickness in its early stage. He made sure Evelyn was bundled into bed and did not rise as strongly as any boarding school matron.

Cholera. In Melanie's mind, the word belonged to the slums of London and Liverpool, the horrid overcrowded settlements that rose together with the giant factories booming with the war. It also belonged to the lands of the Ottomans, which suffered from its bouts almost yearly.

Melanie only managed to fall into a fitful sleep when the sky outside the latticed windows was already growing grey with the expectation of sunset. When she woke up, she woke up to sunlight and silence. The silence did not bother her at first when she washed her face and dressed without care, too eager to check on Evelyn than to think on anything else.

It was only after she entered Evelyn's room and found her lying on the mattress, Wharton sitting listlessly next to her, that she realized, in the back of her mind, that something might be amiss.

'Where are the servants?' Melanie asked, coming closer. 'Why is no one preparing all those drinks you said should invigorate her?' She heard her own voice, the thin, crystal string of hysteria sounding in it.

'They have left,' Wharton replied grimly. 'Together with their master. They have left in the night as soon as they realized what it was that their guest had.'

'Where?' A mad scheme – not so much a scheme as a ghostly vision of chaotic efforts – arose in Melanie's mind. To find their host, to rouse his conscience, to implore him ...

'To some country house or other, I suspect. The countryside around Damascus is a prime place for those, given the water and the greenery. There would be no finding them.' In a quick, tried and tested movement, Wharton caught Evelyn's wrist, feeling the pulse. There was a fleeting change in his expression – a change that did not promise anything good.

It was only now that Melanie managed to overcome the fear of what she might find and looked into Evelyn's face directly.

Her pallor was such as if she had already been a ghost, dead of her sickness centuries ago. Her arm was hanging, trailing in the open air beyond the bed. Only her cheeks were bright with fever, rosy as those of a May Queen.

'Can she hear me?' Melanie asked quietly.

'I very much can,' Evelyn replied. 'And I would really... really appreciate it if you stopped talking of me as if I were already en route to the cemetery.'

'I'm sorry.' Melanie took her wrist. One did not need a medical education from Gottingen to feel how irregularly blood was beating in her pulse. 'But I am frightened. Oh, Evelyn, I am so frightened.'

'Worry not, I will do my best not to infect you.' Her dark hair was spread across the pillow, like a funereal veil. 'If you mean that mishap with the servants, I think we are quite lucky. They could have run off with our money as opposed to just running off.'

'Melanie.' Dr Wharton looked at her, and there was grave earnestness in his eyes. 'I need your help. You've mentioned preparing the drinks.'

'Of course!' Melanie jumped at the opportunity. She hated feeling helpless and listless. 'Just tell me the measures.'

'I will do so. But there is something else.' Suddenly, a kind of bashfulness entered his tone, as though he suddenly remembered the woman he was talking to was a genteelly bred daughter of Yorkshire gentry. 'As you know, Asiatic cholera is accompanied by bouts of sickness...'

'Yes? Do you want me to — hold the vessel when these bouts occur?'

'As a matter of fact, yes. But I would also like to wash the vessel afterwards.'

A life sewn of white linen. How shocked her father would have been to find her even entertaining such a request. But then, her father would have been shocked at rather a lot of things.

'There is running water here,' Wharton assured her hastily. 'A medieval construction, from the times of the caliphs. The water is derived from an underground well and directed into a tap. There is also sand to scrub the thing with. They took their soap with them, I'm afraid.'

'Just show me where that is,' Melanie replied.

The next days became a blur, a kind of evil kaleidoscope of holding the bowl and stroking the hair matted with sweat, of washing and scrubbing, of mixing and heating and cooling. Often, the tasks collided like tectonic plates — one minute Melanie was holding a cup of water or camomile to Evelyn's lips, and the other she had to help her while she retched.

The rare moments of relative peace came when, her body exhausted from the constant fight, Evelyn fell asleep. Still, even during those quiet hours, there was a veil upon the house, warping reality, poisoning it with silence and shushing. In the morning, Melanie went out to the market to get their groceries, especially chicken for Evelyn's broth. Every time, she all but ran home, surer with every step that some unspeakable tragedy has happened while she had been abroad.

Once she established that no changes had occurred – either for the worse or for the better – Melanie sat on the edge of the sofa and silently counted their remaining money. Ottoman piastres, old Hungarian coins, and the silver dollars of Germany. Every kind of money with heavy bullion in it counted for something in this country that didn't trust its own currency; but how long was its supply going to last?

By the evening of the third day, the twilight heavy and murky, Dr Wharton bled Evelyn for the first time, and, once again, Melanie held the bowl, looking at the crimson liquid running from Evelyn's limp hand and staining the white.

By the evening of the fourth day, Dr Wharton, who long since left the harmless spearmint for quinine, gave Evelyn the first dose of opium. He explained it should help with the fever.

By the end of the week, he called Melanie to him with the same strangely embarrassed look that he wore when first asking her to wash the bowls of vomit.

'What happened?' Melanie asked, her hands still reddish from scrubbing the bowls with sand.

'I won't lie to you, Miss Bright. Lady Evelyn is very unwell.'

'But she is going to survive, isn't she?' Melanie's heart beat faster within her chest. 'Or?'

'That's what I wanted to speak to you about. Do you know the story of Cesare Borgia and his French disease?'

'I know that he existed once.' Melanie blinked. 'That is the extent of my knowledge, I'm afraid.'

'No matter. When his fever was particularly foul, his physician forced him into an icy bath to break it with shock.'

'Did it help?'

'If it didn't, I wouldn't have been telling you this story,' Wharton said with impatience, and Melanie noticed the dark shadows beneath his eyes as if seeing him for the first time.

'The idea I have is somewhat similar. Invigorating the body, mobilizing it to fight the disease the way our men are fighting Bonaparte.'

'Why do you need my help?'

'You are going to realize soon. The task is a little personal. It's not that I cannot do it at all by the virtue of my sex, but, I think, it would be better if it were performed by another woman.'

'Why?'

'You would have to rub her body with a mix of mustard, oils of turpentine, and cayenne pepper.' He swallowed, his throat moving. 'Obviously, I mean her naked body.'

The moment Melanie stepped into the sickroom, she couldn't tear her eyes away from the figure on the bed. Evelyn was breathing in strange, shallow gulps, and her forehead was as hot as a working forge.

Heavenly dove, Melanie prayed in silence, disrobing her, *help the one who invokes you so often.*

Undressing Evelyn turned out to be a much easier task than it would have been had she still been wearing the European gown she glowed in in London. She was swathed in the Turkish robes to make her perspire along with shirt and trousers and shawls. Shawls from Malabar, Melanie recalled. Pearls from Bahrain.

Melanie pulled the last garment off inch by inch as if any touch of cold could make her worse – or as if Melanie was unwrapping some sacred statue for a pagan festival.

Evelyn said nothing in response; she merely turned her head on the pillow and emitted a low noise that might have been a moan.

'It's all right,' Melanie murmured, taking the cup with the heat-breathing mixture up. 'It's going to be all right.' She did not believe it, not anymore. But what else could she possibly say?

Evelyn lay upon the bed naked as the day as she was born now; naked as a dead Venus except with heavier breasts than the slender goddess of the temperance-loving Greeks. Melanie stared at her helplessly for a moment, pity, fear, and something unmentionable mixing in her soul. It was unmentionable not because Evelyn was a woman but because Evelyn was dying.

Melanie scooped the mixture up in her fingers and started to rub it into the other woman's shoulders. The skin beneath her fingers was unnaturally, irregularly heated as if in a grip of passion instead of disease. 'It's all right,' Melanie repeated, moving lower.

Her palm slid between Evelyn's breasts, massaging the mud-coloured salve in. Evelyn opened her eyes for a second then closed them again. From what Melanie managed to see in that moment, the world beneath her eyelids resembled murky glass. *Heavenly dove, help her.*

Melanie rubbed the salve into her stomach, moving in slow circles. *Such a thin stomach, after all our travels, after living on beans and rice and chicken broth.* Melanie's gaze fell on the gorgeously dark-haired triangle between her thighs and wondered, for a fleeting second, just how thorough Dr Wharton expected her to be. Then she concluded that a hot, biting mixture of mustard and pepper was likely to do more harm than good in that sensitive place and continued down her legs.

The ritual of anointing took long. Indeed, it seemed to Melanie that time had decreased its pace, dissolving into the slowness of honey, stretching the treatment into hours. By the end of it, Melanie's palms were burning. She wanted to touch Evelyn's face but couldn't for the fear of staining it.

'How is she?' Dr Wharton asked her quietly once Melanie exited the sour-smelling room.

'Terrible,' she said before thinking, before couching her words into a gentler, more diplomatic reply. What use would a diplomatic reply be here? 'What are we to do now?'

'Wrap her warm. And pray.'

'Can I sit with her tonight?' Melanie asked.

'I don't want to subject you to the risk of infection any more than I have already.'

'I doubt that's going to make a difference after what I've just done. Either I fall ill or I don't.'

'You are a brave young woman, Miss Bright.' There was, however, not mistaking some relief in his voice. Dr Wharton's eyes were reddish from the lack of sleep, and his face was almost as pale as that of his patient.

Melanie recalled the smell of sickness in the room she just left and recalled the sight of a single arm hanging in the air. 'I am not brave, Dr Wharton. I am not brave at all.'

That night would be a long one; she knew it as soon as she agreed to it. There was no book to settle with in the darkness, and even if there was, they couldn't afford to waste good wax candles on reading. Everything Melanie was doing now was done by touch alone. Pewter warmth beneath her fingertips: the water-filled cup. Cold: that thrice-damned bowl. Softness: the coverlet that should not, under any circumstances, slip or cover Evelyn to a lesser extent than from the chin to the toes.

The first two hours went by quietly. Evelyn was sleeping, if such a state could be called such a peaceful word, as soundly as she had during the experimental treatment. Then she opened her twilit eyes.

'Melanie?' she murmured, her voice hoarse from the constant vomiting and her fingers icy as northern stars.

'You shouldn't try to speak. Try and fall asleep again.'

'That was you, wasn't it? In the afternoon. I felt the touch, but I thought that was a dream.'

'Yes. It was a treatment devised by Dr Wharton. It should make your body fight.'

'I hope it does, Melanie. I hope it does. I am myself so tired of fighting.'

'I know. I know.' Melanie squeezed her fingers almost the way she had at the Greek church. 'But try to fight a little more, won't you? Just for me.'

'I can't.'

'You can,' Melanie insisted. 'You are the strongest person I know. I remember you teaching me sabre-fencing for the first time, there among the painted ruins of the Temple of the Sun.'

'I remember that.'

It was hard to see in the stone-clad darkness, but Melanie thought she could discern the hint of a smile.

'You were so good. I was even wondering if you might have lied about it being your first time.'

'Most people don't lie and betray one another for such petty reasons as that.'

'Heavy-handed, Melanie. Heavy-handed ...' Her tone was almost dreamy.

'If you mean Dr Wharton, he almost purged himself of health tending to you.'

'I know. I know I shouldn't have exploded with him so much. I am sorry.' She paused, evidently gathering her strength. 'I am sorry about a lot of things.'

'How about almost kissing me beneath the Greek mosaic?'

'No.' Now there was definitely an attempt at a smile. 'I would never be sorry about that.'

'Try to sleep,' Melanie repeated, reaching out and touching her hair. 'Try to sleep.'

To her surprise, Evelyn obeyed. She slid into slumber like into a chasm and spent the rest of the night there, tossing on the pillows from time to time. Every movement of this nature made Melanie raise her head, alarmed, but no horrors came.

Melanie wouldn't have been able to pinpoint the moment when she herself fell asleep if she tried. At some point, the murky waters had simply closed over her head, and she spent the rest of the night in a strange, liminal state, half aware of the receding darkness around her, half moving through the twilit light of dreams, populated by ghosts and giants.

When Melanie finally opened her eyes, her back and neck cramped from sleeping while sitting, it was to a shock of sunlight. The room was drenched in it, the bed whitened in the rays. Melanie looked into Evelyn's face intently but could not find anything but deep, death-like sleep there.

With a jolt of fear, Melanie touched her wrist, afraid to wake her up and afraid she wouldn't be able to. Closing her eyes and attuning her senses, she felt the feeble beating of a pulse.

Thank God. Thank the Heavenly dove.

Judging by the sun climbing high beyond the latticed windows, it must have been closer to the afternoon. Melanie hoped Dr Wharton did his usual market duty today. She was going to need more chicken soup for when Evelyn woke up. If Evelyn woke up.

Evelyn didn't realize at first that she woke up.

For the last few hours, she swayed in a queer dream where she lay in a boat drifting in the middle of a sapphire ocean. The tropical sun was beating down upon her skin, but she had neither the energy not any great desire to move. The world beneath her eyelids was inflamed.

When she woke, it was not immediately obvious she had moved out of the realm of dreams, for the real world was just as stiflingly heated. But now, at least, she could move her fingers.

Evelyn opened her eyes. The room was already tinged red from the light of the sunset seeping from the window. On the seat by the mattress, Melanie was nodding off to her own slumber. Evelyn whispered her name.

Melanie shuddered in a sudden awakening and gaped as she looked at her. 'You are awake!' she exclaimed. 'Oh God, I was so worried. Let me call Dr Wharton.'

Wincing at her own lack of strength, Evelyn brushed her fingers against Melanie's wrist where she intended to grip her. 'Don't,' Evelyn said quietly. 'Stay. Just give me something to drink. I am dying of thirst.'

'How are you feeling?' Melanie asked anxiously as soon as the cup was away from Evelyn's heated, parched lips.

'Weak.' That was the only answer she could give and still be truthful. She was feeling weak as a kitten, as if her body had been emptied of muscles. She was feeling light and bloodless.

But, for the first time in days, she was feeling lucid.

'But not feverish?' Melanie touched her forehead, and Evelyn leaned into the touch like a woman starved leaning towards a crust of bread.

'No,' she replied after listening to her sensations. 'Not feverish.' Evelyn paused. 'You've nursed me back to health.'

'Hardly. That was Dr Wharton's doing. I've only helped.'

'That seems to be your motto. I've only helped.' Evelyn couldn't help but grin. 'We haven't even become lovers yet, and already you have saved my life like the most devoted of Penelopes.'

Melanie drew in a breath sharply. 'Yet?'

She would have lied if she said she derived no pleasure from hearing Melanie's indrawn breath. 'Unless you've changed your mind ...'

'No. Not at all. I never would.'

'Well, then. I am a touch to weak at present to reach you, but if you lean down ...'

Melanie followed her request as soon as the words left Evelyn's lips. Rising slightly on her elbows, Evelyn claimed her lips. This time, properly.

She tried her best not to appear too hungry, to restrain herself for the sake of Melanie's butterfly innocence. But her movements ended up being as unwieldy because of her state as Melanie's were because of her inexperience. It was as if the illness had wiped Evelyn's memory clean and rendered her a debutante virgin with an unkissed mouth yet again.

Melanie's lips were timid indeed – at least, at first. However, it was not a timidity born of the lack of desire but of the enormity of it and the shock of finally getting what one wanted. She froze as if unable to decide quite what to do.

Evelyn was glad to help her. She probed carefully with her tongue and was surprised to feel Melanie's lips parting to admit it. She was even more surprised to hear an urgent whimper – to feel it against her mouth – in response.

Evelyn's head was still light, her limbs still feeling boneless. She had to withdraw for a second after a bout of dizziness, only to have Melanie whimper quietly and lean after her, clearly aching for more.

'You are going to be the death of me.' Evelyn fell back upon the pillows.

'Not anymore. You've survived cholera, after all. I should be much easier.' Melanie paused, visibly catching her breath. 'Is it the first time you kissed another woman?'

Evelyn nodded. 'It's not the first time I've desired one, though.'

'Oh? Who was she?' The notes of jealousy in Melanie's voice were unmistakable and rather delicious.

'Grace Dashwood.'

'The actress? The one played—'

'Yes, she made a wonderful Lady Macbeth. I was scoffing at first – so much praise – but when I saw her ...'

'She is the one with the red hair, isn't she?'

'The very one. A gorgeous, burning crown, I thought. I talked about her for weeks after the premiere. I'm afraid I have a reputation for theatre madness among most of my acquaintances now. I've even written a letter to her, and when I roamed about to find the address, it turned out that she was living with a certain lady playwright for company.'

'Does that mean ...'

'That might mean nothing but companionship and patronage. But that can also mean that we are not lone beasts in this world.'

'Have you ever – acted on these desires? Not with Miss Dashwood, obviously, but with others?'

Evelyn shook her head. 'Never. Neither with women nor, before Robert, with men. I was afraid.'

'Of censure?'

'Of love. Love makes one into an open wound.' A belated panic caught up with her. How could she be so candid? But, like her body, the panic was enfeebled by the disease and the arduous work of healing and faded away.

Melanie touched her neck just where the scar marred the skin.

'Was this done by a jealous lover?' she asked quietly.

'No. By a jealous father.'

'How?'

It was a long story, and Evelyn knew she should start from the beginning – from the sylvan days of her childhood, from the decline and the growing silence of her Greek-reading mother, from her father's first lessons. Or lack of them.

Lord Gerald Prynne, the Earl of Marsden, was a fierce proponent of the principles Rousseau set out in Emile – that lessons of nature were infinitely more important than whatever can be learnt from books; except Lord Prynne took it to the logical conclusion and allowed neither of his children into his library until they turned twelve and thus had learnt everything there was to be snatched from the air of wilderness.

Evelyn didn't think that their neighbours' children lived differently, for no neighbours called upon them; she didn't know her mother's education was infinitely different, too, for her mother had already thinned into pale shadow. She simply orbited her father's glowing planet as though she were a moon, destined to reflect his radiance, and questioned nothing.

She hated herself for that unquestioning adoration to this day.

She didn't question him either when, instead of giving her brother Paul a tutor or sending him off to a public school, he paid for his son's apprenticeship with a blacksmith, binding him in the usual half servitude that such contracts usually entailed. Paul had been insolent and over proud and needed to be taught humility her father said. Evelyn accepted it not without some confusion but accepted it nonetheless; surely there were not many ways in which a boy of twelve could exhibit any great pride.

She was only shocked out of her unquestioning rough happiness when she saw Paul five years later when Father finally allowed him to come home for Christmas. Rough-handed and as quietly miserable as her mother, Paul had certainly learnt his lesson of humility well but no other lessons, however. When Evelyn showed him her careful diary to read, his eyes roamed over the letters without understanding.

The next day after her brother's departure to his place of servitude, Evelyn committed an unimaginable betrayal. She wrote a secret letter to her uncle.

She was not sure Uncle Owen would even read it, much less listen to her pleas – according to her father, he was a blackguard and a tyrant lover, no better than the people whose heads were rolling off the guillotine across the Channel. Besides, didn't her father say that a true citizen of his ideal Republic is rugged and self-sufficient?

She was shocked when her uncle responded with horror that was seeping through the lines of his elegantly written letter and agreed to buy Paul's apprenticeship out and take him in immediately. Evelyn didn't have any plans for leaving her childhood home. Father made a lapse of judgement, she reasoned; he was, perhaps, a little over harsh. But everyone made mistakes. No one was perfect.

She still loved her father. Her father loved her, too. Up to a point. Up to a point, and, unbeknownst to her, she had passed it.

His reaction upon learning of her betrayal – for he viewed it as a betrayal – would have reminded her of Elizabethan revenge tragedies, had she ever been allowed to go to a theatre.

'You were born in an evil hour,' he declared in his usual grand manner, pinning her to the wall. 'You've always been a stranger to fear. Perhaps, I should have corrected that.'

Evelyn was trying to look into his face and not at the thin gleam of a paper knife in his hand. 'I am not going to apologize,' she said. 'I haven't done anything wrong. It is natural to love one's brother.'

'If you truly loved your brother, you would have allowed me to bring him up in his best interests.'

'Uncle Owen is going to send him to a university next year. I think that is going to be in his best interests.'

'Uncle Owen is not the head of this family.' He put the point of the knife to her throat. 'I am. You would do well to remember that.'

If Evelyn really were a stranger to fear, she would have ceased to be so in that moment. The world narrowed to the width of the blade of the paper knife.

'I disdain all heads of families,' she whispered, looking into his eyes, 'unless they also have hearts.'

Something turned inside her then – some quiet, horrid understanding of her adored father's nature. It was as if someone shifted the curtains, and the portions of her childhood that were so far sweetly shaded suddenly became drenched in a glaring light.

She did not have a lot of time to contemplate it, for then the shock of pain came. It was unlike anything she had ever felt. Unlike the cuts and bruises of her childhood adventures, this one was sharp and tinged with malice. For a second, her vision became crimson.

Then, just as quickly as it came, it receded into a pulsing hurt, and the world in front of her eyes cleared.

Her hands shaking, Evelyn touched her neck. her fingers came away wet and red. There was blood on the blade of her father's knife, too. Her blood.

He stepped away from her and spoke to her in the same tone he usually used with her late mother. 'Then go and live with your uncle Owen. This house is closed to you henceforth.'

Evelyn arrived on the doorstep of her uncle's London townhouse, a handkerchief bound tightly around her neck, when the next morning was turning the sky grey. She was sure she iwas going to be turned out, for who would want a traitor to her own family?

But she was not turned out. In fact, she was fussed over and consoled and bathed and combed, and a physician was called to clean her wound.

'I knew my brother was a madman,' Uncle Owen pronounced after a moment of stunned silence upon unveiling her stained handkerchief. 'I didn't know he was also a brute.'

It was hard to recount these things now in the sun-soaked bedroom in a different part of the world.

'I used to think you received that scar in some glorious adventure in a different part of the world,' Melanie said when Evelyn finished her story. 'Eventually. At first, I thought it was a result of your being too headstrong and rushing into danger.'

'Well, you were not wrong with this latter one.' After the agony of telling her story, muted only by exhaustion, there was only emptiness, but it was a blissful emptiness of a cleared glass. 'Though wrong with the former. I have never been beyond England before setting sail for Lebanon. The war took care of that.'

'Neither had I. Though, I think, that would have remained the case whether there was a war on or not.' Melanie grew earnest, her face translucent from the tiring worries of the last days. 'No one who truly loved you would have hurt you like that. And I promise never to let anyone do it again.'

'You promise?' Evelyn couldn't help but laugh a little. 'My brave defendant. My aScythian Amazon.'

'You did say I was showing a promise with the sabre!' Melanie protested.

'So you were, my dear. So you were. We have to resume our lessons once I am well enough for exertions.'

Melanie nodded and her cheeks reddened. Yes, I can imagine you are too exhausted by the illness to exert yourself now.'

'Ah,' Evelyn realized just what kinds of exertions Melanie was likely thinking about. 'That depends on the kind.' Not wasting time, she pulled Melanie down by her sleeves.

'You cannot mean it,' the fair-haired beauty exclaimed, falling on top of her, dazzled rather than frightened.

'Oh, I most certainly can,' Evelyn purred and clasped Melanie close, turning her about so that now she was beneath her with Evelyn rising above her on her elbows. 'Unless you would prefer me coiffed and jewelled?' she teased, stroking Melanie's chest through her shirt. 'Though I wouldn't fault you if you would prefer me bathed...'

'No.' Melanie shook her head with a sudden decisiveness. 'I would prefer you right now.'

'Such hunger,' Evelyn mused. Feeling somewhat languid from the long healing, she could afford now the kind of slowness she would have been too impatient for in the normal run of things. Perhaps, here, with this lover, that was exquisitely for the best. She slid her finger across Melanie's lips and shivered with delight upon feeling the other woman's tongue darting out to caress it.

'Little wanton,' Evelyn whispered, divesting her of her shirt and wide Turkish trousers. 'I promise to sate you.'

'Please,' Melanie whimpered, gazing at her as if she were the rising sun.

Evelyn had no intention to break such a promise. She had, however, a full intention to take her time. She covered Melanie's neck and shoulders with kisses, unable to withstand the temptation to nip on her neck and to feel the lithe body beneath her bucking up a little. Then she finally cupped the blonde's breasts in her hands.

'A little like apples.' Evelyn rolled her thumbs back and forth over Melanie's nipples, delighting in her lover's writhing. 'I wonder if they taste just as sweet?'

She bent her head and lapped at one of Melanie's nipples with her tongue before taking it into her heated mouth fully. She repeated the motion several times. Melanie emitted a thin, high whine, arching up, and then Evelyn covered her mouth with a palm.

'Wharton could have heard you. He can come at any moment, in fact,' Evelyn whispered, feeling wicked. 'So, you'd better keep quiet if you want me to continue.'

Melanie bit her lip immediately, and a delighted charge coursed through Evelyn's veins at the sight of this obedience.

'Now let me please you properly,' she said, stroking Melanie's narrow hips and nudging her thighs apart, shivering at the slick feeling in between. 'Show me where you like it most.'

'I – I have never done it before. With anyone.' Something like panic flickered in Melanie's eyes, and Evelyn thought fleetingly just how deep and visceral it must be, this fear of being thought unchaste and less than – for does an unchaste lady not become a less than?

'I mean on your own.'

'Oh, I – I hadn't ...'

Evelyn merely raised her eyebrows.

Redder than a beetroot, Melanie took her hand and guided it to a point at the meeting of her thighs. 'There,' Melanie whispered, avoiding her eyes. 'Pressing from the right side.'

Evelyn followed her instructions, if slowly, and received a whimper of sudden delight in reward. Spurred on by this sound, she started brushing the spot with her knuckles then stroking in little circles.

What weakness? Evelyn felt heated and golden, filled with some exhilarating elixir from top to toe. Evelyn had done her best to forget how it felt to give pleasure to someone you loved and to shiver in anticipation of receiving this pleasure in return, and she wondered why.

Why had she spent all this time covering her heart with frost or trying to find her redemption in blood? Such things now seemed to be as distant as the Arctic Circle. Breathing heavily, Evelyn slipped one finger between her lover's thighs and finally within her.

Melanie arched up, and for a second, Evelyn was afraid she hurt her. But the sharpness of her movement was that of passion, not of pain, and Evelyn set about moving her finger with the same rhythm as she remembered her first lover moving in and out of her, among the hothouse flowers, the air breathing with sweetness.

'Heavenly dove, someone should paint you like this,' Evelyn whispered, looking down at Melanie. Her blonde hair was dishevelled upon the pillow, her eyes half closed, and her cheeks flamed so brightly as if it were she who was burning in fever now.

'You'll have to find someone who specializes in saucy engravings,' Melanie replied boldly.

'I'll have enough pin money to do that once we return home.' Evelyn's fingers continued working, but her mind, for a second, disconnected from the delectable picture.

Once we return home. Before the discovery of the papers, that notion was as ghostly as Odysseus's vision of Ithaca;

however, now, when their mission had been accomplished, it rose in front of Evelyn in all its reality.

Returning home meant going back beneath the roof of her uncle's house – a beloved house, for sure, but never one of her own. It wasgoing to mean Uncle Owen fulfilling his promise and organizing a glittering season for Melanie.

More likely than not, it was going to mean Melanie finally making her brilliant match.

Evelyn banished those thoughts from her head. It was silly to plan a funeral before someone died; besides, a lot of things still had to be done before they saw the white cliffs of Dover again. For one thing, they had to make it to Beirut.

But right now, on this glorious evening, in the crimson rays of sunset, Evelyn wanted only one thing – to help her lover make it to the peak of pleasure.

Evelyn shivered with delight as she felt Melanie's body tensing up in an unmistakable way. 'Like this,' Evelyn whispered. 'Come for me, my darling.'

As if following her direction, Melanie arched up then convulsed in a sweet spasm, clutching her legs tighter around Evelyn's hand as if trying to squeeze the last bit of pleasure from them.

It seemed never to end. Evelyn didn't want it to end.

When the peak had passed, Melanie fell back upon the pillows, breathing heavily.

Melanie has never felt such bliss.

She had never felt such sweet helplessness either.

Her body, aching and tender in the aftermath, yearned to return the favour. Her heart, for the first time in her life, yearned to assert her power.

She wanted Evelyn be the one to squirm this time.

'Lie on your back.' Melanie stroked her lover's hair, her fingers moving lower, coasting down over her neck, 'I want to worship you.'

Evelyn followed her direction with surprising readiness, her dark eyes burning with curiosity, her breathing heavy with arousal. The sight made Melanie a little impatient, eager to move on to pleasing her – but not yet.

She had always been patient. She wouldn't let that trait fail her now. Melanie kissed down the hollow between her abundant breasts, stroking the left one at the same time. 'Such beautiful breasts,' she murmured against Evelyn's skin. 'Ripe and silky.'

'Do they look even better without any clothes to constrain them?' Evelyn asked playfully, and it was abundantly clear she was loving every second of the caress.

Melanie hummed in agreement, not quite trusting herself to formulate a coherent response now.

Then, she moved lower, kissing a trail over and down her lover's stomach, keeping her hand on her breast still. A wild thought came into her head. If that sweet spot was so susceptible to touch, surely it would be just as sensitive to a kiss. Wanting to test that hypothesis, Melanie bent her head and kissed Evelyn at the same place where her lover had touched her before.

A gasp from above confirmed her suspicion.

Smiling in private triumph, Melanie flicked her tongue up and down on the spot experimentally, and the response was Evelyn's hand in her hair, her fingers curled and tensed up there.

In a wordless reply, Melanie quickened her pace. The taste on her tongue was strange but very far from unpleasant. Then came the mewls in a familiar – and yet unfamiliar – voice, and Melanie raised her head and said, 'Shh. Do you want for Dr Wharton to discover us?'

With a glance devoid of real fury, Evelyn bit her own hand. Not that it stifled the noises completely, and Melanie was grateful for it. Feeling for a moment as powerful as any potentate, as if it were her lover's life and not merely pleasure that were in her hands, she started flicking her tongue horizontally instead of vertically upon the sensitive nub. Judging by the noise from above, that was a right decision.

A brief panic gripped Melanie when she realized her tongue was getting tired. Was that wrong? Was she unable to please her lover after all? Just as that thought came flitting through her mind, Evelyn clamped her thighs around Melanie's ears, trapping her in the warm darkness, her convulsions like the shuddering of the earth.

Some moments passed until her legs fell upon the sheets again in exhaustion and Melanie could rise. She was standing on her knees upon the bed, kneeling between her lover's legs, sensing the wetness upon her lips, and feeling as though she had just undergone some rite of passage.

'How was it?' Melanie asked breathlessly as if it were she who had just been pleasured.

'Incredible.' Evelyn sighed, stretching upon the bed like a cat in the sunlight. 'If I hadn't known the innocent circumstances of your life, I might have suspected that you weren't as inexperienced as you told me you were.'

'You do need to trust people more.' Melanie lay down next to her, the narrowness of the bed almost pleasant, leaving her a small space between the wall and the heated body of her lover. 'People and yourself.'

'If that is something you want to teach me, my gentle mentor, I think I have already learnt the lesson.' Evelyn tucked one sweat-matted lock of Melanie's hair behind her ear.

'Mm.' Melanie took her hand and kissed the reddened teeth marks on it. 'We'll see about that.'

Chapter 13

'What do you mean, there are no ships?' Evelyn asked the harbourmaster angrily.

'Just what I told you, lady.' He shrugged. 'No vessel is going to Malta now. There is a war on. No one is going to trade with a British possession anymore.'

'Officially, I suppose. But unofficially?'

He looked at her angrily. 'I know not the things of which you speak, lady.'

Evelyn sighed. She had a persistent suspicion and was not in a mood for subtleties. 'Do you want baksheesh?' she asked frankly.

'Who doesn't?'

'I don't have much money with me now. I had a spell of sickness in Damascus. The stop ate up most of our reserves.'

'That is your problem, lady, not mine.'

'I need to get to Malta.'

'We all need to get somewhere.'

'Don't bother, Miss.' A man with a strong, clear voice intruded upon the argument, and Evelyn turned, amazed to hear her native speech so far from home. 'I have tried to secure a passage for my cotton a hundred times. These natives are extremely stubborn.'

'Who are you?' The thought that was not how one was supposed to address gentlemen strangers flickered to life in the depths of her mind.

The man, perspiring in his waistcoat, his face blooming with heat, raised his eyebrows but replied nonetheless. 'Mr Josiah Kelley at your service. Perhaps, you have heard of my trading company?'

'I didn't have this pleasure.' Her tongue was finally catching up with her mind, remembering how she was supposed to speak to gentlemen.

'We specialize in procuring cotton from Acre. Plenty of good English bedsheets were made softer with it – if you would forgive me so frivolous a mention.'

It took a second for Evelyn to register the part that was supposed to be frivolous. Ah. Talking to a lady about bedsheets.

'I am glad to hear that. I am Lady Evelyn Prynne; this is my physician, Dr Wharton, and my – dearest friend, Miss Melanie Bright.'

'Lady Evelyn Prynne!' Mr Kelley straightened his shoulders as though a recruit sighting a general on inspection. 'I would have never imagined encountering so esteemed a lady in so wild a milieu.' He was evidently polite enough not to draw any attention to the lady in question's own equally wild appearance.

'I have been accompanying my friend. She is a prolific travel writer.' This lie did not feel like a lie, for all that Melanie blushed her adorable blush at it.

'Remarkable, remarkable. Where are you staying?'

'Nowhere, so far. We thought to catch a ship to Malta today.' The less time they now spent in the territory of the Ottoman Empire, the better, and Lord Howick would certainly find a way to make sure Dubois's papers found their way into the right pocket or vault.

Or so had been Evelyn's reasoning.

'I hope you wouldn't mind my presumption if I invite you to my humble abode? It was some time since I had guests, particularly guests of my own race, not to mention of such a great birth; however, I would do everything I can to ensure your comfort until the travel would be made possible once again.'

Evelyn exchanged a glance with Wharton and Melanie. They were tired and angry at the delay, and the house of an English merchant might prove to be a safer place for their burning treasure than an Ottoman hostelry.

'We would be delighted,' Evelyn said in a tone she now forced herself to remember and gave him a smile worthy of a ballroom.

When Evelyn stepped over the threshold of Josiah Kelley's drawing room, it seemed to her for a second that she had been transported back to Mayfair. The wall hangings the fine colour of clove, the heavy ormolu clock, and the porcelain service already set upon the table all breathed familiarity.

This sensation dissipated somewhat once she took in the details. The wallpaper did not fare well in the moist heat of Beirut, the maid pouring the beverages had a distinctly Greek profile, and the beverage was not tea but the kind of Yemeni coffee Evelyn got used to smelling in the grand tent of a Bedouin sheikh.

'I hope you would forgive me for the absence of pekoe tea,' Josiah Kelley apologized. 'It is hard to procure Chinese goods from here in the best of times, and the war has stopped trade in its tracks.'

'If you are trading an Acre cotton, why are you not residing in Acre?' Melanie asked bluntly.

'Acre is an inhospitable place for Christians, Miss Bright. Indeed, I have yet to encounter a city so full of heathens. I do business there through an agent. Plenty of traders do the same – the French, God sink their ships, the Germans, now even the Russians have moved in. But I suppose you are not particularly interested in the boring details of trade.' He smiled indulgently.

'I am a travel writer.' Melanie's voice was unwavering. 'I am interested in everything.'

'Are you a great letter writer, then?'

'No, I am planning to turn my experiences here into a book. Like Hester Piozzi.'

'Hester Piozzi – that's a battle-axe. Of course, she belongs to a different age. Civilization has changed quite a bit since Dr Johnson's day. Where have you been staying while in Lebanon?'

'We haven't been staying anywhere,' Evelyn replied for her, growing strangely angry on Melanie's behalf. 'We have been travelling through the country. First with the Bedouin tribe of the Ruwallah, then by ourselves.'

'My, that sounds dangerous! One hears about the customs of these sons of the desert.'

'I've found them hospitable and noble.'

'If you say so. Still, I wouldn't have allowed my own daughter to stay tête-à-tête with a Bedouin, if you would pardon me saying so. I suppose you are lucky your uncle is of a more permissive disposition.'

He is not, Evelyn thought. *He simply hadn't heard the details yet. But he is going to hear them by the time I am back in London, if not before.* The thought pierced her not with fear but with unnamed exhaustion.

Perhaps it was better that she encountered Mr Kelley before setting sail from Beirut. It would be better for her to practice before returning to her native soil and a horde of men and women who thought like him, would click their tongues like him, and stare at her like him.

'I haven't thought of any plans after I return to England, to be honest,' Evelyn confessed. At least Melanie had her book to write. For Evelyn, the adventure would end as soon as she sighted the white cliffs of Dover again. She was going to become, once more, not the hope of her country but a glorified housekeeper.

Mr Kelley turned his surprised grey gaze to her. 'Why, what kind of plans can you possibly have, if you don't mind me saying this, but returning to your uncle's household? Unless there had been an engagement the ton hadn't heard about? Mind you, I am about as far from the ton as Acre is from Mayfair.'

Evelyn smiled bitterly and shook her head. What kind of plans indeed could she possibly have apart from disappearing behind the walls of her uncle's house or those of her husband's?

'No, Mr Kelley. I am not spoken for.'

'More is the pity. You are a lady of rare loveliness even despite your age. I am surprised there has been no one enticed by the prospect of spending the rest of his life with you.'

No one enticed by the prospect of my dowry and my uncle's connections, you mean.

'There had been someone.'

'Sir Robert? Yes, I remember that tragedy. Its tendrils managed to reach even my abode. Still, it was years ago. It is hardly healthful for a young woman to waste her tears and beauty on something that shall never come instead of seeking her natural fulfilment while she can.'

'Thank you for your advice, Mr Kelley. I shall take it into consideration.'

'Make sure you are not going to put off considering it until it's too late.' His expression held no malice – nothing but a genuine worry for a woman already not in her first bloom, who could miss out on her sole defining destiny.

'We have some things we would rather keep with us.' Evelyn tried to change the topic.

'I see your possessions here are scarce. I shall have them brought up to your rooms.'

'Oh, I can share the room with Miss Bright,' Evelyn said lightly, a kind of panic flaring up in her chest. 'We are close friends.'

' 'But hardly sisters, nonetheless, I don't think it would be necessary. Or, to be frank, entirely seemly.'

This was how it was going to be, Evelyn realized, once she was back home. Melanie would be in her room and Evelyn in hers; encountering each other at country house parties but never sharing a bedroom again even there.

The wilderness of Lebanon, even its stone cities with their ancient gates and ruins of pagan temples, was the kind of land where time and custom stood still. The kind of Tir-na-Nog land where they could dwell in suspended happiness.

But it was time to go home.

Not if I have anything to say about it, Evelyn thought, keeping her expression ballroom polite. *Not if I still have blood in my veins.*

She finished her tea, took a copper bath graciously offered to her upstairs, and dressed in the travel-stained Turkish garb again. Then she snuck out of the house and turned to the bazaar coffee house she had visited for the first time so seemingly long ago.

'Forgive me for this request,' Evelyn said, smiling charmingly at the proprietor, 'but I have a message to pass on to Joseph Verney. He is likely to pass through this town soon.'

The answer arrived when Evelyn had already lost any hope of receiving it.

She knelt in her room, reading the lines of Swiss German in the latticed light of the window.

Esteemed Lady E.,

I have to concede you are not entirely wrong on the subject of the Emperor having little tolerance for failure. However, if you want me to put my expertise in the service of Britain instead, you would have to give me further guarantees.

For one thing, I would need a British passport to be given to me at the end of the war.

For another, as a personal reward, I request one of the maps of those I know Dubois had hidden at Ascalon to be passed on to me at the earliest possible opportunity. It is going to be entitled La crusade, La croix, *or something cognate. It is supposed to represent the crowning of Dubois' efforts of reaching a hoard left in Syria or Lebanon by the warriors of the Crusades before they had to abandon those salubrious places for Europe. It is going to pose no risk or change to the current interests of the British Empire.*

The exchange can be made at the place we both know.

With high regard,

J.V.

Not losing time, Evelyn jotted down a reply.

Dear J.V.,

I think I have a reasonable chance to obtain the promise of a British passport for you from my contact in London. However, not having been born yesterday, I would refrain from simply sending you the map you requested. I demand to accompany you every step of the way. Should it really lead to an innocuous hoard, I promise not to impinge upon your right to it. I must say, however, that I am surprised by your pecuniary motives. Is the Emperor's pay really so meagre you are reduced to chasing treasures in the wilderness?

With high regard,

Lady E.

She crumpled the response into her small bag, having been made to change into a European dress again at the insistence of her host. Mr Kelley had spent the whole of the first day with his eyes glued to the ground so as not to glimpse Evelyn's legs in the Ottoman trousers, and he finally begged her to consider the gown kept at his home for the sake of his visiting sister. Evelyn did not believe this tale of an innocent relative being the female presence in the house. She had heard too often of British merchants who got rid of their loneliness in the East by purchasing Greek and Circassian concubines in the local slave markets.

Melanie did not think of this possibility, Evelyn realized, tenderness touching her heart. Melanie was initially relieved at finally wearing the kind of clothes her body had been accustomed to since her early days in girlish skirts. She even spent some time in front of the full-length mirror in her room – the room into which Evelyn slipped before dinner solely for the pleasure of seeing her prepare – fussing over her newly washed hair. However, during the dinner in question, Evelyn couldn't help but notice a new apprehension in Melanie's movements, a minute carefulness in her steps and a diminutive air in the way she ate as though she had been bound into iron instead of muslin.

Evelyn felt a similar way – her dreams were still star-studded and wind-blown, and it was impossible to imagine galloping down a sea of grass or sand upon a steed of the Bedouins in a gown made for quiet country walks.

Her thoughts were interrupted by a knock on the door. Evelyn walked to the door and opened it to reveal Mr Kelley, uncharacteristically nervous. By instinct, Evelyn shrank from him, wondering feverishly if Verney's reply had burnt well in the blazing fireplace.

'Lady Evelyn?' Her host coughed as though she could have been someone else. 'There is a ... a gentleman downstairs. He is asking to see you.'

Evelyn's heart leapt. Could Verney have found her?

'I am going to come down in a second,' she said neutrally. Instead of following him downstairs, however, Evelyn darted into Melanie's bedroom and met her confused stare.

'What is going on?' Melanie asked. 'I've heard all this noise downstairs—'

'Noise?' Evelyn frowned. Evidently, she had been too absorbed in her thoughts of intrigue to notice anything else. 'I thought he would come alone.'

'Who?'

'I'll tell you later. I'll tell you everything. But now, it would be better if you stay here in your room.' Evelyn brought Melanie's hands to her lips and, unable to restrain herself, planted a kiss upon each knuckle, feeling a familiar heat burning below her stomach at the sweet smell of linen and soap and the feel of Melanie's tender skin against her lips. Now, beneath the genteel shade of Kelley's household, the reddish hue given to Melanie's skin by the open sun had paled. 'Stay in your own room, and tell Wharton to do likewise. All will be well.'

'Evelyn, you are scaring me.' Melanie made a step as though to form a barrier to her exit, but Evelyn was already outside.

She smoothed her hair and descended upon the ground floor of the merchant's well-made, modest dwelling.

In the midst of the drawing room stood a man surrounded by a whole squadron of armed Turks. 'Lady Evelyn Prynne, I see,' the stranger said, looking at her. 'I am Mustafa Aga, the Kapugi Bashi and the Lord of the Stirrup, here by the gracious command of the Sultan Selim.'

Evelyn froze. She knew this title. The Lord of the Stirrup rarely left Constantinople without a good reason. When a Kapugi Bashi went to the provinces, it usually meant some high official was found to be dishonest – or dangerously prosperous – by the sultan and was now living his last days on this earth.

But it did not have to be a high official.

'I am glad to meet you,' she replied, keeping her poise. 'I know it is not my place to offer you to sit, me not being the hostess, but—'

'But we would rather remain standing,' Mustafa Aga finished for her. 'I hadn't come here to drink coffee. If I wanted to sit around with cups instead of doing my duty, I would have joined these desert savages for a ride. What are you doing in the domains of the sultan, Lady Evelyn?'

'I have business here.'

'Your host has business here. He is buying cotton. What's *your* business?'

'Intellectual curiosity.'

'Bah. Don't play games with me, Lady Evelyn. I am not one of your pet ambassadors. You are here to spy.'

'I assure you I am not.'

'You have been asking the Ruwallah about Vincent Dubois's last journey. You are after his papers. Or, maybe, I should say you *were* after his papers? Have you found them?'

'This is absurd. I have heard his name, that is true,' Evelyn added, thinking that pretending a complete ignorance of this cloak-and-dagger incident would work against her credibility rather than for it, 'but my goals here had nothing to do with him.'

'Have they not? We have ways of making you speak truth, you know.'

'You wouldn't dare.'

'Your country is far away, Lady Evelyn. By the time it lodges a complaint about the treatment of the prisoners of war, you would have lost the use of your limbs.'

Prisoner of war. She was going to be a prisoner of war. She, and the poor, fiery Wharton, and – Melanie. Her Melanie. Evelyn thought of her lover's limbs, the pale hands she had been kissing with such gusto not half an hour ago.

'There is no need for that,' Evelyn said, straightening her spine. 'If you don't believe me, I can show you exactly what had been our goal in coming to Lebanon.'

'I knew you had something in that space between your ears.'

Evelyn turned, led the Kapugi Bashi and his entourage up the staircase, and knocked on Dr Wharton's door.

'There is an emergency, Wharton,' she said in English as the men poured into the room.

'What do you need?' He took a deep breath, looking at them.

'I need your correspondence with Sir Sidney Smith.'

'No!'

'It's either that or we are all going to learn how the rats in the Ottoman dungeons taste.'

'Lady Evelyn, it had been my work of many—'

'Well, then those many would have to work more,' Evelyn whispered, losing her patience swiftly. 'Wharton, we are all going to be arrested for espionage against the Sublime Porte. Is that what you desire?'

'You mean we aren't going to be arrested if we give the Ottomans the proof that we have been trying to go against one of their most beloved trades?'

'It is better than if they find the proof that we have hunted down the papers of the agent belonging to their new dear ally.'

'Lady Evelyn.' Dr Wharton drew himself to his full height. 'These letters contain the plans that can lead to the liberation and happiness of many. I am not going to give them up.'

Evelyn exploded. 'These letters contain the plans that can lead to the misery and civil war! How else do you think an Ottoman emir lending his private army to a Western force would end?'

'Sir Sidney Smith is a master of diplomacy—'

'Sir Sidney Smith is an utter dolt if he thinks his venture could lead to anything good! Give them the letters, Wharton. It's my order as your mistress.'

Behind them were the heavy footsteps of the Kapugi Bashi and his soldiers. The stairs were creaking under their boots.

How many military boots have these stairs withstood in the centuries this house has been standing And in the centuries before it had been prettied up and gilded to the taste of an English merchant?

Evelyn wondered how many stairs there were to the dungeons of Constantinople and how deep the echo was.

'You would better not deceive me, Lady Evelyn,' the Kapugi Bashi said heavily, his gaze darting menacingly between her and Dr Wharton.

'I would never dream of doing so, Effendi,' Evelyn replied, turning to him. 'Our aim in coming to the East had been to negotiate with Emir Bashir of the Druze.'

'What was it you were going to negotiate about? The Druze independence? Were the British offering to help them in an attempt of another conquest of Beirut?'

'God save me, no,' Evelyn tried to laugh. Inside, her nerves were a-jingle like thinned-out strings of a harp. 'We wanted to ask Emir Bashir for help in our fight against the Barbary slave trade.'

'Why would the British even take interest in the Barbary slave trade? The Barbary coast is our waters,' the Kapugi Bashi asked pointedly.

'There are some people whose heart bleeds for the plight of the enslaved.' Evelyn did her best to say it lightly, so as to not allow the Ottoman to realize that she was, indeed, one of these *some people*.

'That's stupid,' Mustafa Aga grunted. 'The strong take possession of the weak. It has always been so. Times were, the Turks were weak, too, and the Greeks strong. The Greeks didn't spare us then. Why should we spare them?'

'Please, believe me. I am speaking the truth. Should you desire it, there is a proof of our intentions. Wharton,' Evelyn added in English, 'bring us the letters.'

For a second, it seemed he was not going to do it; it seemed he was going to defy her to the last, which might indeed become a last for him. But Edmund Wharton, the doctor of medicine, merely threw her a dagger-like glance and disappeared into his room. Without ceremony, the soldiers followed. Mustafa Aga clearly didn't trust the Frankish traveller.

There were plenty of letters. Most of them were written in English and a few in Arabic, for the perusal of the Druze potentates Wharton and his mistress could have met along the route; one of them, the neatest of all, was destined for the hands of the distant Emir Bashir. This was the first time Evelyn had read it – and she had to do that quickly before it was snatched from her hand by one of the Kapugi Bashi's men. It was fulsome in its praise of the warlike Emir's virtues and breathless in its extolling of his likely support for the pious mission.

But just because he allowed the Christians on his lands some freedoms, it occurred to Evelyn it did not necessarily make him their friend, much less a friend to the West. He was a shepherd to them – not the good shepherd of the holy books but one of the earthly sense, a practical man who wanted to gain something from his sheep and thus didn't allow them to starve. Sir Sidney Smith didn't know that. He had never seen the flocks of the Druze sheep protected by the Christian herders or gazed upon the silkworm-abounding mulberry trees in the villages below Salkhad.

'It says you are also carrying gifts for the emir.' Kapugi Bashi frowned, raising his eyes from the letter. 'Let us see.'

'There turned out to be no sense in them. We haven't met the emir, and now we never would.'

'Still,' the Ottoman official insisted.

Silently, Dr Wharton produced the gifts in question – two battered Persian pistols for the emir, a dressing box for his wife, and a black satin abah destined, again, for the potentate himself. Modestly enough, the abah's chest was emblazoned with Sir Sidney Smith's crest.

Mustafa Aga couldn't contain his laughter. 'Is that all? You are no conspirators, it seems – you are idiots! Who on earth brings a Druze weapons made in Persia? English weapons are good gifts; German ones are good gifts. Even the new American ones aren't so bad. Persia? The last Bedouin dog is going to throw these into the ditch. And the abah? It's like gifting one of your gentlemen sauntering around Pera something made of chintz.'

'Are you satisfied, Effendi?' Evelyn asked. She tried not to look at Wharton's face, his expression breathing thunderclouds.

'I know everything I need to know now.' Mustafa Aga raised his paper bounty up as though it were the cut-off head of his enemy. 'But don't think I cannot come back.'

The last Ottoman soldier had left the premises, and the door closed behind him. The silence reknitted itself in the air of the household as though nothing had happened. As though the world has not been turned upside down.

A door creaked, and Melanie stepped out from her room.

'I have heard everything,' she said quietly. Her gaze was not on Evelyn but on Dr Wharton.

Following the line of her gaze, as if clinging to something protective, Evelyn finally glanced at his expression. To her surprise, there was no fury there – not anymore. Only red-faced mortification.

He has failed, Evelyn realized. This had been his great mission just as Dubois's papers were hers, and he had failed it.

Or, rather, she had failed him.

'It wouldn't have worked in any case,' Evelyn said, putting her hand on his arm.

He stepped away, letting it fall.

'She only wanted to protect us,' Melanie ventured.

'I would like to resign from your service, Lady Evelyn,' Dr Wharton said heavily. 'Effective as of now.'

'That would be insane. You are going to be alone in a foreign country—'

'I daresay I am going to survive.'

His expression was set, the line of his mouth hard. *He has decided*, Evelyn realized. *He has decided, and there is nothing I can say to make him change his mind.*

'In this case, I would ask you to complete one last assignment for me.'

'An errand, you mean?'

'No,' Evelyn replied. 'An assignment. I would ask you to take Dubois's letters on the first ship west and pass them either to Lord Howick in London or to Sir Alexander Ball, the civil commissioner of Malta.'

'I can do that, but ...'

'Do you mean you are not going yourself?' Melanie finished his question, her eyes suddenly urgent.

Evelyn shook her head. 'I have a mission of my own to complete.'

'What mission? We have done everything we needed to do.'

We have indeed, Evelyn thought. *From where Melanie stands, we have indeed done everything required of us, and we need to do nothing further. We can return to our genteel homeland, to the normality she craves.*

Something turned inside Evelyn's heart, and it was painful as the feeling of flesh caught between screws. I have written to Verney.'

"You *what?*'

'I have written to him and made an attempt to turn him to the service of our country. He has agreed ... under one condition.'

'Money?'

'Treasure. One of Dubois's maps had nothing to do with great routes and everything to do with valuables. He wants it. Wants them.' Evelyn paused. 'And I am to help him.'

'Evelyn! Why have you done such a thing? How *could* you have done such a thing?'

'You don't understand.' Evelyn shook her head.

'Then tell me, by the grace of God! What on earth possessed you?'

How could she explain it? Evelyn didn't have the gift to put into words this raging fire that burnt within her, this hunger for victories and empires – or, failing that, for a glorious immolation.

'Our mission was a singular thing, wasn't it?' Evelyn asked rhetorically, looking at her lover. 'A way for Lord Howick to use a compromised noblewoman in an urgent situation. Now that it is over, I shall have to return to my place. To my uncle's side. Forever a glorified housekeeper, never an actual mistress of the house.'

'Do you want to marry? Is that what you mean?' Melanie's expression was that of confusion and heartbreak.

'No.' An old irritation was rising within her soul. Was there really no way to make her lover understand? She thought they had shared this singular moment of affinity the moment they saw each other's thoughts. Evelyn might have been mistaken.

'What I want,' Evelyn continued, 'is to do something that truly counts. I might not have another chance for that once I depart these shores.'

'What about your life? You might never return from this journey. He might capture you, double-cross you, kill you—'

'Then he will capture me, double-cross me, and kill me.' Evelyn shrugged. 'You are going to be safe here, Melanie. You can go with Dr Wharton.'

'Never.'

'I beg your pardon?'

'I am coming with you.'

'Over my dead body.'

'I am coming with you exactly because I want your dead body to remain an expression.'

'I've betrayed Wharton's dream to the Turks to keep you safe.'

'But you have chosen to endanger yourself in the daftest way possible.' Melanie pursed her lips. Never before had she looked so exactly like the matronly chaperone her uncle had been advised to get for her. 'Therefore, I have no other choice. This is, after all, what Sir Owen might have wanted me by your side for,' she added with bitter irony in her tone. 'To keep you from making even more daft decisions.'

Chapter 14

The village was an entirely nondescript place, apart from a beauteous white shrine in its vicinity. Shining among the clay-brick houses, it was attractive with its nondescript smoothness. However much Evelyn gazed upon it, she could not discern whether it was dedicated to a Christian martyr, to one of the half-heretical Mahometan saints, or whether it had, perhaps, even started its line as an altar to the ever-grieving Astarte, the tearful precursor to Venus. Years and rains had worn the stones down. The only thing Evelyn could tell now was that it evidently still inspired not-so-covert respect from the locals, judging by the heaps of flowers decorating it and a single cup of milk standing upon it.

She did not have a long time to contemplate it. As agreed, Joseph Verney was waiting for her beside it. Three women in Bedouin garb accompanied him.

'What is the meaning of this?' Evelyn asked without a greeting. 'You were supposed to come alone, not with the representatives of the Anazeh.'

'They are not representatives of the Anazeh. They are labourers who are going to help us with the unearthing of the hoard. Don't look at me with such genteel shock, Lady Evelyn,' Joseph Verney said in German. 'I thought you made of sterner stuff. What do you think these women do in the camps of their menfolk? Embroidering and playing pianoforte? They carry the burdens, whatever their stations. Or have you never noticed that? Do you think the Bedouin way is all songs and stars?'

'No,' Evelyn replied quietly. 'I only thought, for some reason, that throwing oneself into the uglier aspects of their way is something the former knight of St. John might have avoided.'

'Heavens above, and here I thought you a realist. How did you think the Knights of St. John come about in the first place? How did they gain power? There was a day their word held sway across Europe and commanded fleets that made the Sultan tremble. Force and cunning, Lady Evelyn. Force and cunning. The knightly honour came later.'

'Is that why you joined the Corsican so readily? Because of his display of force?'

'Because of his wielding of it,' Verney corrected her. 'When our last grandmaster had signed the Order away, I was as outraged and furious as the others at the betrayal of centuries of chivalry. But what I saw in Egypt made me realize that the ideals I once worshipped were no more than relics belonging to the time of the Crusades. Rusty armour is for showing off to guests, not for donning in battle.'

'So you betrayed your former brothers and decided to join the winner.'

'I decided to join what looked to be the winner in Egypt. That was before the Battle of the Nile, before Trafalgar ...'

'Before your own fiasco. Don't downplay the fear for your life, Verney. I won't believe you otherwise.'

'I cannot give more of a pig's foot for whether or not you believe me, Lady Evelyn. You think yourself different from the missish debutantes with their rose-tinted glasses, but, in reality, you are sisters under the skin.' He nodded at Melanie, who was sitting still upon her mule.

'Oh, believe me,' Evelyn noted lightly, 'we are much closer than sisters.'

'You admit it, then. Much like her, you have no idea of how the world really works.'

'No.' Evelyn shook her head. 'I simply found a different engine.' Her hands calm, she produced the map from her saddlebag. 'Are you satisfied, Herr Verney, or are you in the mood for some more monologues?'

'I am going to be satisfied when the hoard is going to be in front of me. I am not going to allow you to trick me, Lady Evelyn. I am not a fool.'

'Are you suggesting I come with you?'

'No, of course not. I am stating it.'

'The treasure might have been removed centuries ago!'

'In this case, our budding partnership is going to be dissolved. That would be a pity.'

'Very well,' Evelyn conceded. 'We are going to accompany you. But I would need guarantees.'

'I can swear on my honour as a knight, but you know how little that would mean. I can swear on my father's grave, but you have never known my father.'

'Swear on your own life, then. On your life and your standing.'

'If you insist. I—'

'In Arabic,' Evelyn interrupted him. 'Swear your oath in Arabic. I want them to hear and to carry the word to their husbands and fathers, should you go against your word. No Bedouin potentate would deal with an oath breaker.'

'Force and cunning. It seems they are not entirely alien to you, Lady Evelyn.' Joseph Verney pulled his sabre out of its sheath. 'I swear upon my life that this blade shall never know your blood.'

'I swear on mine, too,' Evelyn nodded, mirroring his gesture.

'Then we have a deal.' Verney extended his arm.

Without dismounting, Evelyn shook his hand.

'I know this place.' Verney frowned when Hisn el-Nasara grew on the horizon.

'You do?' Melanie asked him, not without surprise.

'It's an old Seljuk castle.'

'Is anyone living here now?' Evelyn asked.

He shook his head and opened his mouth as if to answer, but one of the Anazeh women exclaimed, 'This is an unlucky place, this black shell. Just look at what happened to the ones who lived here before.'

'It happened because they have killed one of the Smātiyyeh Arabs in a row over cattle stealing,' Verney addressed them sternly. 'If not for the habit of picking quarrels, they would have been alive now and the castle populated. If anything,' he added, 'their loss is our gain. Imagine what it would have been like to search the place with the family still in residence.'

Melanie gazed upon the grand construction beyond the gates. The castle looked like one of the places where even the stones were tired. The towers were greyed out with exhaustion from the brunt of all the events they had to witness.

'Has the government not requisitioned it?' Evelyn enquired.

'The Porte is wary from digging their fingers too deep into the territory of old Bedouin clans. It has always been.'

They rode slowly beneath the gate of black stone and into the courtyard. In the ordinary times, Melanie imagined, it would have been filled with the smells and sounds of activities unchanging since the days of the Middle Ages – hammer falling upon anvil, hunters bringing in the prey, and the butcher's cleaver falling upon the stripped flesh of hares.

Now, there was nothing but silence and the wind.

'The interior was likely stripped over all these years,' Evelyn said, sliding down from her horse. Melanie followed suit.

The dark rooms inside the castle made her shiver. They really were almost pristine of furniture: not a single carpet, not a single sofa, and not a single cushion or cup had survived the years of looting. The whitewash on the walls had in some places grown half translucent, like the skin of a sick man, and partly chipped away to reveal brownish flecks underneath.

Every tracery of the windows in the banquet hall had been blocked with stones to keep the night cold out. The great, cavernous room must have once been lit by candles and the red glow of the warming brazier. Yet even then, in those better years, the whole company must have had to huddle about these sources of living light like moths.

'We are going to search the western part of the castle,' Evelyn proclaimed, taking Melanie's hand. Beneath the notice of strangers, her thumb run warmly along Melanie's palm, soothing and igniting at the same time.

Melanie peered into the dark, crumbling corridors leading into the sleeping heart of the citadel. They seemed to have grown like thorns straight out of the pages of Ann Radcliffe with her Italian horrors – the kind of Gothic fortresses where young maidens shouldn't venture unless they want to en-counter danger and dishonour. Melanie as she had been but a year ago would have recoiled.

But Melanie as she was now knew there were worse things in the world than dishonour – certainly worse things in the world than a little darkness. Seeing a cavalcade of Bedouin warriors streaming down upon you, for instance. Or watching the woman you loved battle deadly fever.

'I'll come with her, Verney,' she said.

'Suit yourself.' he shrugged his shoulders. 'But one of my ladies is going to accompany you to make sure you don't try something. I doubt you would mind. As a good girl, you must be used to chaperones.'

They spent hours combing through the empty rooms light-ed by pointed windows with rosettes and mouldings round the arches. Diligently, Melanie, her lover, and the Bedouin woman Ferideh had knocked on each wall, hoping to hear a hollow sound, and explored each floor where the layout of the stones seemed to be in the least queer.

Nothing came of it as Hisn el-Nasara stubbornly refused to give up its secrets.

'What are we going to do?' Melanie asked, lighting the candles. The sun beyond the narrow windows had completed its circuit of the sky, and soon enough, it would be a time to bed down in the banqueting hall.

'Search,' Evelyn said stubbornly. 'We must have missed something. Dubois couldn't have been wrong.'

'What if he was?'

Then you have led us all into a deadly trap, Melanie thought before she could restrain herself. *We could have been sitting in ease and warmth in the cotton merchant's drawing room now or even sailing towards Dover with the sea churning beneath our ship. Instead, we are at the mercy of a former French agent whose fingers are trembling with avarice.*

'Then we are all as good as dead,' Evelyn said lightly and crouched beside one wall.

'We have already checked this one,' Melanie called out, but it was as though Evelyn hadn't heard her.

Melanie looked at the wall. In the concentrated light, the old whitewash looked semi-translucent, like an egg white. Suddenly, Evelyn chipped a few small pieces away. Greyish dust settled beneath her nails. Some patches of colour were bared beneath.

Melanie brought her candle closer, and the close light resurrected the patches into crimson. *This was once a vivid paint*, she realized. The kind of paint that was once worth gold and spices, and used only for precious religious frescoes. The dust beneath her lover's fingernails thickened; Evelyn gathered more chips into her left palm.

A faint, black trace of a line appeared among the colour. Was it a drawing once? Melanie squinted. An arm? A sword? A decayed fresco signified nothing but age, but a whitewashed fresco signified an intent and a purpose.

'The castle could have been built by the Crusaders them-selves during their brief glory' – Evelyn turned around excit-edly – 'and lost to the Turks together with the other strong-holds in the Holy Land.'

'And the Turks?'

'The Turks have whitewashed the frescoes of the warriors and saints and carved the archways with flowers of insentient beauty. Do you understand?' Evelyn stood up and clutched her hands. 'If the castle was initially built by a Christian order, there is a great chance that the castle mosque was originally a chapel, repurposed later. Like the altar of Astarte in that village was once repurposed into the shrine of a saint. The Seljuks were pragmatic people; they wouldn't have let a great structure of stone go to waste.'

'If there truly was a chapel,' Melanie said slowly, 'then, in so great a fortress ...'

Evelyn finished her thought, as though they shared one mind and body '...it was bound to have a crypt.'

This is all so horribly cliched, Evelyn couldn't help but think as she descended the staircase through the night with a single candle in her hand.

The amber light flickered unevenly on the steps of crum-bled stone. She was walking slowly and carefully and clinging to the wall as she spiralled downwards.

Melanie was walking behind her, her shadow on the wall stretching forth and touching Evelyn's skin. Verney and the other two women were waiting for them at the bottom of the staircase. The candlelight was turning their skin unnaturally bright in the dark.

Without a single word, Verney gestured for them to follow him into the courtyard.

When the esplanade ended, it revealed a sky luminous with stars. The heaven was crowded with light, spilling the milky moonlight onto the world below, and Evelyn was startled by beauty.

But she had no time to enjoy it. The end of their journey awaited. One last effort, she promised herself, and then she was going to have all the time she wanted to gaze upon the stars.

The group crossed the courtyard silently to the northern end where the mosque – the former chapel – stood. A small fountain for ablutions was silent near the flowery archway. The door, of course, was closed.

'Your pin,' Verney ordered, opening his palm.

Wordlessly, Evelyn pulled out the pin that held the coil of her hair and passed it to him despite cringing internally at his tone. She would only have to suffer it for a while now. Just for a while.

In no time at all, the pins clicked softly, drawing back and releasing the wooden bolt. After a short fumbling, the door was drawn back.

It opened onto a black, cavernous space, clearly designed once to house hundreds of knights and give spiritual suc-cour to great households. The world it served had long since retreated to the distant shores and then died out, but the church-mosque remained in all its stone enormity. The blackness swallowed the light of six candles as if they were fireflies.

'We need to separate,' Joseph Verney decreed.

Evelyn could not help but agree with him here - the dark universe in front of them was too great to be explored in a group effort. He briefly described the architectural elements they should look for, and the group dispersed.

Evelyn picked her way into the farthest area. Her steps were almost soundless upon the stone. After a long circling of the bare walls, she finally encountered a niche. It was not decorated with inlaid gold or ivory as those in the mosques of Constantinople on the engravings she had once seen, but it was still, unmistakably, what she was looking for.

It was a mihrab located in the direction of Mecca, and this must have been the qibla wall. The part of the prayer hall where the qibla wall was located was usually set beneath the dome, the earthly vault of heaven. Evelyn had read of the arrangement in regards to Turkey, and she doubted the faithful of Syria would be radically different in that regard. If so, then, in its earlier incarnation as a church, this part was probably the apse, the traditional setting for the entrance into the crypt, set beneath the semi-circular dome. She walked quickly to the extremes of the former apse, feeling for a door, or at least a hollow sound, but the walls were thick and blank.

'I've found the transepts,' Ferideh said when they reconvened, six flames floating in the pool of darkness.

'Did you see a corbel of beams in the wall there?' Verney asked impatiently. 'It should have been left after they removed the gallery.'

'Yes. Nothing like an entrance.'

'It can be in the nave,' Melanie said.

'I've never seen a crypt entrance located in the nave,' Verney replied.

'I've read about the Grotto in the Church of the Nativity in Jerusalem, where Jesus was born. The stairs are in the chancel, near the altar, but the crypt itself is under the nave. Maybe they've put the entrance in the nave itself here?'

'Maybe.' Joseph Verney nodded. It was clear he was not in the mood to discount any sort of maybes.

Another, much smaller area was sliced for patrol - the part of the prayer hall that stretched from the entrance to the transepts. Melanie's breath caught when the dull sound of filled walls that had accompanied all her attempts before this suddenly changed. 'Come here!' she called. 'I think I've found something.'

In a thrice, five people were by her side, breathing down her neck. Out of the corner of her eye, Melanie saw their excited faces, but she kept her attention focused on the wall. 'It's hollow on the other side,' Melanie explained.

Verney didn't take her at her word. He spent a lot of time making sure she was not mistaken and not lying either. 'Very well.' He raised his head. 'Ferideh, bring the hammer.'

Breaking the wall down took strangely less time than ascertaining the need for this action. Dust and the shards of whitewashed clay-bricks were soon spilling upon the floor, staining her garments.

Evelyn was clutching her hand with a painful, heated grip as though the demolition could hurt her, as though the hammer was directed not at the mute wall but at her flesh.

Soon, Melanie stared down a spiral staircase, its steps drowning in the darkness.

'Ladies first.' Verney gestured to them – not, however, to the women of the Anazeh.

'Are you afraid there is going to be a trap?' Evelyn asked tensely.

'I am afraid of very few things, Lady Evelyn. I am merely taking precautions.'

Suddenly, the chapel-mosque seemed almost cosy. Melanie threw a last glance back before beginning her descent into the subterranean world. There was a smell of damp and mould and a smell of wet stone and ancient dust. When Melanie entered the first burial chamber, her candle snatched several glimpses from the dark.

'See these columns with the lilies of Byzantium?' Evelyn whispered, her barely lighted expression that of awe. 'It seems the Eastern influence has flowered even in the austere abode of the knights.'

Melanie nodded, looking around at the imposing tombs of the Crusaders, centuries having softened their features into anonymity.

'I see no vessels,' Evelyn said, and the implications of her words sank in deep to Melanie's bones. If there was no treasure after all, they were not going to be getting out of there alive.

'You are not looking very well in this case, Lady Evelyn,' Verney observed. Then he walked to the nearest tomb, nodded for Ferideh and the two others to follow him, and, with their help, shifted the lid of the tomb.

'You cannot do this,' Evelyn cried out.

'Of course, I can. It would simply take a little collective effort. Would you like to join in, perchance?'

'You cannot defile the tombs of the dead!'

'What exactly do you expect, Lady Evelyn? That I would simply turn around and leave the way I came? No. I have walked too long a road to reach this chamber.' He returned to his task.

Her heart beating fast, Melanie walked over to the tomb. Within the depth of the carved stone, a skeleton in rusted armour was lying – not the pristine white bones of a Gothic engraving but a fragile mess. And at his feet stood a neat coffer of darkened silver. Verney took it in his arms as though it were an infant, raised it with a visible effort, and placed it back. Something clinked within.

'Coins of the time of Crusader states would fetch an astronomical price at any antiquarian,' Evelyn said tensely. She did not let go of Melanie's hand. 'Is that a good enough reward for you to change sides?'

'An adequate enough reward,' Verney said. Verney's hand dove into his cloak and brought out a pistol. He swung it up, pointing it at Evelyn's chest almost lazily, almost as if it were an afterthought. He pulled the trigger.

Evelyn's hand was torn violently from hers with the force of impact. Evelyn stumbled backwards and fell, her head hitting one of the columns crowned with Byzantine lilies.

Time froze for Melanie. Then, in the crackling aftermath of the shot, all was silence.

Joseph Verney put his gun away, and time resumed. 'Run, little mouse,' he advised. 'Unless you want to join your friend, of course. I suppose I don't have to tell you that you are to tell no one what happened here. To anyone who enquires, our caravan had been set upon by the Smātiyyeh Arabs. Lady Evelyn didn't make it, for all our efforts. Good girls always do as they are told, don't they?'

'Perhaps, I am not a good girl anymore.'

'Don't be stupid.'

With numb disbelief, Melanie gazed at her lover's body and took in the crimson stain spreading upon her shirt and the heavy weight of her fallen eyelids. Melanie drew her sabre almost instinctively and pointed it at Joseph Verney. 'I challenge you to a single combat.'

'This is not a time or a place to play Boadicea, little girl. Haven't you seen what just happened? Are you tired of life?'

'No, but I know you are not either. If you shoot me after I have issued my challenge, the word of it is going to trickle back to Anazeh. As Evelyn said, these women have husbands and brothers. Women have tongues, too. You won't be able to slaughter us all.'

'Don't throw your life away. It would be better for you if we reach an understanding.'

'Understanding?' Melanie threw her head back and laughed, her laughter like shards of glass. 'There can be no understanding between a man and a wounded beast. If you come close enough, I'll savage you.'

'Let it be your way.' Verney bared his sword. 'In the afterlife, don't tell her I hadn't warned you.'

At first, they merely circled each other in the darkness. Melanie recalled all the principles of footwork and guards Evelyn had taught her over the months they spent together. Verney was probably getting the measure of her. Melanie could almost feel it physically, this sense of having been weighed on the scales and found wanting.

His first lunge at her was almost lazy. She parried it in a frantic, harsh movement, then let the tip of her sabre circumnavigate his and extended her arm, trying to stab him in the chest. All but chuckling, Verney dodged the blow.

There were only six sources of light in the subterranean room, six candles weeping their bridal-white wax. Recalling Evelyn's advice, Melanie cut the air with six swift diagonal cuts, defending herself from any lunge. It worked but only marginally. She couldn't do it constantly; despite the light grip, her wrist grew tired easily.

They continued to circle the room, Verney lunging and Melanie parrying or –occasionally – the other way around. Her heart was beating in her throat. She had to do this. She had to avenge the woman she loved. She had to rid this world of a monster. She had to, and damn the sweat that was causing her grip to slip and her arm growing tired.

The pommel of her enemy's sword darted in her face, and the world tilted in front of her eyes. Verney tripped her at the heels. Melanie barely managed to roll away from the line of the next blow. Her sabre clattered to the stone floor.

'Getting tired, little mouse?' Verney taunted her. 'I am giving you one last chance. Throw down your weapon and leave her here. I won't pursue you. My word.'

She remembered the sleepless nights she spent when Evelyn was fighting with cholera. She remembered holding her hand, her feelings in turmoil, and silently begging for Evelyn to fight, not to give up. If Evelyn managed to conquer a deadly disease for her sake, then Melanie could damn well defy a man of flesh and blood.

'No." Melanie gripped her sabre again, stood, and raised it to be almost in line with her shoulder. The hanging guard. The fruit of foreign *Fechtkunst* that Evelyn specifically told her not to use.

There was a quirk in the corner of Verney's mouth when he perceived her movement – a movement, to him, probably breathing with the overconfidence of an amateur.

Paying his condescension no heed, Melanie advanced. She lunged at him. And lunged. And lunged again.

Evelyn had told her the hanging guard tired one out. Melanie felt no such thing, not now, when her whole being was on fire. She felt a flaring up of pain when Verney managed to throw her attack off. It was quickly followed by two more sharp pains.

Melanie focused on her attack. She didn't aim for his chest. She had nothing so fine as a sense of symmetry on her mind. She simply kept her sabre of Damascene steel on the level of her shoulder and lunged. She didn't have to push it. The fine, well-honed steel passed into his pale throat like a knife into warm butter.

Blood spurted out of his neck as he opened his mouth for the last time, looking at her not with horror but with utter shock. Blood flew down his robes and stained the ancient stones brought here by the knights.

Melanie withdrew her sword. Like a puppet whose string had been cut, the thing that had been Joseph Verney fell upon the floor. Melanie lowered her arm.

The fiery, decisive confidence trickled out of her as if it were she and not her enemy who had been bled. She gazed at the fallen form by the columns. What was the point of killing a man in a duel if it couldn't bring back the woman she loved?

Unheeding of who saw her, Melanie knelt by Evelyn's side and put her head upon her lap. Her heart screaming with pain, she stroked her dead lover's hair, almost recoiling at the unpleasant warm wetness of blood. If the shot hadn't killed her, the nasty fall certainly would have.

Where was the justice in that? To live such a life, to make such a way, to realize a great love, only to die in a crypt at the hand of a despicable enemy?

Tears boiling in her eyes, Melanie put her head upon her fallen lover's chest, and winced at the crack she heard. *Wait. That doesn't sound like the crack of bones.* With quick, eager movements, Melanie raised Evelyn's shirt, felt her chest, and drew in her breath at her own sudden pain. She had cut her fingers on something.

Slowly, carefully, Melanie took up the fine golden chain hanging on Evelyn's neck and pulled the locket out. It used to be an exquisite construction of glass and gold. Now the glass had been shattered, its edges crimson, while the golden part was disfigured beyond belief by a small bullet that had wedged itself in it.–

'The wind changes quickly in the Ottoman Empire,' Lord Howick said, leaning on his walking stick. 'Despite the ancient nature of its pedigree. Now that our boys took Alexandria, peace is going to be a matter of time.'

'I hope so,' Evelyn replied. Hyde Park was astonishingly peaceful – so much so that riding here seemed a miracle now. 'I want to return to Lebanon, after all.'

'Why?' Lord Howick glanced at her with curiosity. 'Hungering for glory again?'

'No. Or, rather, not quite. I simply fell in love with the place.'

'East does have a tendency to get into your blood. One needs to have a strong constitution to sustain it, though.'

'I think my constitution is strong enough.'

'Your physician has brought me the correspondence you have uncovered.' It was safer to refer to Dubois's papers as correspondence. Curious ears abounded here on the Rotten Row. 'Remarkable. Very remarkable.'

'Even despite the fact that I have failed to bring our friend for a visit?' Evelyn leaned into the foggy terminology.

'I've never asked about it in the first place.'

'But his expertise in ... ornithology could have been useful.'

'There are plenty of birds in the sky, and some predators are better off shot.'

'I will tell our keen huntress. She had been quite out of sorts.'

'Worried about crime and punishment? Plenty of Frenchmen perish in the East these days. Lebanon, in particular, is just crawling with outlaws.'

'No, she rather feels guilt.'

'Despite the fact that our ornithologist tried to dispatch you to kingdom come? Your friend is remarkably tenderhearted, Lady Evelyn.'

'So she is.' Evelyn smiled her own private smile.

She had spent the morning of the same day meeting with Dr Wharton. His decision to remain in London until the gunpowder fog over the East was going to clear did not surprise her. The threadbare state of his lodgings did.

'I thought I gave you remuneration enough,' she called out from the threshold then.

Edmund Wharton turned around, startled, but quickly regained self-possession .'I cannot know how long I would have to stretch it out for. It is better to be prudent.'

'It's strange to hear a talk of prudence from a man who wanted to entice the Emir of the Druze into a war on slavers.'

'Have you come to taunt me, Lady Evelyn?' he asked tensely.

'No.' He could have hardly stopped her if she tried to step inside the room, but he wasn't inviting her, so she didn't. 'I have come to apologize.'

'There is no need for apology.' His words rang hollow.

'I think there is. I have ruined your plan.'

'My plan had not a chance of success. You've said it yourself.'

'I can be wrong.'

'You weren't this time. Lord Howick explained it to me.'

'You've tried to complain to him about my conduct, then?'

'What can I say? I made an attempt.' A smile touched the corners of his lips. 'He explained to me, in no uncertain terms, what a fool I have been.'

'I have been worse than a fool. I have used your own secrets against you and opened you to the danger of being dragged away to the Turkish dungeons.'

'Had you not done this, we would all have been dragged there.'

'Still. I have a plan to ...'

'To make up for it?'

'No. Better. To make things right.'

Silently, Dr Wharton gestured for her to come inside and sit.

Evelyn did precisely that, lowering herself into a well-worn armchair, before starting on her explanation. 'I have recently come into the possession of an independent fortune,' she said.

'Congratulations.' For all his courteous words, it was clear he hadn't completely forgiven her quite yet.

'I am going to put some of it towards starting a new life in the East, but I also want to direct it to a good cause.'

'What kind of cause?'

'I cannot be the only person in the whole Ottoman Empire who holds slave trade to be an abomination upon the earth. I am going to create a network of searchers who are going to find such illicit markets and buy the Greek and Circassian slaves – and these are usually women, refugees from domestic disasters – out. I am no Wilberforce. I cannot command debates in Parliament,' Evelyn added, 'but I can do something.'

'What if you find no such people? No such allies?'

'Then I would have to do everything myself. Fortunately, that would not be for the first time in my life.'

'These are noble intentions, but I suspect you hadn't come here only to inform me of them, Lady Evelyn.'

'No.' Evelyn shook her head. 'I have come to offer you your old place by my side. If you would like to accept.'

Wharton looked at her for a long time before finally nodding. 'I would.'

This brief encounter somehow left her simultaneously elated and exhausted, so Evelyn didn't relish meeting with Lord Howick in the afternoon. However, some appointments one really didn't postpone.

'Our job sometimes requires the suspension of the kind of principles implicit in the ordinary life,' the foreign secretary continued.

'M-Miss Bright didn't hire herself for this kind of job.'

'I know, but you have. Unless I misunderstood your intention?' The man looked upon her enquiringly.

'No, your lordship. You have guessed it correctly.' Evelyn paused. 'May I ask how?'

'Had you been filled with the kind of disdain and apprehension plenty of ladies – and gentlemen too – feel after fulfilling a task of that sort, you would not have agreed to this meeting. Knowing you, we can also rule out politesse and propriety as your reasons. Therefore, you are interested in our ongoing collaboration. Am I right, Lady Evelyn?'

'You've read me like a book, your lordship.' Evelyn laughed and watched the sunlight playing upon the leaves of orange trees.

'Well, this is my job. I have sent a word of your willingness upstairs.'

'Already?'

'I am rarely mistaken, Lady Evelyn. I have recommended you as a gifted amateur whose manner is somewhat flamboyant but efficient.'

'A gifted amateur?'

'It was not meant as an insult. We are all amateurs in this trade, and you are better educated than most. Your knowledge of the language alone is a rare thing, especially in its current polished state. I have also taken it upon myself to recommend you for a discreet but generous government pension under the condition of your continued service.'

'Your lordship, this is ...' Somehow, she had been transformed into a schoolgirl whose principal finally recognized her for her achievements. A schoolgirl she never got to be.

'A gratitude would be misplaced. This is not charity, Lady Evelyn – this is a wage.' Lord Howick gazed beyond the greenery of the gardens. 'I feel we are going to do great things together.'

Epilogue

T**wo years later**

Melanie never quite understood the necessity of a desk inlaid with mother-of-pearl. Nevertheless, she couldn't help but admit that working at one felt rather nice.

Evelyn is going to make a hedonist out of me, she thought, looking at the fruits of her labour. The clean copy of *The Cedars of Lebanon: Diverse Recollections of the Land in Question, Its Nature, Customs, and People, as Written by Miss Melanie Bright* was almost finished. She stroked the pages as if they were a lover's back, imagining the glorious frontispiece and the lovely engravings her publisher was going to adorn it with. Provided, of course, the manuscript wasn'tgoing to be lost in the sea en route to London.

Hearing steps at the door, Melanie almost jumped. With great surprise, she turned around and saw Evelyn stumbling in, her pristine white Bedouin robes greyed out with dust.

'You are back already?' Melanie exclaimed.

'What a fine greeting.' Evelyn raised an eyebrow. However, her still heavy breathing rather spoiled the effect of ironic nonchalance. 'I hope you are not hiding a lover in one of the castle's niches?'

'I wouldn't have had the time to pay him court even if I wanted to,' Melanie parried. 'I have been busy with *Cedars*. How did your ride with the Ruwallah go?'

'Splendid. It's a shame you were too busy to join us. We might have given you some new material,' Evelyn teased.

'It's a little too late for that. For the next book, perhaps.' Melanie nuzzled her neck, not put off at all by the tang of sweat and sand.

Evelyn fell straight upon the floor where a carpet and cushions of Aleppo silk awaited them, and pulled Melanie down with her. Melanie exclaimed in a delighted yelp, knowing the softness was going to muffle the impact, that the hardness of the stone was now forever encased in silk.

Had Ferideh or any other woman of the Anazeh been there now, she would have been hard-pressed to recognize the black shell that was Hisn el-Nasara. The castle itself had been bought after a protracted negotiation with the Ottoman government in the months that followed the peace treaty; the agreement to yield a half of the Crusader hoard to them had smoothed the conversation a lot. Remembering her promise to Wharton, Evelyn only used her own inheritance for the restoration and furnishing of the edifice but use it she did. The room where they were now tumbling on the floor boasted calico and brocade, large lanterns of bright brass to ward off the evening darkness, and a painted door carved with star patterns leading into the next chamber. The remainder of the sunset light was streaming in through the panes of stained glass.

'No tickling.' Melanie laughed. 'It's unfair.'

'Oh, is it?' Evelyn purred, pinning her to the floor. 'How about this?' She kissed by Melanie's ear, then allowed her teeth to graze her earlobe gently. Something contracted within Melanie with unutterable sweetness, and she wrapped her legs around Evelyn's waist.

'This is fair enough,' Melanie whispered, looking up at her face.

'I need a bath after all of my exertions. Would you like to join me?'

'For some more exertions, I take it?'

'I am nothing if not honest.'

'Wait.' Melanie kissed her quickly on the lips and crawled, rather ungainly, out to the desk again. 'I only need to finish the dedication page.'

'Come before the water turns cold. I will be waiting.'

'You won't have to wait for long,' Melanie called out before sitting down.

On the clear page prefacing the volume, she wrote:

'To my dearest mother, whose love has always been a consolation for me and whose esteem I will daily labour to deserve.'

***

Have you enjoyed this romance? If so, check out the next book in the series – *Her Vixen Actress.*

One has a fiery temper. The other is governed by rigid self-control. Will an unexpected pair become a comedy of errors or a legendary love story?

9 783982 550022